To S...
here's y...
love
Robert Gibson

KROTH 1:

THE SLANT

First Published in Great Britain 2012 by Netherworld Books

First edition: 2012

Any reference to real names and places are purely fictional and are constructs of the author. Any offence the references produce is unintentional and in no way reflects the reality of any locations or people involved.

A copy of this work is available through the British Library.

ISBN: 978-1-909224-30-8

Netherworld Books
Mirador
Wearne Lane
Langport
Somerset
TA10 9HB

Kroth 1:

The Slant

Robert Gibson

1: Holiday Mood

It is rarely mentioned out loud. But on occasion you do hear it, tersely. *"Got the Slant?"*

"Yeah."

"Sure?"

"Yeah."

"Good. Let's march."

You will understand when the time comes.

I was lucky. Without knowing what I was letting myself in for, I blundered my way into legend, I took part in a revolution led by a great man, and I lived to tell the tale. To repay my debt to Fortune, I have named my narrative after that survival skill which you must acquire if you are to venture south of Sixty.

Remember, you won't hear it often named. Far more frequently you'll hear the word "Slope". After all, on the basic Earth, questions of life and death, peace and war, personal success and failure, depend literally on where you stand upon its down-curving Slope.

But the Slant – it's inside you. Or at least, you had better hope it is.

Yet none of us knew it, on what we used to call "our world", when my story begins.

*

Nothing can beat the sheer relief you feel when a batch of exams is over.

That morning, from 9.30 to 11.30, I had sat the last one – a History paper – and there were no lessons for us sixth-formers in this "study week", so the school let us go.

I trudged happily through rain-dampened streets back to my house. The dullness of the weather did not depress me at all. In fact I was in such a good mood that every dripping tree and sodden bush in the gardens of the semis gave off a scent of mild excitement. *Who needs sunshine, anyway, if what's on your agenda is just to flop, to collapse in exhausted freedom!* It was a tonic for me to walk that familiar suburban route at this unaccustomed time. The grey, wet day, in my drained-out state, soothed me with the pleasurable fact that an empty house awaited me, and a stress-free, uneventful afternoon.

I felt "in my bones" that I was in for a reasonably good result in all four of my AS-levels. However, even more important, right now, was the prospect of this selfish afternoon, lounging and mooching to my heart's content, blissfully binning my revision plan. My few friends lived not in Crickham but in the adjoining ex-villages of Lade and Foxton, and I felt sure that no social demands would be made on me that day. In fact I was then somewhat of a loner, partly out of necessity but also out of choice. My parents were dead, my stepfather was locked up and my uncle, theoretically my guardian, left me to myself most of the time. To a moderate degree I enjoyed company, provided that it wasn't too exciting. I'd had enough drama from the days when my stepfather used to chase after my late mother wielding a breadknife. More than most seventeen-year-olds, I valued quiet.

A minute after I had let myself in, the phone rang.

A bit surprised, but assuming that it would be my uncle, I picked up the receiver and heard a voice that shocked my pulse into a faster beat.

"Duncan?" it said. "That you?"

I hedged, "Yes, hello...." I knew who it was but I found it hard to believe the evidence of my ears.

"It's Elaine. Elaine Dering."

"Yes, hi. I didn't think you were the *other* Elaine." That would indeed have been too much to believe. A tinkle of laughter down the phone line showed that my caller agreed – we both knew, we didn't need to spell it out, that the other Elaine, Elaine Swinton, would hardly trouble herself to phone anybody; she'd more likely be waiting for people to call her while she languidly admired herself in the mirror.

By contrast, Elaine Dering would look less spectacular on the catwalk but was far more adorable in my opinion. But why was she calling me? We hardly knew each other.

"Thought I'd catch you just as you got back, before you go out celebrating...."

"Little do you know," I said.

We were now several sentences into the conversation and I had not yet messed it all up. What a day this was turning out to be. I would have been even more thrilled, were it not for my realistic streak which pointed out that she wasn't likely to ring me up for the pleasure of it. She must want something from me. This isn't meant as a criticism. Elaine D. was a glorious extrovert, a bubbly personality full of overflowing good nature, and I was thankful for my bit of the overflow; it's just that I, being threatened by happiness, naturally became cautious, and warned myself not to read too much into it.

"Fortunately," she went on, "there aren't that many Wemyss's in the phone book...."

"We're a rare breed," I acknowledged. "By the way, you're supposed to pronounce it 'Weems', not 'we miss'."

"Sorry! So anyway, I found you, and I can buttonhole you."

She sounded, as she said this, as though she feared she might be about to say something slightly cheeky. Odd, that this splendid person should suddenly lack confidence. She continued as though she had to make excuses: "I couldn't delay calling you because my Chemistry exam is at half past one. I want your advice."

"Go ahead, Elaine; if you think I can advise you, I'll gladly help all I can, as soon as I know what you're talking about."

"This is a long shot, but.... Look, you see, Duncan, I think you're quite brainy, but that's not all of it. It doesn't explain it – doesn't explain, I mean, how you get by."

"What on Earth...."

"I'm talking about these exams! I think you've got some secret! Haven't you?" She heard my silence and became bolder. "Come on, admit it."

"Oh," I said. "So that's it," I added, playing for time. "Well.... Don't you think it's maybe a bit late to ask, a bit late to apply it to this afternoon...."

"Aha. AHA!" (I imagined her eyes flashing, her arms waving in actressy gestures. At the same time, with the phone receiver it was as if her lips were pressed against my ear.) She said throatily, "Hohoho, you do have something, don't you? I thought so." Full of certainty now, she continued: "You never seem to worry, never seem under pressure, always seem to know just how much and what to read up on, whatever's most useful.... If I just thought you were a genius I wouldn't bother with you, but I think you're something else and I want to know what. So there!"

"I'm not psychic," I protested.

How could I explain to her that at this stage in my life my great determination was to avoid stress of any kind; that I had just about made a science out of it; that I had been determined from the start that I would not leave anything to chance.... how could I tell her all this without risking further enquiry?

Well, maybe I could give her a little, provided I made it sound sufficiently boring so as to put her off questioning me about what started it all.

"All right, I'll tell you my exam technique," I said. "For a start I take sensible precautions, such as going in for subjects like English and History, and avoiding incomprehensible stuff like Chemistry...."

"Oh ha ha."

"Sorry. I'm only saying how it seems to me. I know *you* don't have anything to fear from Chemistry."

"All very well for you to say that. Come on, get to the point."

"Right, I will! But I warn you, it's nerdy."

"I dare say it is. Keep going!"

"I designed what you might call a voucher system."

"Now we're getting somewhere. Tell me how you do that."

"Listen, then. This is the core of it: you survey what you have to do, then write yourself out a series of revision vouchers on slips of paper. One voucher per hour's or half-hour's or quarter-hour's work; anyhow, one voucher per stomach-full, if you see what I mean. Got that? You have to 'spend' them, so to speak, by doing all those lengths of revision, but there isn't a rule about when you do them, or which you do, so long as a certain number get done every week...."

I droned on, imagining the glaze creeping over her eyes as she realized that I wasn't telling her anything that she could possibly use for the exam coming up at half past one today. I finished, "So there you are, that's about it. You asked for it."

"Hmm. Yes, I did, didn't I. Pity we didn't have this chat several months ago...."

"I wish we had."

"Still, I'll be able to use your words of wisdom for next year. But I'm not looking forward to this Chemistry, I must admit."

"Um...." I said, helplessly.

"Ah, well. Think of me, while you're living it up this afternoon...."

"Elaine, you seem to think I've got big ideas about celebrating, but I haven't. I'm just going to sit down and *be.*"

"Wish I could right now. What about the hols – got anything interesting lined up?"

Now the tone had changed; she was just being polite, asking the sort of question one uses just to finish off a normal conversation.

"Nothing planned, but Uncle Vic has hinted he'll come up with something. Take me here and there on some of his scientific conference trips. A few week-end jaunts."

"That all?"

"Uncle's a sport; he lets me mooch on my own. I'm used to it. Shouldn't be too bad."

"Hope you enjoy yourself. 'Bye, Duncan."

"'Bye, Elaine."

Click.

Well, that was quite nice, I thought. In fact, more than quite nice. It had bathed my entire awareness in a golden glow; yet I didn't "whoop" out loud, for absolutely nothing must be permitted to breach the no-stress rule. Happiness was risky. If allowed to take hold, it could get one dancing along the edge of a cliff.

My survival technique applied to more than just exams.

*

The crisis with my stepfather had begun with a car accident which altered his personality. Previous to that, we had got along fine. Afterwards, he was a violent case – a different person. He was put away after a few months but not before my mother had been turned into an invalid, so that just at the time when I had to study hard for my GCSE's, I also had to do a lot of extra work round the house and looking after Mum. I developed The Philosophy: if I didn't have time or energy to do a thing, such as homework, well, it just didn't get done. That was that. No strain; extras just go down the chute and into the bin.

Then my mother unexpectedly died. That shock threatened to crack my new armour. But still I carried on with my routines of living. I was in a smooth kind of daze in which I did not really think of her as gone, for I still sensed her presence quite strongly in the silent house; a reassuring presence as if she were co-operating with my denial. "All right, Duncan, a big change has happened but there's no law that says you have to crumple up." So I didn't.

My new guardian, Uncle Vic, was a dry, undemonstrative type, just what I needed. He provided stable support and otherwise let me work things out my own way.

I perfected The Philosophy. "Pressure," I told myself, "is inevitable in life, and I can cope with it so long as it's smooth and even and steady. But as for the other sort: I'm not having it. I cannot, will not cope with hassle. Unforeseen irregular stuff is, therefore, unacceptable – I've had enough of it; it's out! I refuse to accept any more violence from the universe, and in order to enforce this rejection, *I* will control the pressure dial, *I* will apply the pressure to myself, feeding it to myself at a steady rate, averaging out in such a way that I am always buffered by a safety margin of accumulated power."

This, alas, is not the philosophy of a brave man. But you might say I had some excuse.

The phone rang again. *This* time it will be Uncle, I said to myself.

It was. The dry, sardonic voice said, "How did it go?"

"Not so bad! No nasty surprise questions. I think I did all right."

"Of course you did – I expected no less." He paused. "Listen, Duncan, I have been summoned to the Boone demo at Imperial College tomorrow morning. Remember I told you about it?"

"I expect you did," I said, racking my brains.

"Well, do you want to come along? I'm going up to London this afternoon to do a quick bit of prior research. If, as I believe, the demo is a flop, at least you get a couple of days out with all expenses paid. If I'm wrong, you get not only that but an opportunity to witness history being made."

Uncle was generous on the expenses side. And he treated me like a responsible adult. Besides, one never knew, the thing might even be interesting.

"I'd be glad to come along," I said. "Thanks."

"How about this, then: I'll pick you up on my way home, Reen meanwhile will prepare us a spot of lunch, then the three of us will shoot off without more ado."

"So we'll get there with about ten hours to spare," I said dryly, for Uncle always was so keen on speed.

A chuckle. "Right then, you get packed and I'll see you in about half an hour."

Click.

I'd forgotten all about this demo thing, whatever it was. So I wasn't going to have a quiet afternoon absolutely to myself after all. Still, lounging around in luxury London hotels was at least as good as loafing at home. And as for the event itself, the doings at Imperial, I would be a mere spectator. No need to bestir myself.

My mind was running more on the topic of Elaine's phone call as I went upstairs to bung some things into a case. It occurred to me that it must have taken quite a bit of courage on her part to ring up someone she didn't know at all well, just for the sake of a "long shot" idea. I wouldn't have dared to try so long a shot myself. I hoped that she wasn't too disappointed in the result.

Soon after I had descended with the suitcase, I saw, through the leaves outside the lounge bay window, Uncle's car draw up. I went out, locked the door and sauntered down the path, in holiday mood. Uncle watched as I swung my case into the boot.

"Ready for high adventure?" he asked, with quirked eyebrows.

I played up to it. "I've said all my goodbyes," I said, "to everyone else that lives in the house – that's to say, the cacti and the geraniums. You may gun the motor."

He snickered and pulled out from the kerb. The engine purred – it was actually a powerful car. A new one. I glanced at Uncle, wondering, as I often did, what made him tick. He bulked in his grey suit, looking like a prosperous slightly pear-shaped businessman with a somewhat grimly handsome face and lanky black hair; he could have starred in The Godfather Part IV, but what lay behind those keen eyes?

Some things I was fairly sure of. For example, that to him and to Aunt Reen I was the son they never had. And whatever else he was, he certainly wasn't mean. I had a lot to be grateful for. But it was very hard to find out where he stood on any issue: he delighted in building up a case for something and then knocking it down. He seemed to enjoy confusing people. And he didn't seem to care for anybody except Reen and, to a lesser extent, myself; everybody else was the object of his amused contempt.

His real name was an embarrassment. Being not only a quarter Italian but also a quarter Russian, he had been christened Vladimir, thence shortened to Vlad. In my younger, more sensitive days I had put my foot down to stop the news spreading at school that a relative of mine shared a first name with Dracula. Reen took my side in this, and we eventually persuaded him to call himself Vic. He had snorted, "Very well! Vlad the Victor! I shall do my best to live up to both names."

By profession he was a freelance science journalist, and by all accounts a good one, highly regarded in his field. He had won a string of awards for articles which set out to tame the big themes of modern science and make them accessible to the ordinary reader. Reen was proud of his accomplishments: at lunch recently she had told me he'd won a prize for a piece in *New Scientist* about "carbon nanotubes", whereupon Uncle Vic had smiled cynically and added, in the tone of a TV advert, "Want to dazzle your friends with nanotechnology, astrophysics, palaeoanthropology? Go to Vic Chandler; he'll bluff you through."

This time, though, the topic was going to be some other big polysyllable, and I heartily wished I could remember what it was, for I was most reluctant to disappoint Uncle Vic by admitting that I had forgotten what "the Boone demo" was about.

Glancing at his profile as he wove through the lunch-hour traffic I sensed his keen zest and determination to make a professional job of this latest assignment, and though my own understanding of it all could hardly make a difference to the outcome, I very much wanted to be on his wavelength. If only I hadn't forgotten the topic! How could I draw it out of him without letting on? Vlad the Victorious wasn't an easy man to fool.

I finally thought of an approach.

"So, what'll be the title of your next article?" I inquired.

"Oh, doubtless something with a question mark in it."

"Like?"

'PK – The Clincher?' Or, 'PK Pinned Down At Last?' That sort of thing."

"And when will it appear?"

He grinned. "I could write most of it this evening."

"Hang on, Uncle – you said the demo is taking place tomorrow."

"Well, so what? Just another one for the *Observer* – I ought to know how to pitch it by now."

I realized he was just being cynical again. Meanwhile I hadn't solved my problem. I was about to give in and ask point blank, "What's PK?", when chance or luck came to my aid.

We were hurtling along a stretch of the St Albans Road, and I was getting jittery about the speed of Vic's driving. It wasn't the first time my nerves had suffered from his tendency to treat any long straight bit of road as though it were a motorway. But I remembered a helpful fact and said aloud, "Speed camera coming up, Uncle."

He didn't respond.

"Er, look," I went on, and then my voice died away because it was plain that he had seen the camera. His narrowed eyes shot a fierce glare at the oncoming post – he wasn't going to slow down!

Well, he was rich enough to not mind paying the fine, but –

Next moment we were past it and I had not noticed any tell-tale flash. The speed camera was therefore not in working order. Clever Uncle to have known this, to have known that he didn't need to do what he doesn't like to do, namely, slow down. What I then saw on his face – a smirk of utter squashing contempt, compressed into about a second of time – randomly gave me an idea for a story. Imagine someone who could influence speed cameras by *willing* them not to work. Someone who had the power of psycho-whatsit – I knew the word, I knew it – psycho*kinesis – PK!*

I was so pleased I had retrieved the word, I made haste to use it.

"This Boone demo – is Boone the one with the psychokinesis?"

"Yes, and in fact he's a lad of about your age. Poor chap, he must be tired of being a freak."

I dared to say, "Just then, I had the idea *you* might be one. Using your mind-power to put the speed-camera out of action."

"Ha! I'd do that to all of them if I could! Dratted machines...." As if deliberately emphasizing his hatred of all restraint he zoomed round a corner much faster than I liked, so that I was scared enough to let my irritation show.

"Uncle – speeding in an urban area is not funny."

I suppose my brains were still addled after all the exams, otherwise I would never have made such a blunder. My only advantage was that I was one hundred per cent in the right. That was a small point to set beside Vic's far greater advantages of age, experience and personality. Hastily I added, "Sorry to sound priggish – but...."

He smiled. "Refreshing role-reversal! We oldsters can sit back now, and let teenagers do the telling-off!"

Sarcastic though this may seem when read in cold print, it was spoken in an amused tone that reassured me. I had got away with it. I had worried unnecessarily, merely because I had momentarily forgotten something important about Uncle. He *liked* cheeky opposition, provided it was articulate. The thing that really put him off was a sulky refusal to argue. Knowing that this was so, I had learned, over the past months, to express myself quite a lot more than I would otherwise have done. Now I told myself that it would be better to finish what I had started.

"Thanks – in that case, Uncle, I'll lecture you some more. Life isn't a James Bond movie, you know! No matter how good your reflexes, some day some child or idiot youngster is going to dart out in front of you and you won't be able to do a thing about it."

I half expected him to make some remark about reducing the surplus population.

What he actually said was, "Here we are. And there's Reen with the stuff."

For we were pulling up at his house. Reen must have seen us through the front curtain; she was already coming down the steps, suitcase in one hand and handbag dangling from the other. The best one-word description of Aunt Reen is "sweet". Gentle through and through, she was the perfect antidote to Vic's aura of ruthlessless. It was impossible to imagine her angry. I got out of the car, gave her a kiss on the flawless skin of her ageless cheek while Vic opened the boot, and put her case alongside mine.

"You got here quickly, dears. Have you been speeding again, Vic?"

He threw his head back and laughed heartily, then gave her huggable figure an enthusiastic hug. "Got it in one! I got told off by Duncan."

"Well done, Duncan. Keep it up."

"Perhaps he won't need to," said Vic. To my surprise he said it quite seriously. He always did have an unusual respect for argument, and I had one of my spells of feeling suddenly proud that he was my uncle; I had a mysterious sense that here was a person who might be on the way to something big. We went in for our "spot of lunch" and I was relaxed and happy.

When we came out again and zoomed off towards London, I thought the speed issue was over and done with. Once we had got onto the A1, however, he turned to me and said, "Shall I really open 'er up?" – nodding at the indicator.

"Now, Vic," warned Reen. "Don't start that again. Control that urge to be a spaceship pilot."

"I just thought Duncan might be interested to see what the car can do...."

"He's seventeen, not fourteen!" said Reen with finality.

"Right-oh! I accept what you say. That's what we men need, a good woman to keep us on the ground. I'm a lucky man."

"That you are," Reen confirmed.

Looking at his calm smile I wondered if there was anything that could disturb his composure. I thought back and couldn't remember anything that ever had. And somehow the result of these trivial conversations was that the feeling crept into me that he could, if he wanted, be a dangerous man.

Of course it wasn't his fault that he had a somewhat sinister face, but still, if he should ever decide to go in for politics or crime, and if he could steer people like he steered the car, then he might go very far indeed, in directions that were hard to imagine.

I wasn't worrying about it, though. I was too relaxed and happy to have premonitions. Besides, there was one fact about Uncle Vic which made all this fanciful speculation useless: namely, that he was – to put it mildly – a complete fence-sitter. He never took sides; and you don't get to be a world-shaker by never taking sides.

2: The Experiment

From my viewpoint in the front passenger seat, facing the monotonous flow of the motorway landscape, it was quite hard to believe in the approach of any world-shaking event; and yet, Uncle Vic had hinted that the result of the Boone demo might – just might – show up as important in the annals of science. A breakthrough of some sort, maybe; but, I thought, probably not sensational – not immediately. The sort of thing that starts by forcing changes in theory which then has an effect on technology which in turn, eventually, alters everyday life; hardly an overnight process. Not likely to plunge anybody's life into immediate chaos. But on the other hand – nowadays there was always the media frenzy to take into account. Journalists *might* whip it up into the big story of the season. In which case, goodbye to my idea of a quiet holiday….

I said out loud: "This experiment we're going to see.... You said something about it possibly making history…."

A playful smirk spread across Vic's profile.

"You're too young to remember this, but there used to be a series on TV called *The Saint.*"

"I've heard of it," I said.

Reen said from the back seat, "Always liked Roger Moore, I did. Nice soft-spoken man, biffing the baddies."

"And quite often he got biffed back, didn't he?" amplified Vic. "Amazing, how often he got knocked on the head without suffering concussion. And how many times the baddies captured him and could easily have killed him, except...." He glanced at me. *"Except...."*

"It would have put an end to the series," I finished for him.

"Precisely. You get the point, I see. And it's the same in the never-ending saga of *scientific issues*. The good old themes crop up again and again only to get knocked, but not fatally, on the head."

"You're trying to tell me that nothing's going to get biffed permanently on this trip."

“Well, after all, it would be such a pity to kill off this kind of dispute by settling it. A pity for all concerned. Think how sad it would be, for example, if homeopathy – which is unscientific because no one knows *why* it should work – were accepted by the medical profession merely on the footling grounds that it *does* work. A pity for the medicos who could no longer sneer, a pity for the homeopathic crowd who could no longer whinge about the establishment, and a pity for *condottieri* like me who would no longer be able to blast away first on one side of the dispute and then on the other.”

“Like if they found the Loch Ness Monster.... end of mystery.”

“Quite! There you've picked an even better example! The press would enjoy one short field day and then, forever and ever, no more pantomime ding-dong oh-yes-it's-real, oh-no-it-isn't. The Monster would become familiar. What a tragic end to a richly productive saga.” He tut-tutted, giving his head a solemn shake.

A voice from the back of the car: “Come on, Vic, I bet you wouldn't pass up the opportunity, if Nessie emerged from the loch and posed for you.”

“Trust you, Reen, to see through my pretensions. Yes, I admit, I couldn't afford to miss a genuine monster. However, as far as tomorrow's experiment is concerned, I doubt there'll be much to get excited about.”

*

We checked into the Rolvenden Hotel, Kensington. Reen went out shopping and Vic set about collecting some notes and photocopies; he told me he was headed for Imperial College library. “A bit of research,” he explained, clicking a briefcase shut.

“Rather last-minute research,” I remarked.

“Like last-minute revision. Nice and fresh in the mind.”

“Ha,” I said, “you wouldn't catch *me* relying on last-minute revision! A mug's game. Still, you know your business,” I added, remembering that Vic didn't have my phobia about stress. On the contrary, he thrived on it.

“And judging by your success in exams, you know *your* business, so now you can enjoy your reward! Don't paint the town red,” he grinned. “Early start tomorrow.”

He had explained to me that “The Experiment” was scheduled for 10 a.m., so that if anything big were to happen it would be in good time for the evening news. Calling 10 a.m. an “early start” was a typical Vic dig at teenage habits, but I was far from resenting this. I followed him out of his room and gazed appreciatively into mine. It looked as though I was going to be left to my own devices for the afternoon, and that's just how I wanted things to be. "I'll have a flop, a read, a stroll, and then, guess what, I'll.... go and eat some scones at tea time," I declared. "The town will stay unpainted, at least by me."

"Ah, what it is to be young!" sighed Vic, and left.

I didn't care whether he thought it funny or not – I was grateful for the opportunity to rest and just be me. Anyhow, teenagers are reputed to be lazy, so why fight it? But as I relaxed on the bed, my thoughts wandered, not always keeping to holiday things. They began to flow as if in a dream-jumble, mingling my own affairs with public events that should not have anything to do with me. For some reason I was ceasing to believe in my holiday. In fact I could almost sense "holiday" slip from my grasp and make a dash for the horizon, so I tried to steer my thoughts around to prevent its escape. What, I demanded, was I worried about?

It was, I admitted, just possible that what I was going to witness tomorrow might involve some stress. But surely it would be other people's stress, not mine. I would see to that. It was up to me, how much I got involved in Vic's schemes. He wasn't demanding anything of me. And after what I had gone through the last year or so, even if he did demand something, I was entitled to be selfish and to refuse. Not that I seriously regarded Vic as the problem. Life was the problem. So –

Any bothersome events that came my way, I'd shunt them aside for someone else to deal with. Fair enough, eh? By adopting this attitude I was avoiding the alternative, which was to crack up. Thus by being "selfish", by looking after myself, I was sparing the world the nuisance of having to look after me. Thanks to this enlightened attitude on my part, society would not have to accommodate yet another problem teenager.

Therefore – no worries, as the Aussies say! Here was I, stretched on the bed in my hotel room, with some reading matter within reach and a bedside lamp behind me, and downstairs a restaurant to which I could go down whenever I wished and spread butter and jam on some scones and read my book while sipping tea. *A heaven to treasure up in case history is made and I can never be cosily bored again.*

*

I love hotel breakfasts; I reckon I ate more bacon and sausage and toast and marmalade than Vic and Reen put together. Reen reminisced about her childhood on the Isle of Man and the breakfasts she had then (her parents ran a guest house). While we talked about food, Vic sat lost in thought.

Reen waxed nostalgic about her childhood and said how much she would love to go and live on the Isle again. Vic shook himself a bit in sudden surprise and said:

"You never told me that before."

"Yes I did, Vic, loads of times. Could we ever do it, do you think? Move back there?"

"Maybe, someday."

"You look a bit put out, dear," she said, placing a hand on his arm.

"Only that if you really have mentioned it so often, I am sorry I have taken no notice. The fact is I just can't remember. So I must have ignored you. I must not have been listening."

"Don't look so uncomfortable," she reassured, squeezing his arm. "Men don't listen; they're not built that way. At least you're sorry."

What with all this, we finished breakfast without having chatted at all about what we were going to see at ten o'clock. Then it was time to get a move on. Reen waved us goodbye; I don't know whether she could have obtained an invitation to The Experiment if she had been interested – anyhow she definitely wasn't. "I can think of better ways to spend a day in London," she said.

"So can I," said Vic. "See you later."

In contrast to yesterday, the weather was fine though breezy, and not too hot for London in June. I enjoyed the short drive to Imperial College. This was the first time I had seen the place, and I liked its spacious, modern look as Vic and I threaded our way along concrete walkways past big glass windows. But our first destination turned out to be rather cramped: a surprisingly small room in the Department of Metallurgy.

It was nothing like the lecture theatre I had expected from once having seen a famous painting of Faraday performing experiments in public. It looked like a cross between an office and a laboratory, crowded with about a dozen people besides Vic and me. I didn't feel like asking questions; I felt heavily out of my depth.

I heard some chatter but it wasn't loud. A shortish, tanned, bald man in a blue jacket was supervising four younger men working in pairs as they disconnected some leads and began to lift machinery off tables. The blue-jacketed man was in turn watched by others as we all trooped out, following the men carrying the stuff. The procession turned a corner and went through a door and now we indeed were in a proper-sized lecture room, able to seat hundreds. The Faraday scene after all. Except that the audience was thinly scattered; perhaps twenty-five or so.

In a very low tone Vic explained to me: "Checking for fraud." He nodded at the blue-jacketed man who was standing over the machinery while others connected it all up again and examined it. "That's Professor Glover; he's a total skeptic, or he thinks he is. Not a *real* skeptic like me." Vic's voice had sunk to a murmur; I strained to hear.

In an attempt at conversation I, too, murmured: "Not many around yet."

"There won't be. Matt insists on playing it down."

"Matt? Matt Boone?"

"Yes. Nervous lad. He wants – he insists – on just a few key figures present. Ah - here he comes now."

A scrawny, gangling youngster of about my own age had made an entrance accompanied by a couple who I guessed were his parents. Several people immediately converged on him. As he greeted them he looked subdued, with a slouchy, droop-shouldered posture – until he caught sight of Vic. He then straightened and waved. He detached himself from the group that had clustered about him and came towards us.

"Glad you could get here, Mr Chandler," he said to my uncle in a tone of great respect.

"Glad you could, too, Matthew! I wasn't absolutely sure you would! This is my nephew, Duncan Weemys."

The youngster nodded to me and said, "Hope you enjoy the circus." Switching his attention back to Vic: "I'm not happy with all this, Mr Chandler. I didn't want to come."

"The pressure of being a celebrity," said Vic lightly.

"I hope for a final result today," the boy went on.

"I can't promise to give you any breaks, you know that, Matthew."

"I know that, Mr Chandler. That's why I trust you. Oh, well, I'd better get back to work. Mears and Glover are watching to see you don't pass anything to me."

"They know better than that, Matthew. Besides, cheating would be impossible. It's not that sort of test."

When the lad had gone back to the group of scientists, and Vic and I had sat down in one of the middle rows of seats, I asked: "What kind of test is it?" By this time I was seriously regretting my ignorance. If I had paid proper attention in advance, right from the beginning, to what this was all going to be about, I would – I now realized – be enjoying it much more. However, I could still hope to keep sufficiently on track to have a chance of appreciating the show.

"It's actually a series of three tests," Vic explained. "All to do with affecting scientific instruments remotely. Boone is trying to demonstrate, under controlled conditions, that he can use PK to deflect the needle of a gaussmeter, the needle of a Geiger counter and the scale of an electronic precision balance."

With a jolt of surprise I realized that the experiment had already started. I had expected an introductory speech from someone, but no, there was no showmanship here at all. This was a businesslike gathering restricted to people who were in the know. It was now obvious that there wasn't going to be anything much to see, as far as the science itself was concerned. Then, by a sudden long link of ideas, I remembered something different yet in a way comparable – some astrophotos Vic had once showed me, consisting of "before" and "after" pictures of the expanding remains of a supernova. The differences had been small, just a slight increase in size of the shell of luminosity from one still to the next. But, wow, when you related it to the distance and the size of the thing, the fact that you could see any change at all in real time – well, it was enough to boggle the mind. The evidence itself was un-dramatic; what it *implied* was very dramatic indeed.

"Here comes Mears," Vic nudged me.

"Erm – " said I.

"Haven't I mentioned him? Zeb Mears from the SPR."

A slightly overweight man had detached himself from the group around Boone and strode into the row in front of us. He sat down and turned, to confront us with his thick glasses, wild curly hair and thick parted lips, panting a bit. "Well," he murmured, "look who's in at the death. Might turn out to be a good morning's work, I'd say, eh, Vic? No one can say we haven't been thorough. Yes, reckon we may prove something today."

"What if we do?" asked Vic, provocatively.

"You mean, people won't take any notice?"

"I mean, what if it's only marginal?"

I sensed these two were old rivals, if not enemies. The SPR – Society for Psychical Research – must have an axe to grind, and Vic was trying to blunt it.

“Ha,” said Mears in a “gotcha” tone, “what then of the widely admitted point, that it only takes one successful breakage to destroy a scientific law?”

“That's the case if you're being hierarchical about it. But what if reality isn't hierarchical? A majoritarian or coherentist structure could keep orthodox science as the mainstream whatever happens today, leaving your 'Paranormal' as mere froth.”

“Pah! The 'froth' as you call it would soon start chipping away at the mainstream!”

“Chip away, like in the Sorites – ”

“Forget your Greek paradoxes. This isn't a game.”

“Oh, you reckon not?” smiled Vic. “I often feel I might as well be a sports correspondent.”

Mears turned away, with a sniffy expression, but then he turned back for just a moment with a look of triumph as one of the instruments honked BEEEEP and the whole room stiffened to attention.

“The Geiger counter! It has registered.”

I heard some cheers. There was jostling up front. People were striving to look at the readings. I heard someone call, “Try it again, Matt!” – and then I heard a second, confirmatory wail of the Geiger.

I sat frozenly thinking: The Saint *has* been given his final knock on the head. Then, without knowing why, I shivered.

Vic was patting Zeb Mears on the shoulder, “There you go. Congratulations. History made.”

Mears, however, did not gloat. He did not respond at all to the congratulations; instead, he moved fast along the row of seats, kicking at some of them in his haste.

It gave me something to say, something to shake my thoughts out of their paralysis. “Look at him,” I said to Vic; “he's leaving the room.”

“Who? Mears? Yes, I dare say he wants to make sure he gets his own version out first.... But old Zeb's a neurotic; really there's no point in hurrying now. Come on, let's congratulate Matthew. And while I'm about it I had better review the setup. Then – back to the Rolvenden for lunch.”

Vic made notes as he talked to the staff and to the star of the show, while I stood around dazedly, aware that something big had happened but not sure of my personal reaction. Matt Boone was responding in monosyllables to all the congratulations and the high frequency of excited discussion; I didn't blame him at all for withdrawing into his shell. I caught his eye, gave him a thumbs-up sign and he grinned wryly back at me. It was as if he had read the thought behind my gesture: good luck, mate, you'll need it. I left it at that. Imagining myself in his shoes, I retreated to give him space, or what would have been space if the rest of the mob had done likewise.

Eventually, the gathering began to disperse and Vic and I joined the drift towards the door. As soon as we stepped outside the building, cameras flashed in our faces. Vic was thronged by half a dozen reporters. "Mr Chandler, do you have a statement?" "What's the verdict, Mr Chandler?"

"You people aren't supposed to be here, you know."

One woman said tartly, "They said no reporters at the meeting. They said nothing about no reporters afterwards!"

"Mr Chandler, can you tell us if Matt Boone has disproved the laws of physics?" asked a bespectacled young man.

"Ask him when he comes out," Vic evaded.

"Come on, Mr Chandler, you know he hates talking to us!"

Vic threw out phrases: "You'll hear from me later today.... Positive result.... Yes, I said, a positive result.... Er, that's all I intend to say at this stage."

3: Circling Shark

“Let's get out of here,” muttered Vic when he had pushed his way past the reporters. They weren't following us; they wanted to keep watch on the exit door. “Back to the hotel for lunch.” It was, in fact, rather too early for lunch, but I didn't point this out. We drove back in silence.

At the hotel he disappeared into his room, which was what I expected him to do, as he had his notes to write up and a statement and an article to compose. Working to a deadline, he wouldn't have time for sociable chit-chat about what had occurred. This was the excuse I made for his preoccupied air. On another level I sensed a different explanation; I could tell he was worried and I could guess why:

Vic had been forced, at last, to come off the fence.

At lunch, which we ate in the hotel restaurant (just we two; Reen, it seemed, was out for the day) he appeared reluctant to talk about the result of the Experiment. I made one or two comments about it and he shied away from the topic as though it were Top Secret even though we both knew it was going to be in the evening news and all over tomorrow's papers. He talked *round* it, alluding to moments of historic decision such as Caesar's crossing of the Rubicon or Hitler's declaration of war on the USA.

I quoted grandly, “'There is a tide in the affairs of men',” and then dug into my cannelloni.

“Ah, so Crickham Secondary does *Julius Caesar*. That's something anyway.” He brooded for a moment and then added, “As for me, I'd rather quote from the movies.”

“Go on, then.”

“'If you don't grab life, life'll grab you.'”

“The point being....?”

“I intend to be the grabber.”

After the meal we repaired to the lounge for coffee, but he had only got through half a cup when a waiter came to say there was a call for him.

“Thanks. I'll take it up in my room.” Vic left the lounge with an energetic stride. It was about ten minutes before he reappeared with a kind of bloodless expression I had never seen on his face before – an astonished dismay, as though he had come off worst in an argument which he had not expected to lose. "Duncan," he said, "I want your advice about something. Not here, though. Let's go back up."

"Right," I said slowly, and "right, right," I repeated under my breath, feeling stupid yet proud as I followed him to his room, where we sat at the table on which he had strewn his notes. For a couple of moments he directed his scowl at those notes.

"I am not permitted to tell you who has called. I promised to keep it confidential. However I can give you the gist of what he said. He argued, quite persuasively, that to release a favourable report on Matt Boone's PK claims would do great damage to science."

Vic paused and I said, "Oh. So he wasn't convinced, this caller of yours."

"On the contrary, he *was* most definitely convinced! Not for one moment did he attempt to deny that Boone had been vindicated. And he admitted that science ought to be sufficiently robust to take a knock now and then. The point he made – now listen carefully – was that, in the present state of education, the public couldn't be trusted with the truth; they'd go berserk and snatch back the funding from countless worthwhile projects just because all science *seems* to be discredited if Boone is right. Never mind that this public attitude will be short-sighted, question-begging, philosophically inadequate and so on; it's nevertheless what will actually happen if the news gets out. The caller then requested that I do something to save the situation. He said that if I threw my influence on the side of minimising the Imperial College experiment results, my action might save lives. He said that he knew he was asking me to do something that was dishonest by normal standards, but he argued that if the truth cannot be received properly, if the truth is bound to be taken the wrong way, then it's the *truth* that is effectively dishonest and a lie. Now, I hate that kind of twisted argument yet I see his point. I thought I'd get your opinion. What do you think I should do?"

"Go for the truth, the real truth," I said without hesitation, utterly certain I was on firm ground. "Otherwise you're letting Matt down, you're letting the College down, you're letting yourself down and ultimately you're letting science itself down." I was in fine preaching mode just then.

Vic's face contorted into a guilty grin that unscrewed again after a few seconds and I saw he looked much relieved. "I do like your black and white approach. Ah, the vigour of youthful thought! You've given me just the injection I needed. *Fiat iustitia et ruant coeli.*"

"Uncle, please, I've told you often enough, I didn't do Latin."

"Never mind," he replied happily; "it has a grand sound, don't you think?"

I left him to get on with his press releases and his articles. Though I felt good that he had confided his doubts to me, I felt no sense of responsibility about the advice I had given him, for I could not believe that he had really needed it; instead I interpreted his request as a favour and a compliment to me. It was his way of educating me in the ways of the world, giving me a taste of involvement in the big stuff. That I actually might have pushed him towards one conclusion or the other was an idea which I dismissed out of hand.

That evening, after he had emailed his articles, Vic went off back to Imperial College to appear live in a TV newsclip which I watched from my room. The programme gave him about thirty seconds to convey the bare bones of what had happened in the Experiment. It didn't amount to much. The voice-over commentary was in a breezy tone that almost made a joke of it all. He had warned me not to expect more than this; it was too soon for a more serious response. Tomorrow morning's papers would be where the coverage got properly underway.

While he was out I went into his room (he had left me his key and told me I could have the use of his laptop) and I went on the Net to look up *fiat iustitia et ruant coeli.*

As the translation floated on the screen before my eyes, my thoughts became cushioned in a great quietness; not a muscle moved in my body.

"Let justice be done though the heavens fall."

*

Doubts then began to swirl in my head like sharks circling a diver's cage. I needed to reinforce the bars of that "cage", quick; I had to firm up my anti-stress stance.

I switched off the laptop, went out of Vic's room and locked the door, went down and left his key at reception, went back up to my room and locked the door from the inside, and lay down.

Let justice be done though the heavens fall.

Even now, as I write this, my mind boggles at the idea that, if I had acted differently, I might have prevented what afterwards happened. What consoles me, a year later, is that I turned out to be in a position to do something about it *after* it had happened.... but at that time I could not face the responsibility, or rather, the mere possibility of being responsible for what might ensue from Vic's decision – encouraged by me – to go ahead with the historic announcement of the PK breakthrough.

The reader may wonder at this point why I did not seek the comfort of human contact. Above all, why did I not try to phone Elaine? She had phoned me in her hour of need; I would have been justified in doing the same. But I did not have her address, and her number was ex-directory, and I had not asked her for it when I had the chance, because I was an over-cautious cowardly fool. Or to put it a bit more nicely, I had lacked the necessary presence of mind.

So I switched on the TV. It's not just that I needed to relax – I could have done that with a book. I needed to be *bored.* And that is why, even if I had had her number, it would not have been any use to phone Elaine. You can't banish a small, distant, closer-creeping threat merely by placing good things in front of it to block the view. Horror can grin over the shoulder of Good - whereas boredom, which kills good and evil alike, is incompatible with fear.

I flicked through the TV channels, inventing names for each one: the bunk channel, the twaddle channel, the yuk channel.... until I happened upon something that seemed not too repulsive. I found myself watching a documentary about Monticello – Thomas Jefferson's house. A topic that linked the ordinary and the extraordinary: the home life of the Great. Good, I thought, this is how to get away from it all and keep calm. The only trouble was, it wasn't really boring enough. Not boring at all, in fact. Being ignorant of American history, I felt the kind of mental pleasure that is the equivalent of taking a shower – when you're all hot and sticky with a mess of questions, take a shower of new facts from a different world. So this was all right, I thought: although it wasn't boredom, it was *irrelevance*, which did the job just as well. A more pleasant defence against those circling sharks.

I ought to have known better.

The presenter toured Monticello exhibiting the bizarre fixtures which the third President had installed in it, and which made me think of the eccentric inventions of the White Knight in *Alice Through the Looking Glass*. I especially liked one feature of Jefferson's design: the bed that was placed between two rooms, so that you could get out of bed either into one room or (from the other side) into the other. Most of all I liked the fact that Jefferson and Monticello and the early-1800s USA seemed as far as one could get from anything to do with me and my problems.

What I failed to take into account was the way the unconscious can *create* links. That night I sank into a dream which must have been influenced by the documentary.

I was in a bed like the one at Monticello. I was dithering as to which side to get out. Into which room should I emerge?

Should I do what I wanted to do and get out into the familiar room on the right, my own? Or should I obey a blob of growing darkness which was reaching out with the intention of pulling me into the other room on my left? The amoeboid blob, billowing like a weightless liquid, was also in some sense a hovering curtain on which was embroidered a graph, a steepening curve, which told me that the blob was gathering force to compel me to choose the other room, and as I felt the pull begin I clutched at the bedclothes, sat up and shouted at tomorrow to go away. It wasn't courage that I showed, as I raged at the nightmare; it was despair, the cornered rat in me lashing out with all it had till I sank back, exhausted with my efforts.

Had I impressed my views on the enemy? Had I altered what it was going to do with me? Sadly, no. My protest merely made the dark grin wider. *The* nightmare, the unfaceable one, was opening its jaw to receive me for keeps. With my last ounce of will I found the strength to roll over, out of bed and into the room I knew, rejecting the unknown.

4: The Slope

After a dream like that it would not have surprised me if I had found myself on the floor. But, though the duvet was twisted and askew, showing that I had thrashed about, I hadn't actually got as far as falling out of bed. Maybe I missed a chance there; maybe the bump, if I had fallen, would have woken me sooner.

My pyjamas were drenched with sweat, and in some disgust I lurched in the direction of the shower. I had taken maybe three strides when I stumbled against an object that had not been there before – a bathtub. No shower? No shower. Come to that, all the rooms of the suite impressed me vaguely as being smaller and simpler than I had remembered them.

Aha – so ran my thought – I am not awake after all; this must be one of those con-dreams where you think at first that you've woken and then you find you haven't. And if you *try* to wake up you just find yourself in yet *another* layer of dream. In these tiresome situations the only thing to do is to wait for the natural vigour of body and brain to break one's self out of the pesky illusion.

Meanwhile, though, I threw off the sweaty pyjamas and bathed in the tub, ignoring the yapping inner voices that told me I would not need to do this if I were still in a dream; that I was therefore not in a dream; that something had gone frighteningly wrong.

I got dressed. Noting that my possessions were still around, including humdrum things like my toothbrush and a copy of the Radio Times, which oozed all the reassurance of dullness, I became quite cheerful on the surface of my mind. Next stop: a nice dream breakfast! But wait! I hadn't opened the curtains. Opening curtains is a natural reflex to the start of a new day. To glance at the weather – a normal thing to do. So, why not?

As I hesitated, I heard the silence. No continuous growl of London traffic. In which case, maybe the window was not such an inviting prospect after all. Maybe it would provide me not with a first-floor view over part of South Kensington but with a view of something else, something I'd rather not see.

So maybe I should forget the window and just go out through the door, which should only take me into one of the corridors of the hotel.

It's quite natural, in a dream, for one's analytical side to take a back seat; thus I contrived to hope that although my room had changed, the rest of the building would be the same, and I could stay in it until.... until the outside became acceptable. Better still, why not restrict myself entirely to this room, for a while? It was bearable, and – *it would be stupid to face the corridor now. Better tackle it when it's in a better mood.* This was dream-logic with its emotional laws.... and yet once I had my hand on the doorknob, suddenly it was all no use. My realistic self simply took over, and in sticky slow motion I could not retract my turn of the knob, the command from my brain, posted into the system of my nerves, wending its way towards delivery, was unstoppable, and while the timid side of me kept bleating that I should have stayed in bed, the door began to open under the pressure of my hand.

The first inch of opening let in a shaft of direct sunlight. In some hard and precise way, from the intrusion of that light I knew that I was awake: the long run of denial was over.

I pushed the door fully open.

Here are the facts of what I saw.

I was facing out from the front porch of a bungalow. The house appeared to be surrounded by the ingredients of some ordinary English suburb or village. My front garden had roses, irises (a bit late for irises, I thought), and a well-kept lawn; the concrete path ran out to a gate in a privet hedge. Through the bars of the gate I glimpsed a pavement and kerb. Beyond, a half-visible motorcycle leaned against a tree on the other side of the road. The street was lined with detached bungalows similar to mine, all built on a hillside, sloping quite steeply upwards to my left. The road climbed the slope, curving gradually back towards the rear of my house as it did so in order to skirt a pine-wood, while to my right, on the down-slope, my view was obstructed by some tall oak trees belonging to my neighbour. From where I stood on the front step I could not yet see people, but my ears caught a distant trace of ordinary voices.

Yes, I knew I was awake. But how did I know? First of all, the scene was so *crisp*. Its sheer hardness and clarity obliterated all thought of dream.

But secondly, and more powerfully, for the sake of survival I knew I must cut out the fooling. A trick, a big trick had been pulled and I must take it seriously. A shock was impending and I must brace myself for it. The most dangerous strategy of all would be to accept the all-round pleasantness of the scene at face value, for only a mug would be optimistic after having found himself transferred during the night to an unfamiliar location with no explanation as to how or why he had been taken there.

What gave me a really bad feeling, was the strong hunch that what had been done to me was not a crime in any normal sense of the word. A foreboding of something worse than crime, worse than spooky, pawed at the threshold of my understanding as I nerved myself to take a step forward.

This peculiar fear, that hampered my movement like a river of mud, was of a kind I had never before experienced or even heard of. Until then, if anyone had asked me what is the worst kind of fear, I would unhesitatingly have answered, "supernatural terror – of ogres, vampires, things that go bump in the night". I now know that there is another dread which can match it. Call it *universal* fear. All other horrors seem mere drama *when the stage itself starts to tip.*

You may wonder what I mean; but if you ever meet that ultimate outrage I think you will find that it is recognizable to your innermost self, and you will agree that dream logic turns out to have some application in a waking nightmare. I, at any rate, knew "in my bones" perfectly well what I would find when I reached the gate.

I knew; but I had yet to admit it consciously. To get it over with, I walked down the path, and, nearing the gate, I began to see some people on the pavements: a few pedestrians, someone entering a corner shop, a woman with a child in a pushchair pausing outside a hairdresser's. Even with my senses keyed to a high pitch I could detect nothing unhealthy or weird about their faces or their movements, but I did consider that they appeared to be rather subdued, as though bad news had just been announced over the radio, and a frivolous part of me wondered if in this dimension England had just been knocked out of the World Cup yet again. It's a marvel how the brain can babble away with its stupid chatter even in the face of the most appalling truth.

I reached the gate, opened it and stepped onto the pavement. I gazed to my right, down the road. From the eerie clarity of my distance vision I might have been on an airless world like the Moon, despite the plentiful signs of life and the blue sky and the fact that I could breathe. Let blunt language now suffice for what I saw.

The whole world was tilted about fifteen degrees to the horizontal. Down-slope the sky, un-obscured by cloud or haze, reached *all the way down* to fifteen degrees below where the horizon ought to be, and thus showed that the slope went on forever into the blue.

Convulsed with vertigo I slumped against the gate-post.

Run back into the house, I urged myself. Sleep it off. Perhaps I've been drugged. Not unheard of, surely, a drug that plays tricks on the eye? That has got to be the explanation.

But my house, and all the other houses, were bad news as far as this drug theory was concerned. For when I say the world was tilted, I don't mean that a normal horizontal scene had just been tipped over fifteen degrees. The houses did not stand perpendicular to the slope, which they would have done had that been the case; instead they were sensibly built to compensate for the slope, to make their floors level, which was why I had not known of the tilt while I was still inside. In other words the houses stood just as they would have stood on a hill on Earth, only *this* hill went on forever. If you stayed indoors with the curtains shut, you could hide from the truth, but outside there was no escaping it, no disbelieving it.

Turning my back upon the unacceptable sight I took the opposite direction and began to plod along the pavement up-slope. Don't get lost, I warned myself. When you've finished your walk you'll want to be back at your house. Well then, if you just keep left you'll manage to do that easily, you'll just go round the block. But that means you'll have to face the down-slope on your way back. Well, so what? You can get used to it. You better had get used to it.

The road, as it veered gradually leftwards to skirt the pine-wood, came at length to a sharper corner, with a house on the corner-plot. It had the look of a new-built house. I noticed one window with Venetian blinds pulled down and another blank without curtains. The garden was bare earth. It had no hedge or boundary wall. I jumped to the conclusion that the place was uninhabited, and I suddenly wanted, for some emotional reason, to feel that bare earth under my shoes. So I trespassed; I cut across.

Certainly during those moments I was in a state of bewilderment, under the mental bombardment of my delayed reactions to fantastic events, and this must be why I set out to do something so incautious as to walk over that garden.

"Corn salad! C-o-o-o-rn sallud!"

The scratchy voice made me jump. Freeze. Gulp. Then slowly turn around.

"You're treading on my c-o-o-rn sallud!" insisted the owner of the voice, a very short lady in her fifties, with bright snappy eyes and an underslung jaw that made her upper lip protrude. Embarrassed by her crossness I felt natural shame at having stepped on ground which someone had planted and in which, I now noticed as I looked down, some seedlings were pushing up.

"I'm very sorry," I mumbled, and stood confusedly wondering in which direction to step. "I'll pay for the damage...."

"Hey, young man, are you all right? Come here!"

I obeyed. She was looking hard at my face.

In a softer voice than before she said, "Don't worry, it's all right. You look as though you could do to sit down. Wipe your shoes properly, there now, good lad. Come into the lounge. Take a seat." I accepted gratefully.

We faced each other in armchairs in a partly furnished sitting room. The windows lacked curtains; she must have just moved in or maybe the curtains had been taken down to be washed. "You live just down the road, don't you? I am Miss Tyler."

"I'm Duncan. Duncan Wemyss."

"Of course, I remember. Duncan, I admit I was rather irritable just now, but I suppose, looking at you, that you had a worse awakening than most of us did."

I sat up straighter. "Awakening?"

Miss Tyler said gently, "From the dream of Earth."

I slumped. She went on, "You poor boy, have I shocked you? I suppose I am rather blunt. Some people can't stand it being mentioned directly. I saw Celia Hammond early this morning – she's next door to me – putting out her wheelie bin the same time as I was, and I said, 'snap!', meaning to congratulate both of us on our promptness, and when she just glared, I said to myself, I'm not having this, and so I added firmly, 'So we both coped, that's good, isn't it, Celia?' and she gave me a look, a really resentful look."

"The dream of Earth," I repeated in a strangled gasp.

"You see," she approved, "that is a good sign, that you can manage to get the words out all right. No sense in repressing these things. As long as you keep the memory in its proper place and don't let it become an obsession, it's good to.... Duncan! Yoo hoo! I say, do you want me to fetch a doctor?"

"Doctor?" I echoed, slack-jawed.

"Dr Hatton might do you some good but I don't know if I could get him; there must be plenty of calls for his attention at the moment. You won't be the only one who is finding it hard to adjust to finding yourself back on Kroth. But since you're young it shouldn't...."

"I'll be all right," I said hastily. The message had sunk in, from this lady's ramblings, that everybody was in the same boat, but that some of us were taking it better than others. I loathed the idea of being one of the weaker sort. "Uh.... I'm still a bit groggy, that's all. Kroth is...."

"The world."

"Ah. Of course. Thank you, Miss Tyler. Well, I'll pop off now. Thank you for your kindness. I just need to find my way around."

"Drop in any time."

"I will. You're right, I haven't adjusted as well as most; I need all the friends I can get, but at the end of the day it's down to me to, er, adjust. Anyhow, I shall do my best."

"Goodbye for now," she said. "And welcome back to the real world."

*

The next corner of the "block" turned out to be a crossroads, a very wide crossroads in the middle of which stood a stone "island". Dominating the "island" was a structure like that of a four-branched market cross. A sign placed on top of it said, in letters big enough for me to read without going any closer, GUTHTIN - 75° NORTH.

Near to hand, on the corner next to me, stood a shop with a sign, GUTHTIN NEWSAGENT AND GENERAL STORES. I lingered in front of it, attracted by the idea of going in. For one thing it would postpone going round the corner and facing that awful dip in the sky gouged out of where the horizon ought to be. Furthermore, it made sense to buy a newspaper; it might tell me a lot. That raised the question of whether I had any money. For the first time on Kroth, I thought of looking in my pocket wallet.

Standing on the pavement outside the shop, I opened the wallet and took out a coin.

It was about the size and shape of a British pound coin. One face had two concentric circles and YEYLD engraved three times around the area close to the rim. The other face had a finely detailed picture of a fountain soaring above a city, both topped by an arc forming the name SAVALUK. Underneath the city was the coin's value: ONE TESG.

I rummaged for other coins and found some thinner ones – seven ONE MYNINU pieces, three SIX MYNINU and two EIGHTEEN MYNINU. From the most likely common multiple of these numbers I suspected that there were thirty-six myninu to the tesg, but I couldn't yet be certain. It struck me that I might learn quite a bit about this society from its coins, just as numismatists study the Roman Empire, and in my state of general shock I welcomed the thought of such scholarly discipline, its close boundaries, its defined limits.... The pictures on the smaller coins were as intriguing as the design on the one-tesg piece. One looked like a representation of a hill with rays coming out of it or spears stabbing down at it, I wasn't sure which. Another portrayed a city built on a thirty-degree slope, with a huge fortress wall facing the downward side. Then I realized that in playing guessing games with all this I was merely finding an excuse for inaction. It wasn't a matter of looking for clues about a vanished culture; I was in the midst of a living society. Surely I could pluck up the courage to enter a shop. My poor staggered self could manage that much.

A bell klinged as I pushed open the door and went in. There was no one behind the counter. I gazed at the news-rack. On its top shelf was printed SAVALUK TIMES, and on the lower shelf GUTHTIN GAZETTE, but both shelves were empty.

The sound of footsteps brought my glance back to the counter behind which there now appeared a dumpy, slab-cheeked woman in her sixties. This sight gave me the further shock of meeting someone I actually knew. *"Mrs Nott!"*

"How may I help you?" she said, frigidly. The old sourpuss gave absolutely no sign of recognizing me, but there was nothing spooky about this: it was just the way she had always behaved on Earth. She ran the corner shop in my part of Crickham and for years I had been a regular customer for her tinned groceries, light-bulbs and other convenience items and never had she given me a greeting or a smile. Her one role in the scheme of things, as far as I could ever tell, was to fill a vacancy for Grumpy Old Woman. So although, actually, I was glad to see her, I could not bring myself to say so.

"Er.... papers all sold out?" I ventured.

This turned out to be the wrong thing to say.

"Of course they aren't 'sold out'," she spluttered with typical contempt. "None were delivered! Did you imagine they'd be able to put out an edition *today?*" Her tone made it clear that I must be the stupidest dolt who ever lived.

Mrs Nott's hostility didn't bother me too much; in fact I would have felt more uneasy if she had changed her personality so as to be nice to me. Still, better not fan the flames of her ire. I therefore decided not to attempt any probing remarks about the big awakening; rather I would profit from Miss

Tyler's experience with her neighbour Celia. So instead of saying something like, "Bad night, wasn't it, Mrs Nott?" or "Bit of a shock to say goodbye to Earth, wasn't it, Mrs Nott?", I beat a retreat from the shop.

Now, if I was to keep to my idea of going round the block, it was time to face the down-slope stretch. Or if I wasn't going to do it, now was the time to chicken out. Except that there wasn't much point in chickening out unless I was prepared to continue up-slope forever, in which case I would never get back to my house, and would it not be rather silly to make myself homeless in addition to my other problems? Grimly I muttered, "What goes up must come down," and rounded the corner.

From then on, along that stretch of pavement, I kept my eyes down, way down, and doubtless I must have looked a funny sight as I tottered along. The few other pedestrians seemed to take no notice of my difficulties. They knew, and I knew that they knew, of the great change from Earth to Kroth, and they doubtless understood, as Miss Tyler did, that it hit some people harder than others; at any rate they let me alone to work things out in my own way. Alternatively perhaps they just thought I was drunk.

Once or twice, since I could not always prevent my glance from straying forward, I did glimpse that awful sagging horizon, or rather – since you can't really call it a horizon if it's not horizontal - the bite taken out of where the horizon ought to have been. When this happened I squeezed my eyes tight shut for several moments. I couldn't take it, even though I did my best to argue myself out of the terror by comparing it with going on a space-walk. I had always loved the idea of being an astronaut, hadn't I? And you're even more surrounded by infinity when out in space, aren't you? So where's the difficulty? No use – the argument didn't work – my terror was linked with ground and sky rather than with sky alone. Nor was I any more successful in parcelling it all up with some science-fictional catch-phrase, though part of my mind kept chattering on about alternate dimensions and what not. It all came back to the soft thud of my shoes on that sloping pavement. And the need to concentrate, with bowed head, to avoid the piercing blue stare of infinity ahead of me. And so all my efforts at making sense died away.

At length I rounded the third corner and now the down-slope was on my right, hidden for the most part by houses. I could breathe easily again except when I passed the open space of a school playground.

Now the fourth corner – left turn again – up-slope once more – and I could hope I was plodding back towards my house. Having successfully got this far, I could dare to admit that there was delight as well as terror in this adventure. Whatever the reason behind it all, at least I could never complain that real life was humdrum. However, my stress-avoidance training reminded me not to get carried away. Play it cool! Walk that tightrope between excitement and fear!

Was it really my house up ahead? Wow, I had done it! I had got round the block. My own little achievement.

I noticed something else. The bungalow just before mine had its front door open. As I came further up, to the point where I had a full view of both my down-slope neighbour's house and mine, dream-logic reared up and whispered to me a comparison between these two houses and the two rooms Vic had booked at the Rolvenden Hotel, London, Earth. One room for him and one room for me. So, here, one house for him and one house for me? The pair of hotel rooms and the pair of bungalows might somehow be reflections, counterparts, of one another!

In which case Uncle Vic and Aunt Reen might be in that next-door bungalow. They might be there at this very moment.

Looked at in one way, it was a daft hope. On the other hand if did turn out to be true, what a boon it would be to be reunited with real family! Besides, if anyone could be expected to explain what had happened, Vic was surely the one. And if I wasn't going to continue forever being forced to accept the crazy reality-flip from Earth to Kroth without any reason given for it, I had better find him, or someone like him. I could ask Miss Tyler, of course, but I feared to press the issue with her, and besides she probably didn't have Vic's extra helping of brains.

*

I stood in the doorway and knocked. No answer. I called out, "Excuse me-e-e!" No answer. I advanced into the hallway and knocked again, this time on the lounge door which was also wide open. "Excuse me-e-e! Hallo-o-o!" Borrowing some courage from somewhere I walked into the lounge.

Uncle Vic was lying on the divan.

It was obvious at a glance that he was not merely resting. He lay untidily as if he had collapsed or been pushed down; his face was frozen into an expression of slack dismay, his eyes wide open.

"No!" I cried out fiercely, rushing forward. *Don't you dare be dead. Don't you dare.* I was right to clamp denial onto my feelings of horror, for when I examined him closely I saw that he was, after all, breathing.

Had he been coshed or mugged by some intruder? Unlikely, I thought. I doubted it was that sort of neighbourhood. If it were, my uncle would have had the sense to fasten the door. My guess, rather, was that when he had woken in this new reality he had immediately flung the door open and found that he could not face what he saw. His greater intelligence could well have made him more open to the truth, and therefore more vulnerable to it, than I was.

I could picture him staggering back and collapsing on the divan, his consciousness overwhelmed by the shock. Anyhow, rather than stand around playing guessing games, my duty was to get help. Where was the phone? Come to think of it, what use would a phone be to me? I knew nothing about the emergency services in this dimension. What I needed was people. Helpful people. People who weren't like me; people who had woken properly, who had fully reverted to their identity as Krothans, rather than being stuck, as I was, with my memories of "the dream of Earth".

Try next door. I ran out and down the path and turned right to the next bungalow down-slope. I ran up its path and knocked loudly and was about to knock again when I heard a woman's voice inside:

"Someone at the door, Elaine!"

My heart bounded to the joyful conclusion that this was dream logic working again, that the people I cared most about were thronging around me due to some kind of gravitational pull exerted by the emotions, and that therefore the name couldn't be coincidence: it had to be *the* Elaine!

The door opened and she stood there, tall and beautiful. Too tall and too blandly beautiful. My heart sank: this wasn't Elaine Dering. It was Elaine Swinton.

So much for dream-logic. The vapid, colourless, toothpaste-ad Elaine stood there like a mere pun on the girl I had hoped to see.

But at least it was someone I knew, if only by name and sight. And she certainly was a magnificent sight. From sleeveless white blouse and short tweed skirt her pale limbs radiated elegance; her face was lovely as ever despite its habitual blank look.

"Hello, Duncan," she said with a trace of a frown. "What's up?"

"Sorry I knocked so loud. Look, it's my uncle – I need help for him – he's been taken ill – can you help me get a doctor?"

"Come in." I followed her into her lounge. Her mother lay on a couch with her head propped up by cushions; she looked wan and feeble, and for a moment I wondered if the "end of the dream" had got to her in the way it had got to Vic. But no; she looked "normally" ill.

E.S. was speaking into the phone. Then she turned to me. "You're in luck; Dr Hatton is available. You can speak to him."

"Thanks." I took the receiver. "Doctor?"

"What can I do for you?" said a calm, reassuring male voice.

"I need you to come and see my uncle. He's collapsed."

"The address?"

I turned to E.S. "What's the name of this road, Elaine? And the number?"

She raised her brows only slightly at this imbecile question.

"Kennan Road. We're at number 19, Mr Chandler is at 21, and you're living at number 23."

"21 Kennan Road," I said to the doctor. "Can you come? It's worrying. My uncle's eyes are open and staring but he's not conscious."

"Is it a dream case?" the doctor asked. I guessed what he meant.

"Yes, I'd say it looks very much like a serious dream case."

"I'll be there in a few minutes." *Click.*

I thanked E.S. and her mother, and got up to go. E.S. said, "Hang on a moment. Mother, I'm going to see how Mr Chandler is."

"All right, dear. I hope he gets well."

"Elaine," I said as we went out, "I really appreciate your support."

"That's all right," she shrugged. "It's not much trouble. It shouldn't be long to wait."

We entered Vic's house, pulled up chairs and sat by the divan to keep watch on him till the doctor arrived. The conversation during those few minutes did not sparkle. E.S. sat with her hands in her lap and a patient expression on her face.

"How is your mother, Elaine?" I asked politely.

"She hasn't been well for some time, but considering she's so weak, she coped with last night quite well."

As did you, I thought to myself. *What an advantage it must be to have a mind like yours. The reality of Earth melts away in a single night and you remain quite unruffled, not even sufficiently impressed to give it more than a glancing mention. Talk about stress-avoidance! You're an admirable clod, Elaine Swinton. Perhaps I ought to become one too.*

"I found it rather a shock," I said dryly.

She nodded. "I thought you didn't look so good, Duncan. It wouldn't do you any harm to have a word with Doc Hatton on your own account."

"Is he good?"

"Certainly he is. He's done a lot for mother. Our village is lucky to have him. Ah! This must be him."

"Come in!" I shouted.

The doctor was a gently dignified man in a big flappy jacket adorned with biros; his confident voice and manner inspired trust from the moment that he bustled in. After an examination in which he tapped Vic lightly on the forehead, looked in his mouth and made passes over his eyes, he said: "Your uncle's condition is not dangerous, but it is serious in the sense that it needs to be seen to by the experts. He's in deep post-terrestrial fugue and I can't bring him out of it here. I have to refer such cases to Savaluk."

"Who, what or where is Savaluk?" I asked, edgily. "Oh, sorry – " for I had just remembered the name of the newspaper. "Savaluk is a place."

Doc Hatton looked at me in surprise that turned to quiet pity. "Ah, so you're a case too." He smiled, kindly. "Yes, Savaluk is a place."

"Er, where is it?"

"You really don't know, do you?" Doc Hatton appraised me with professional interest.

"No, I don't!"

"It's at the North Pole. You can't miss it – the capital of the civilized world."

"Oh," I said in a small voice, not only miserable at my ignorance, but awe-struck at the hefty parcel of mind-boggling ideas which I would have to open and try on for size. For instance I had just learned that there was a Pole to this world, so the Slope didn't go on for ever, not towards the North anyhow, and what other huge things must I learn? I looked pleadingly at the doctor as the silence lengthened. "Well, I didn't know," I said.

"No, you didn't, did you? But don't fret about it and don't sound so despondent. If your memories of Earth are strong enough to *prevent* you from recovering your knowledge of Kroth, well then, um...."

"Then it shows I'm retarded?" I interrupted, bitterly.

"No, it shows that you must have a special reason of your own to go in for this clinging to one set of data and rejection of the other. Tell me, have you recently undergone any – ah – particular therapy?"

I thought of my clever-clever techniques.

"I made a big thing of stress-avoidance," I said. "Too big. It's led me to reject the real world." What an idiot I felt, confessing this stuff within Elaine Swinton's hearing!

"Interesting, most interesting," said the doctor. "You have a problem; but you can learn to get round it. In fact you may find your condition to be in some ways an asset. People are going to value someone with a really clear, sharp, well-preserved set of Earth memories. You'll get a lot of support, you'll see. And with regard to your uncle, no decent person will refuse help to a fugue case.... You two will lack for nothing on your journey to Savaluk."

"How far is it, Doctor?"

"Just over a thousand miles."

"What about the practical arrangements?"

"If you're wondering about an ambulance service, forget it – the Government can only afford that for cases where the illness is life-threatening. But transport shouldn't be a problem. Stand by the Royal Road and you'll hitch a lift pretty soon. The Royal Road," he added before I could ask, "is the main North-South road. Go West for a couple of miles and you'll strike it; no trouble."

"But how will I get Uncle there? He can't walk; he can't even sit up."

Doc leaned over and gave Uncle's head a push, so that it lolled on his neck.

"Nah. He won't stay like this for long. Wait a couple of hours and I guarantee he'll be able to walk, and to look after himself to a limited extent - you won't have to nursemaid him round the house, though you'll certainly have to guide his steps outside. I suggest you set off tomorrow morning. I'll write you a note for the Royal Fountain Hospital at Savaluk."

"But I'd better move in here for tonight, I suppose."

Doc Halliday shook his head. "You'll see that won't be necessary." He straightened, scribbled some words on a pad, tore the sheet off and gave it to me. "I must be off. As you can imagine, I have plenty of other patients today! Have a good journey and don't worry. Take it from me – you'll get help, support, guidance everywhere you go."

"Well, thanks for coming, doctor."

He went, and Elaine Swinton also got up to go. "So that's all right," she said; "and I'll be getting back now." Placidly as ever, her neighbourly duty done, she bade me farewell and glided off.

I waited for the doctor's prediction to come true. Mostly I sat in the lounge; occasionally I went from room to room. Vic apparently lived alone; I saw no sign that Reen inhabited the house. I wondered if in this world she had gone back to the Isle of Man like she wanted to do. Or rather, to some equivalent. Ridiculous; there couldn't be any islands, couldn't be any seas, on the Slope.... I tried to keep my wandering thoughts in order as I looked around for clues about this world of Kroth. I saw no radio or TV. I did find an old newspaper in the bin; I shook the potato peelings off it and spread it out on the kitchen board. The *Savaluk Times* turned out to be quite frustrating. Suggestive though its stories were, without a background knowledge of the culture and geography I could not make much sense of them. For example:

GALAST'S BLUFF CALLED

Ninghestund, .34:

The Galast of Hanamao in a speech yesterday declared he would consider the option of a tax strike if the empty seats in Parliament were not filled. A member of the audience, Li Zang, then asked him if that meant that the Galast would himself be willing to lead an expedition to Hudgung. The Galast replied, amid widespread laughter, that he was needed at home.

TV IN EVERY TOWN BY .00

Savaluk, .35:

A Government spokesman affirmed that the communications target for the dechemeron would be reached provided that no hitch developed in the Forty North Hydro Project. "We must remind the public that hydro power increases with the cosine of latitude, and that therefore the goal of 'A TV in every town hall' is dependent upon good relations with the Tribes of Forty. If they demand protection against the South, our commitment becomes open-ended."

All as clear as mud. And the person whom I most relied on to explain things was in a state of "fugue".

Daylight began to fade as evening drew on. I switched on the light – normal electric light. Performing this action, it came to me most clearly that a large part of the trouble with this new life was not its strangeness but its areas of persistent normality. I could have seen some sense in being pitched into a totally alien dimension, or into a human culture that had developed in its own completely separate direction, but what was I to make of Kroth with its impossible mixture of the familiar and the strange?

Whatever the answer was, I would not find it covered by my reading of science fiction. SF stood me in good stead insofar as it had given me a general elasticity of mind, but none of its standard props (alternate time-tracks, parallel universes, artificial dream-tests) were any good at providing me with an explanation of this particular set-up. I *might* have believed in any of them – were it not for the Slope.

I was thinking in circles. I wished something would happen. Something did – Uncle Vic stirred.

I stood up and called his name but he did not answer, nor did he so much as glance in my direction. Slowly he levered himself up and managed to stand, and then, shuffling like a zombie, made for the bathroom.

Minutes later I heard the toilet flush and then the tap run and then he appeared again, making for the kitchen. While I watched, he put the kettle on and with sure and careful movements began to make preparations for a snack.

There was a loud, confident knock on the front door.

I went to open and saw a very tall fellow standing casual and loose-limbed in a dark green sweater and corduroys. His face, tanned and bearded, was of a man about forty. He said, "Just thought I'd pop round and see if things are still all right. Elaine told me the doctor had been to see Vic."

"You're her father? You're Mr Swinton?"

"Yes, Duncan."

"Nice of you to come," I forced myself to say, squirming more than ever at my lack of Krothan memory. "Do come in and see for yourself how he is."

We went into the kitchen-diner and watched Vic tuck into a sandwich.

"He's like a sleepwalker," I remarked, "which I suppose is not so bad – at least, on that level he seems to know what he's doing. Doc Hatton says it's safe to leave him for the night."

"Then it must be so," said Mr Swinton. He then turned to look me in the eye, and in a tone that was pleasantly self-assured he added: "I'd say that *you* are the one in the more difficult position. You're still stuck in the Earth dream, so I hear."

"I suppose I am. That is – I'm not sure what to say – I mean, I know *this* is real, but...."

"But you don't remember any of it."

"No. And why must I alone lack memory?" I wasn't being honest here; I knew the answer to my own question – I had brought it on myself. Stress-avoidance had led in my case to world-avoidance and to the state of inadequacy which I now suffered.

Mr Swinton answered, "Different people react in all sorts of ways for all sorts of reasons. I managed all right, but then I'm a businessman. Elaine's all right, but then, well, she's Elaine." He smiled. "She always knew what she wanted."

"Lucky girl," I said. "What does she want?"

"To be a geologist," he said. I was so astonished (and skeptical) that I didn't respond to this at all. He went on, "And do you know what you want, Duncan?"

"To get out of this mental fog," I promptly replied. "To find my way. Uncle Vic used to tease me about teenagers; about how they all want to defy authority by being different, and how at the same time they want to do it by being the same as every other teenager. Well, I don't care about being different; I'm not defying anybody; I'm on the conformist side! I want to belong."

Wow, I thought, that was quite a speech by me. Mr Swinton was the sort to induce one to confide.

He replied: "Looking at it from your point of view – you who know virtually nothing of Kroth – let me ask you this: how long would you say it should reasonably take, to get to know a world?"

I thought about it and then grinned sheepishly. "I suppose I am being a bit impatient."

He nodded, his point made. "Things will sort themselves out." He turned to go. "Drop round for dinner sometime...."

"Thanks, Mr Swinton."

"And a game of chess too. I'll miss our games, while you're off on your jaunt to Savaluk."

Hastily, to get his opinion, I remarked: "Doc Hatton expects Uncle and me to hitch a ride there."

"Should be no problem. Well, I'll leave you to it."

He went, and I was alone again – except for my zombie-like relative, who, after his brief supper, went off to bed. I stuck around for another half hour or so in the empty lounge, recalling all the voices – Miss Tyler's, Doc Hatton's, Mr Swinton's – who had told me not to worry and that things would sort themselves out. Then I drew the curtains of the lounge, and went to the front door. There was no key. I could not lock up behind me. Evidently this was a very safe neighbourhood. Another reason not to worry. I recalled the voices again, the reassuring voices of people I respected. But the first thing I saw as I stepped outside made me forget all reassurance.

It was a violet light winking at me from across the road. It shone between a chimney pot and a poplar tree. At first I took it to be artificial; a tiny bright lamp on a mast, perhaps. Then from its pointed brilliance I realized it was a star, but one that outshone even the planet Venus as seen from Earth, and its beauty prompted me to look for more, to crane my neck and admire, for the whole sky was ablaze with unfamiliar stars. All of them were telling me, by their brightness and colours and the patterns they made, that not only my old world but my old cosmos was something I must unlearn.

Sighing, with contradictory feelings of awe and complaint, I turned and plodded up the path to my house, went in, had a quick supper and went to bed. I had maybe seven hours' sleep, not too bad a total but it was punctuated – inevitably – by bouts of restlessness in which my imagination grated and churned like a malfunctioning cement-mixer. The hour came when I awoke and knew I was awake for keeps, so although it was still dark I got up and got dressed. I wanted to face that sky again. I wanted to see those stars again and somehow make friends with them in my mind; be reconciled with the universe in a way that was peaceful and certain. Stars, after all, are pure, clean things, symbolising all that is peaceful and beautiful and holy. You can't be led into nightmare by stars.

I stepped out onto the porch and immediately knew I had taken on too much. For there it was again, that violet star, low in the sky across the road, between that chimney pot and that poplar tree. This, I knew, could not be right. It could not be right but it was. *And all the other stars in the sky are likewise in the same position, though most of the night has passed.*

There was no end to un-learning.

The conclusion was inescapable.

This world does not turn.

5: Northward

In the cheerful light of the morning sun I guided Vic's steps down his path and through his gate. He co-operated like an obedient child. The rucksack I had packed for him, he had shouldered without complaint when he saw me put on mine, though I could not tell how much he understood what we were doing.

Still holding his left arm, as though I were helping a half-blind old man, I steered him to the left along the pavement. With my other hand I waved to a score of well-wishers who had gathered to see us off, for the word had spread around the village that my uncle and I were off to Savaluk. Although many (such as Mr Swinton) were not present because they had gone off to work, or had duties or illnesses that kept them, those who could had turned up, and it seemed quite a crowd. I didn't feel up to making a speech but with many nods and thank-yous I expressed my appreciation as well as I could.

They accompanied us up to the corner where Miss Tyler lived, then to the left as far as the crossroads. Traversing, we continued west, the crowd dispersing now, leaving us alone.

Soon we reached a point where Guthtin Village petered out into the fields and hedgerows of what might (but for the relentless Slope) have been a pleasant English country scene.

If someone had offered us a lift as far as the Great Royal Road I would have accepted, yet I was just as glad that no one had. I wanted to start the day with some exercise in the sunshine and the open air, especially as I knew that once we had reached the Road and faced north there would be less occasion for walking; for no matter how much time we were allowed it was out of the question to attempt our journey on foot up a continuous fifteen-degree Slope. When we reached that northward road, we would have to hitch.

The sky was an absolutely cloudless blue, but the land wasn't dry. I could smell moist freshness; the fields glistened as if after a shower. Partly through the weird human ability to get used to just about anything, I found I could get round the awful fact of the tilted world, and just enjoy the walk, most of the time. Our lateral westward road was, of course, banked on its south side; it had to be. And this helped. If I looked ahead rather than to left or right, I could pretend I was hiking a level route across the flank of some slope in the Chilterns or on the Downs.

But for me the really important strategy, inspired by the wise words of Mr Swinton, was to *postpone judgement.* In order to keep terror and vertigo from seizing hold I must *live without knowing and without understanding.*

In other words: *let things jolly well BE.*

This decision was so liberating! Reality – let it be! It would certainly continue its merry way whether I understood it or not. Maybe in good time I might figure it out, or I might not; but there was absolutely no sense in wearing myself out over the mystery. For it wasn't as though I were on some utterly alien planet on which a newcomer's first mistake is likely to be his last. Here there was some kindness, some tolerant leeway for the ignorant beginner.

And so what if this world didn't rotate, so what if the Sun wanted to orbit the world instead, so what if all the astronomy I had ever learned was wrong, and Copernicus had been wasting his time – not my fault! Don't blame me! I'm not the Manager, thank heavens!

I could have skipped for joy, except that I was holding onto Vic's arm, and his presence reminded me: the idea of this mission to Savaluk was to get help for him. And supposing it was successful, he would wake, properly wake, and then.... Knowing Vic, I had the vague but powerful suspicion that I ought to enjoy my ignorance while I could.

*

We came upon the Great Royal Road quite suddenly, for where we were it ran along a cutting that concealed it from ground level until close approach. Our own side-road continued over it via a bridge. We went as far as the middle of this bridge, from which I gazed along the upward sweep of a thoroughfare that seemed to be about the width of a dual carriageway on Earth. At the present moment, as my eyes followed its slightly wavering course up to the northern limit of vision, I could not hear or see any traffic, though I had been told that the GRR was the main north-south artery of the Krothan economy.

In the silence we turned back and descended a grassy embankment to sit on one of many benches by the roadside and wait for a lift. The existence of these benches, half a dozen of them, suggested hitch-hiking was a popular idea, since I couldn't see any other reason why people would want to sit at this precise spot, though so far this morning we were the only ones here. Similar empty benches stood on the other side of the road. I had noticed that vehicles drove on the right, so I knew we were waiting on the correct side for northbound traffic.

So as to be able to spot a likely lift in good time as it came towards us, I had to keep watch on the road South, and this I did not like. Carefully shading my eyes with my hand, so as to shield them from that sagging blue infinity fifteen degrees below where the horizon ought to be, I limited my sight to the road-surface itself.

Minutes passed; still no traffic. Out of curiosity I also sometimes turned to look the other way but I found that there was a disadvantage in staring North, too. It wasn't quite as disturbing as the sag South; nevertheless the bulking continuousness of the upward Slope was oppressive if you allowed the thought of it to catch hold.

Then came the first test of my "don't-ask, let-be" attitude.

A dot appeared under the next bridge northwards, about two miles off. I watched it grow and gradually resolve itself into a car. No, two cars, one very close behind the other. I heard no sound of engines – of course, come to think of it, they could just roll down the Slope under gravity, saving their petrol for the return journey! I waved as they rolled past me. The lead driver, an ordinary-looking man who might have been an accountant on his way to work, waved back. Then a couple of minutes later came more cars, but this time they came up from the South, and of course *their* motors were running (doubtless in low gear!). Again it was two cars in close formation. They were both full of passengers so I was not surprised that they did not stop. But after this had happened several more times, I began to wonder: why always in pairs? I could not help but think it odd that I had not so far seen a single solitary car.

Back in the village it had been different; there I had seen some lone vehicles, but out here on the great north-south avenue – never alone, always in pairs. Often one of the cars was towed.

It was one of these tow-pairs, finally, who stopped for us. The driver, a smallish man in a grey suit and tie, had no passengers. I nudged Vic into the back seat and got into the front beside the driver.

"And where are you headed?"

He spoke with a Welsh accent. Fine, I thought, so Welshness exists in this world; let it. Why not?

"To Savaluk, to the Royal Fountain Hospital."

"Quite a distance! Is it your father that is unwell?"

"My uncle. He has a case of fugue...."

"Ah! That is special! Worth the journey, then."

I could not quite get the tone of this. Not only courtesy, respect and genuine concern but also a kind of *admiration* for Vic's type of illness. I had also noted this attitude in those who had bidden us goodbye a short while before.

"So I hope. The doctor, he referred me...."

The man nodded, "You will see, in Savaluk, they will cure him. I hope you were not waiting long?" I assured him we had not been waiting long. "That is a good sign," he continued. "Indeed the traffic is getting back to normal, after The Night Before Last. The disruption was worse in bigger towns and worst of all in the City. Where I live, in Cylchcoch, things stayed mostly quiet, but there were three cases of fugue, quite a lot for a small village." Again, something in the tone I didn't understand: a touch of pride.

Now for my little experimental manoeuvre:

"I have not come through undamaged myself," I admitted. "I lack my Krothan identity. I remember only Earth."

I said it in a casual tone but I had carefully thought out the pros and cons of it and had decided that by and large it would be easiest if I got into the habit of confessing my ignorance, so that people knew where I stood. That way they would not expect of me things which I could not know or do.

"Is that so? You remember only Earth! That means, you remember it properly? Like it was real?"

"That's it."

"So! I have heard on the town-hall news, that there are people who can do that. Not many. It is a wonderful gift, though I can see it must lead to problems."

"The big problem," I said just a trifle dryly, "is that I don't have the right mind for where I actually am."

"Then you are doing the right thing in going to Savaluk," the driver said, reinforcing the notion that Savaluk was where things got sorted out. I could have questioned him further on this point, but the trouble with asking questions is you sometimes get answers, and then you have to absorb and perhaps act upon the answers. I didn't want to push things.

After a minute or two of thoughtful silence he mused softly: “Earth is the world that is real for you – fancy that.... I remember a valley in Pembrokeshire.... And what county was yours?”

“Hertfordshire.”

He shook his head in wonder. “For me, my Earth home is only a vague dream, like an imagined colour. Not like your recollections, seemingly.”

“Mine are sharp, all right,” I agreed, though for the first time I began to wonder how long they would remain so. And how would I feel if and when my Earth memories went blurry, and Kroth became my familiar world? Overall would I lose, or gain? I'd gain a lot of ease and convenience and knowledge, but I'd lose the sense of adventure that comes from being in a new world of complete surprise. I'd lose a past that seemed to be an essential component of my identity, but I'd also lose the sense of loss itself, which might well turn out to be a relief.... not that I yet suffered much from nostalgia; the adventure I was in was all too new and absorbed my whole attention; but when I considered the case of the driver of this car and his no doubt beautiful Pembrokeshire valley, vanished now in the limbo of the never-was, I reckoned he was probably better off *not* having memories that were too clear.

Enough of this. I was supposed to be “letting-be”. As the car droned up the Slope I sat back in silence for a while, with my head on the headrest, staring north at the line where sky met land, and seeking to trick myself into viewing it as a normal horizon.

The driver's voice recaptured my attention.

“By the way, I shall have to drop you off at the turning to Sisk. That is as far as I go on the Royal Road. You will soon find another northward car. And you will be about fifty miles closer to your goal.”

But as it turned out we had to stop sooner than that.

The motor suddenly coughed, burped, stuttered for half a minute while the driver brought the car and its towed twin onto the grass verge, and then conked out.

Instead of fishing out a mobile phone and contacting a breakdown service, the driver sighed: “Here we go. Time to change round.” He got out and so did I, ready to lend a hand as I realized what he intended to do.

It was simply a matter of switching cars. I didn't ask what was supposed to happen if the other car conked out as well. My current grand theory of everything said: in any society, stuff happens, and other stuff evolves to deal with it. Call that Wemyss' First Law. From it is derived Wemyss' Second

Law, which states that Duncan Wemyss doesn't need to bother his head about stuff that's way above it.

So I just helped to push the back car to the front position and then the driver re-fixed the towline and I got Vic into what was now the front car (I preferred not to leave him in the back one), and we set off again.

About ten minutes later the driver let us off at the Sisk junction.

*

Traffic was heavier by this time, but we still had a wait of about half an hour before the next lift. I dare say it would have helped if Vic had looked more obviously ill, instead of just looking sleepy. And if I had thought to bring a placard with "FUGUE CASE" written on it, then we might have got really quick results.

It must have been the boring, frustrating side of hitch-hiking that triggered in me a spell of total disbelief in the entire scene. I caught myself thinking, "I'll need warm clothes if we get much higher up this mountain" – as though it *were* a mountain and not a tilt of the world itself. Likewise I caught myself assuming that somewhere far to the south the slope must level out into a plain, much too far down for me to see, but still firmly there somewhere beyond the blueness. But I had the sense to knock these thoughts away. Dalliance with delusion would only set me up for a stressful awakening later on. *You're doing all right. You've made a good start. You know what to do. Accept the great change. No point in fooling yourself. There's no going back.*

The chug-chug of a labouring motor alerted me that something bigger than usual was ascending from the South. It was a convoy of three long lorry-sized vans. On their sides, in dramatically oblique lettering were the words:

SAITTA – BELLINI DROGHE NATURALI

I had plenty of time to note this as the convoy was decelerating. As they slowed to a stop I mis-read the situation: I assumed this was a breakdown. The lead van, I thought, would now have to be towed, so I expected that one of the others would chug round to the front to do the towing. But this did not happen. Instead, to my great surprise, a youngster of about twenty poked his head out of the window and said, *"Vuoi passaggio?* Want a lift?" This great convoy had stopped for us!

"*Grazie!*" I nodded vigorously, making use of one of the few Italian words I knew. A long-distance outfit – which the size of it must surely indicate – was just what I needed. "*Siamo per* Savaluk! Royal Fountain

Hospital! *Mio zio* – fugue!"

The man turned his head and spoke to someone in Italian. I made out the words, *"Si, si, ma non direttamente,"* and then this young fellow turned back to me and said, "We are going to Savaluk but not directly. We shall probably take two days. You might find someone else who gets you there in one day, but maybe not. It is for you to decide."

I decided that a sure thing was better than more waiting. "I will go with you, thanks again, *grazie molto*."

A hum – a door slid open in the mid-section of the great vehicle. I nudged Vic and we approached this opening. A typically fine-looking Italian who looked to be in his forties appeared in it and said, "*Ciao.* Make yourselves comfortable. I am Fabrizio Saitta. You said 'fugue'."

"Yes, *signore*."

"I guessed it." He paused, as if weighing the options. "Well," he said, "it is important, but I cannot go any faster. However I can assure you this *furgone* is reliable. It has four engines, any one of which can pull the entire convoy at need. And the same is true of the others." He spoke with quiet pride. "I hope what I do for your uncle is good enough."

I assured him it was.

The middle bulge of the vehicle turned out to be wider than I had thought. Judging by the spacious interior it must have spread almost all the way across one half of the road. A corridor ran down one side and the other side had compartments like those of a sleeper train, as well as storage for cargo. Vic and I were settled in the most forward of these living-compartments, which were provided not only with couches and tables but also with cupboards well stocked with food and drink.

The hours passed, the day wore on and I greatly enjoyed the ride, which became especially interesting when the convoy left the main road to make deliveries of herbs and tinctures amongst the villages and small towns that lay scattered to either side. Vic and I were treated to the hospitality of the Italians, who seemed pleased to feed us well; nothing was too good for *un malato speciale* like Vic, and when they learned of my memory lack they included me to some extent in that category of "special ill person".

During our breaks, Fabrizio was keen to hear me talk of Earth. I would have preferred not to – but I couldn't very well refuse. After all, Vic and I were being looked after so well that I could just sit back and regard the whole journey as "in the bag". So I obliged my host's curiosity and rambled on about my Earthly home, my school, my holidays.... *holidays.* That was a mistake. All of a sudden he asked whether I had been to Italy.

"Uh, yes," I said, rattled.

"*Il bel paese,*" he remarked with a dreamy smile.

"*Uno stato d'anima,*" his son's voice called out, in a tone of impatient rebuke, from another compartment.

"Ah, yes, a state of mind, as Ugo reminds me," Fabrizio mused with a tinge of wry regret.

Nervously I studied the face of my questioner while my mind raced in a whirl of awkward questions.

As with the Welshman, so with this Italian, I couldn't see how his country, with its well-defined coastline, could ever have existed in this sloping world, where no sea could exist, and which obviously was not a mere alternate or parallel Earth. In fact I doubted that it was even a planet in the normal sense. This being the case, what was I to make of the presence of Earth nationalities in such a physically alien dimension? If Englishness had been the only one, I could have dismissed it as some kind of egocentric illusion, a sort of mentally convenient translation, like the way everyone in the Galaxy speaks English in episodes of *Dr Who*; but my recent encounters ruled out that explanation. Mad though it seemed, Earth nationalities quite obviously did exist on Kroth. Again I faced that immense underlying problem: the mixture of the familiar with the strange. The standard SF explanation – that over the centuries people from various countries must have blundered into Kroth via trans-dimensional gateways or thin spots in the continuum – simply didn't fit, for only just a couple of days ago, prior to The Night Before Last, we were *all* in the "dream of Earth"....

All this flashed through my mind in a lot less time than it takes to express in words. I didn't dwell on it. There's nothing more stressful than a lurking fact that does not fit, nothing more fearsome than a truth on the prowl. So I shelved the problem, as usual, by accepting things, by remembering Mr Swinton's point that it would be unreasonable to expect me to understand what's what at this early stage. But I didn't like talking about Italy to Fabrizio.

During our delivery stops I took Vic out to stretch his legs, and because I too wanted a walk; and when I did so the bystanders would congregate to show a curious and respectful regard for my silent uncle. Sometimes one of them would touch his sleeve and say, "We have a person like this, too," or "We sent so-and-so to Savaluk," but "not as good as he, though". I was starting to wonder if some kind of superstition was at work.

Occasionally, scarier moments occurred. These happened when some neglected aspect of the scene, some visual fact which had capered for hours in front of my eyes yelling in vain for my attention, belatedly clicked.

I experienced this kind of shock in one small town while I was looking at the people in the street, where some of the faces were African. Such had also been the case in the previous two or three towns, but here, suddenly, I twigged that the Africans of Kroth were not black! Neither were they white, and neither were the "whites" white! It crashed upon my consciousness that everyone whom I had seen so far in this world was the same uniform grey of skin, myself included. Race existed – but without variation in colour.

An inconsequential fact in itself, yet frightening because of the way I had ignored it for so many hours. What else might be about to spring into obviousness?

Evening was drawing on when I suffered the next jolt.

This time my stupidity, or rather my emergence from it, really made me shiver. I knew by now that we must have travelled a sizeable proportion of our journey north. We came to the outskirts of a sizeable town, where a sign stood that proclaimed:

SWURK – 80° NORTH

It was a quiet, pleasant enough place, nothing special, with dignified stone and brick buildings one to three storeys high. We parked in a commercial district of everyday dinginess, in the banked-up levelled ground of a bus station. It was getting late but business wasn't over; we had a fairly heavy delivery to make in Swurk.

I helped Fabrizio and Ugo and men from the other vans with their unloading. Then while they spoke to their customers I strolled off, alone, out of the levelled area and back onto the through road. Something was nagging at my mind and I wanted to face it without anyone seeing the effect it had on me.

Then – it hit me: *The Slope was not what it was.* Gradually over the hours it had been getting more gentle, and now that my awareness had suddenly caught up with what was going on, I experienced that unbalancing let-down you get when you miss a step and tread on empty air, except that here the shock was world-sized: for it wasn't just what I knew, it was the *reason* I knew. The Slope had decreased from 15 degrees to 10 degrees exactly. How did I know this? 80 degrees North, the sign had said. Therefore we were 10 degrees south of the Pole. That, you idiot (I sneered at myself) is why the slope is 10 degrees. *And at the Pole itself the Slope will be no more.*

Because I would then be on top of the world.

So that was it. *You are living in a universe with an absolute up and down. This ought to have been obvious from your first hour on Kroth.*

I held onto a lamp post and closed my eyes and drew ragged breath.

I was a mite on the surface of an enormous ball. North was *up*, South was *down*, not only on maps, but for real. As I crept up the side, with every mile the land would get more level, more like what I craved as normal land, and in another.... let me see.... in another six or seven hundred miles it would be quite flat.

Certainly, flatness was something to look forward to, but all the comfort in this idea was obliterated by my grim understanding of what must happen in the *other* direction.

Worse than an eternal Slope, southward must run an *increasing* Slope.

Steeper and steeper until....

Aspects of a frightful picture rose to mind; I hacked at the images, I hurled them off their scaling ladders, and even as I hewed and smote in defence of my sanity I also had to smooth my face so as not to look too sick when I presented myself back at the van.

I must get used to standing on a world, the size and shape of Earth, which one might *fall off*.

I won the battle against panic because I was able to snatch at a saving thought:

Bigness. World big enough, yes, yes. Not only would I find Kroth to be flat at the Pole, it would surely give the impression, in that region, of being flat everywhere. In a circle maybe a couple of hundred miles across the gradient would be unnoticeable and it would be possible to pretend on a gut level that I was somewhere on Earth. There was my haven, provided that I could reach it safely. Maybe I would be allowed to settle, make a life in Savaluk; at any rate the notion was enough to calm my vertigo.

One thing's for sure, I thought as I trudged back to the van: at least I can say, as far as gut-churning revelations are concerned, that I must have had the lot. There can't be any worse shocks waiting.

*

Relaxed, I watched the log fire that crackled and flickered in the grate in the common room of the *Traveller's Rest* – an inn a few miles north of Swurk.

The night that had fallen outside also lurked indoors, in alcoves and recesses and in shadows thrown by the armchairs drawn up around the fire. Hammer beams along the ceiling loomed like the thick branches of oak that they once were; I could imagine myself in Old England, if I shut my ears to my companions – most of the personnel of the convoy had seized the opportunity to take their evening meal here, away from their *furgoni*.

My silent uncle sat in the leftmost armchair of the rough semicircle around the fire; I sat next to him and about a dozen others completed the gathering, some in other chairs, others perched on stools further back, all of them focused on what *I* had been saying.

They had got me to talk yet again about Earth.

"Clouds," I had said; "huge white shapes, the size of mountains, floating like ships in the sky; remember?"

They searched back in their memory of the dream, and I heard sighs.

"Ships!" called a feminine voice. "Hey, Duncan, tell me about ships and the sea!"

This request came from an extremely attractive girl who sat close to the other end of the semi-circle. I had seen Ugo greet her with an embrace and clip a glittering bracelet around her slender arm; with perfect poise she had accepted the gift, and her smile of gracious delight would have done credit to a princess. Evidently, here in the inn, the innkeeper's bonny daughter was equivalent to a princess although the admirers paying court to her regal presence were allowed to address her as "Flo".

Obedient to Flo's command I talked about ships and the sea, about waves and beaches. She listened with enthusiasm to my every word, and kept prompting me to say more, and although most of the rest of the audience were happy enough with this, I became concerned about Ugo. I didn't like the look on his face as I monopolised his girl's attention.

I excused myself and wandered over to the bar. In this place there seemed to be no rules about what age you had to be to get served beer: hereabouts if you behaved like an adult you were treated as one.

I took my time about returning to the group with my refill, postponing the move till a general buzz of conversation had resumed. Under cover of this I circulated till I was placed to speak confidentially to Ugo. "I could do with your advice," I said to him.

He looked sullen but his manners were impeccable. "Please, go ahead and ask."

"You have been here before?"

"Many times."

"You know that young lady?"

"I know her, yes." His face was thunderous now.

"I have a girl friend," I said, stretching the truth somewhat, "and I want her to react to my memories in a good way, like Flo. I need to train this girl of mine. What, in your view, is the secret?"

His teeth flashed in a sudden grin, whereupon I knew I had defused his jealousy.

"You wanna know how to treat girls?" He tapped his brow with his finger. "I give you a clue. Danger."

I waited. "Is that it?"

"It is the thing. They like – I mean, Flo likes it that I have been South to Gonoss, to get the herbs for my father's business. But I don't suggest you go that far."

"No?" I had achieved my aim in this conversation and now I wished to end it but I wasn't sure how. So I asked for knowledge I did not want. "What do I do, then, to give Elaine the, er, danger?"

"Take her to Gonoss theme park," he suggested with another grin. "It is all fake, but it will do. The smell of fake danger will be enough in your case, to win respect."

"Gonoss theme park?"

"I hear you come from Guthtin, no? The Theme Park is not far. It is a good replica, in some ways, of the real Gonoss. The forest is real, and every now and then, Bzzzzt! they shoot the swaash. Of course they cannot do the gradient. Or the avalanches. Or the Gonomong Fingers." He made gestures, a clutching and tearing, and then a tipping with his palms, and his expression became gleeful as he saw the change in mine.

Then he looked a bit sorry at his words. He added, "No, Duncan, forget all I say. I don't say I am better than you. I say you are different. Write to your Elaine to join you in Savaluk, and stay there."

6: Savaluk

A hand nudged my shoulder, shaking me out of my doze. *"Siamo arrivati!"*

I murmured some thanks. But next, I almost said an ugly word, in the bitter realization that I had missed the approach to the city.

I heard Fabrizio say, "We cannot park at the hospital; they do not allow space for private vans there. But it is only a block away, and it is clearly signposted."

I repeated my thanks. Things were happening too fast; I wished I could wake up more quickly. We had arrived at the Top of the World and I urgently needed to be alert and in proper control of myself.

Fabrizio added the welcome words, "I suggest you have some breakfast with us before you go."

"That," I quoted, "is an offer I cannot refuse," and then a new thought, better even than breakfast, made me feel so good that I no longer minded having been overtaken by the speed of events.

Rubbing the sleep from my eyes I went to the window and drew the curtain aside. I saw rows and rows of vehicles, some of which looked even more massive than ours. A few skyscrapers loomed beyond, against a sky that was no longer absolutely cloudless; some wisps of whiteness floated in the blue. A couple of men in darker blue uniforms walked past my field of vision. Other than this, there was (not surprisingly) not much to see from the midst of the lorry-park. And yet my heart sang as I went to the door and jumped down onto the tarmac.

The air was not cold as at Earth's north pole, yet it was noticeably cooler than it had been at the start of my journey, and in it hung some tang which excited me. But trumping everything was the great blessedness, *zero gradient.* A banquet for the eyes, the feast of flatness spread around me; *level ground* enfolded me; what tremendous relief it gave, to stand upon a normal surface encircled by a decent horizon!

I re-entered the van and expressed my warmest thanks to Fabrizio, who, I realized, must have put on some extra speed, or cut corners somehow, despite having said that he could not accelerate his schedule, for the journey had ended hours sooner than I had expected. Yet it was already light. 'Already'? *Of course, dumbhead, this is the North Pole. Never any night here.*

After breakfast, as I did not wish to presume any longer on my hosts' good nature, I refrained from last-minute questions, shook hands with Fabrizio and Ugo, and set off, guiding Vic by the arm, to find the Royal Fountain Hospital. Sure enough, starting from the exit from the lorry park, the route to the hospital was signposted.

In many ways it was like walking through central London, with its hefty office blocks, its traffic, its shops and news-stands, but what made it different was the seaside taste in the air and the *thinness* about it all – the avenue was a good deal wider than Oxford Street, and it was so long that it seemed open to infinity at both ends; the buildings were much more widely spaced, and the proportion of motorised traffic lower, with many more people riding bikes. Also I had the usual sense of 'this is not all', the sense that I was yet again seeing some important extra thing without knowing what it was, but I didn't worry. I trusted the good feeling I had. If necessary I would fight for this place!

At a news-stand I bought the *Savaluk Times* and ran my eye over the front page as I ambled along. Unfamiliar with the social and political background, I expected to find the paper heavy going though not completely incomprehensible. And so it turned out to be. "SALIENT SIN BIN" said the headline, while the subheading added, "Penalty for violent crime: transportation to 65 N, 180 W". *"While resisting calls for martial law, Parliament has suspended some civil liberties on the grounds that the courts cannot cope with the number of criminals taking advantage of the recent disturbances...."* Another front-page article – PARACOPS FORESTALL VIGILANTISM – concerned hastily improvised additions to the police force.

"Recent disturbances": that must connect with the trauma of emerging from the Dream of Earth. Or so I assumed. Be that as it may, as I guided my silent companion along the peacefully bustling streets I saw not a trace of violence anywhere, whereas the newspaper seemed to be full of it. This discrepancy, between the picture of society painted by the press and the evidence of my own eyes, reminded me so much of England, it helped me to feel at home.

Following the signs, I took a right turn along a cross-street towards the next avenue, and stopped to admire what I saw. Right down the middle of this second avenue, and reflecting the bright blue of the sky, idled a leisurely river. Floating leaves demonstrated how slowly the waters crept along.

Numerous bridges spanned the river, but to the left – northwards and upstream – it was straddled by a huge arch, set in the stone bulk of the Royal Fountain Hospital. So the waters flowed through and under the hospital.

The structure's confusing sprawl caused me to take quite some time to find my way in: it had one entrance for ambulances, one for equipment vans, one for taxicabs and (needless to say I found this one last of all) one for pedestrians. Inside, I was still confused. There appeared to be several reception points, and the place was as crowded as the concourse of a central station on a bank holiday. Should I ask for help? Whom should I ask? Everywhere I looked I saw injured folk walking around or being wheeled around, and an even larger number who seemed physically whole but had a vaguely bleary look, perhaps a milder version of Uncle Vic's "fugue" condition. It had become easier to believe in the "disturbances" which the newspaper had mentioned.

Depressed by the immensity of it all, I joined a queue. With diminishing expectations I waited and waited, but when I finally did get to the front and showed Vic to a receptionist, things happened fast. We were taken along a corridor to an examination room; a doctor – a sharp-eyed fellow in his twenties – asked me some questions and then assigned Vic to a ward. And that was that.

"We'll put him right in a few days," the doctor said as my uncle was taken away. "Meanwhile, how are you fixed?"

I replied: "I've got some money with me. I'll just have to find a hotel at first, then lodgings if I can."

He nodded, satisfied, so I knew then that he hadn't been asking whether I could pay for the treatment. He had merely voiced compassionate concern about me, about my situation as a new arrival in Savaluk. Yet I wanted to be sure, myself, on the subject of fees.

"Doctor," I said, "this may seem like a stupid question.... but is the treatment free?"

"I don't know about 'stupid', but it's an odd question," he smiled. "As a taxpayer, your uncle's already settled his score with us. Down in Guthtin, haven't you heard of the Health Service?" He read my expression closely.

I made the quiet decision to be blunt. "I knew the Health Service in *my* country, Britain. I didn't know how much to assume beyond that."

"Oh – aha – your mind is still anchored in the so-called Dream?"

"Yes." I felt glad to give him the truth.

"So. You remember Earth better than Kroth...."

"I don't remember Kroth *at all*."

"And by contrast, your memory of Earth is perfect?"

"Well, it's just normal for a, you know, actual inhabitant of Earth."

"I envy you that! Must be really interesting to have that. I'd like to run a few tests on you, while I'm about it. Don't you worry at all; you're obviously coping fine. It's just that you've roused my professional curiosity."

I could see, indeed, that he was excited as he went to a filing cabinet and pulled out a folder. For the next ten minutes he fired general-knowledge questions at me, mingling themes from Kroth and Earth. At the end he said that there was no doubt; I was an especially clear case of "oneirogeocentricism", or to give it a more down-to-Kroth term, "Earthdream". "Of course," he added, "that rather begs the question of what a 'dream' is. There's quite a literature on the subject; fascinating stuff if you ever want to go into it. In fact it's quite possible you may contribute to it: by that I mean that if you can hang onto your Earth memories as clearly as you've got them now, I and some colleagues would like to record them, once this crisis is over and we're not so busy – if you can spare the time. We'd make it worth your while: we'd offer you a proper job, under contract." He shoved the drawer shut and added, "Meanwhile – why don't you treat today as a holiday in the big city? And come back tomorrow during visiting hours, by which time I'm sure you'll see some progress has been made with your uncle."

*

Now for some time on my own!

I was rested, I had had an ample breakfast and I had been relieved of my charge. And here I was with a day in front of me and a city to explore.

At the hospital exit I turned right and headed for the upstream end, where the river must flow into the tunnel that ran through the great building. From there I continued northwards.

After a few hundred yards the line of buildings on either side drew back a little to make space for a rectangular park bordered by flowers and shrubs. I wandered onto a lawn. Walking past some birds which were pecking at crumbs, I reached an unoccupied bench. Here, on a whim, I decided to sit down for a minute or two.

Well, what next? I could try to make sense of my *Savaluk Times*. Not the front page with its concentration on law and order. The inside pages. I extracted the paper, opened it.

Most of the stories covered the Great Change, or the Awakening, from the individual practical angle, with anecdotes about how Mr and Mrs so-and-so, or little Tommy and Emily, coped with the sudden end of the dream of Earth. I read through all this stuff (there was a lot of it) and I marvelled at the public's attitude of acceptance. Why the Earth-dream had existed in the first place, was a question which no one seemed to bother about, as if it did not require explanation. For that matter, why had *I* never asked? Staring around me at the bright park and the blue sky and the people on other benches reading their papers and feeding the birds, I confronted that question for the first time: why had I never asked anyone, point blank, for the reason for it all? The answer came to me: some things are just too *big* to ask.

I leafed further through the paper in an attempt to find some political commentary. That might give me some handle on how things worked around here. I found plenty on law and order, quite a bit on defence – the need to resist incursions by something called the Gonomong, in the far south – but little on what was happening in Parliament or the Cabinet. Well, in a way it was refreshing to be given a break from the never-ending partisan sloganeering of my Earthly country. And of course, good heavens, the paper confirmed that there *was* a Parliament, there *was* a Cabinet – again, that fantastic mixture, that juxtaposition, familiar institutions in a re-formatted cosmos.... Just for a moment it was too much. Holding the opened broadsheet up in front of my face I grimaced violently, then smoothed my features.

I rolled up the *Savaluk Times*, stuffed it into my rucksack and went to look for a hotel.

*

The Nistoom Hotel was just opposite the park exit. I checked in and lightened my rucksack by unpacking most of the things in it, and then I was ready to roam. An idea hit me and I asked at the desk: did Savaluk have a Tourist Information Office? Yes, said the clerk, it's not far, here's a map. One thing led to another and within the half hour I was boarding a bus for a guided tour of the city.

This was a better plan than trying to wander about on my own. Get the experts to show me what this place has got; after which I could wander more profitably.

The tour guide, a jovial fellow with sideboards, lounging beside the driver as people got on the bus, asked each of us passengers to tell him what part of the world we were from, so that he could build up an idea of the cultural complexion of the group.

"Guthtin," I answered when my turn came.

"Where's that?"

"Er, it's where it is."

"Can't argue with that!" he laughed. I climbed to the top deck and heard him on the intercom as the bus started up:

"Hello ladies and gentlemen, I'm Gary Verly your guide for today's tour of Savaluk. Of course we have to be selective! It would take a lifetime to cover all that there is of importance to see, but we'll see what we can do between now and tea-time! I note we have a good selection of folk from many latitudes and longitudes, and over half of you have never been to Topland before. Those that have, please excuse me if I repeat what they already know!

"Our first stop is the Parliament Building.... then we'll disembark for a short stroll around the section of the Palace that is open to the public.... then a quarter-hour peek at Hirrax Arcade (ladies had better set their watches, ha-ha).... followed by other points of interest such as the Barracks.... the Radio Observatory.... the Yeyld Museum.... and finally the climax of our tour, Nistoom and the Fountain itself.

"Now as we set off you will note on our right an odd shape familiar from countless postage stamps, the terraced pyramid of the Suzz-Edd Hunnurao, from which we get our verb 'to suzz'...." The bus swayed around the next corner and the flow of historical anecdotes continued.

This, I soon realized, was going to be a day that fulfilled its promise; a day to remember. Two scenes stick in my mind most of all. The first of them I encountered as my fellow tourists and I tramped through the great echoing hall of the Parliament Building, where I was enormously impressed by the rows on rows of empty seats, full of haunting possibility, the potential power-house of a world. The majority of the seats had not been filled in ages – so the guide informed us. Only a small section of the hall was ever occupied, and then only on those infrequent occasions when the members from Topland and Upland met to debate and to legislate upon issues of rare importance. Legend, or tradition, motivated the staff to continue polishing and dusting the empty seats so as to keep them ready for the members from Slantland and Hudgung, should they ever turn up. The meaning of "Slantland" was one I could picture only too well; I was reluctant to ask, or even guess, where Hudgung was. I did ask how frequent general elections were. The guide turned to stare at me. He could see I was not joking. "Ah, I get it, sir. You've lost your Kroth memory in the recent you-know-what, haven't you?" he said sympathetically. I nodded, and told him that in compensation I had kept my Earth memories bright. "Wow, good for you, that's really something," he said, and went on, "To answer your question: we haven't had general elections for donkey's years. By-elections only, nowadays. At least, that's how it is in Topland."

"What about Upland?"

"That's what I meant really. Like when people say 'England' when they mean 'Britain', or 'Holland' when they mean 'the Netherlands', in the dream of Earth, as you know! All the area north of 60 degrees latitude is, collectively, Upland. Topland is the special bit of it," he added proudly. "Our part – the part where it seems flat. I might add, young sir, that you made a very sensible decision when you chose to come on our tour." My fellow group-members turned to nod at me and say, "hear, hear", causing me to feel touched and embarrassed at all this good will that was being shown towards the ignorant amnesiac of the party.

Now that my secret was out, the guide was happy to dumb down and show off his knowledge at a more elementary level than before. At our next stop, the Palace grounds, he commented, "Upland is an elective monarchy, perched on top of a pyramidal democracy. In their capacity as the Electoral College, the Lords meet in secret to choose the next Sovereign upon the death or abdication of the previous one. (Just like the cardinals used to elect the Pope in our dream world of Earth, as our young friend here will attest!) Furthermore, the Electoral College uses the same secret voting procedure to recruit its own members whenever a vacancy occurs, so it's self-selecting. Theoretically, anyone could be asked to serve! It could be you! It could be me! In practice, membership is restricted to those who have some outstanding achievement to their credit – and those undeserving cases who have tried to bend this rule have become the laughing stock of history! Plenty of funny stories on this theme; we've all heard of 'Tuppence Tiffley', haven't we? I've met people who doubt he ever existed, yet the records are quite clear – Tiffley was a real historical personage, who not only yearned to get elected, he actually went around *canvassing for the job.* Imagine that, folks! Imagine going around and saying to people, 'Vote for me'! What a Wally, eh! Now, the story goes, the Lords decided to make an example of him, not by rejecting him but (this showed fiendish cunning) by accepting him. By the time he realized how out of place he was, he had clowned his way into folklore.... so in a way, I suppose, he *did* have an outstanding achievement to his credit, hahaha...."

As we traipsed around the lawns and the statues, listening to the guide's funny anecdotes and admiring the architecture, my mind was elsewhere. The Palace and its grounds were splendid enough, but they didn't "get to me", they didn't haunt my imagination like that big unused space in the Parliament building had done, with its hint of some Arthurian-style link between past and future glory.

Dwelling on that theme, I failed to guess that the most staggering encounter yet lay ahead of me. Nothing I had seen so far would equal the climax of that tour. It became apparent that we were approaching it, or rather the edge of it, at a point where one of the long radial avenues of Savaluk came to an end.

"Officially," said the guide's voice over the intercom, "we're not really going outside the city. Savaluk's built-up area is ring-shaped, and – you can guess what I'm about to say – we are crossing the inner edge of the ring. Ahead of us lies the area inside the ring.... the top of Topland.... the Pole itself.... Nistoom."

Underneath a column of thin white cloud a couple of miles away I could see a line of blue, that broadened and expanded to right and left as the bus rolled towards it. Then I shivered with gladness, for I recognized the meaning of that spreading blue, and knew I was looking at what I had feared I might never see again. A gorgeous stretch of open water, with real waves. In this one utterly level place on a world that was almost all slope, the lake was a dream come true, wonderfully, securely real, and it invited me to rush out, splash in it, plunge into it, but even while still out of reach, from where I sat on the bus, it offered brimming satisfaction for the soul.

"Four miles across," spoke the guide, "Nistoom exists in the only location it can exist – centred upon the exact North Pole. The island of the Fountain marks the precise position of the Pole. The Fountain, of course, is the source of the world's water. It is where water is continuously created, to flow forever down the sides of Kroth, making life possible. Are there any geophysicists present? No? Too bad. Pardon me, madam? Oh, don't ask *me* the science of it! Anyway the main thing is, it happens; and because it happens, we happen too. I don't know about you folks, but that's good enough for me...."

He went on to talk about timetables, toilets, the Visitors' Centre and the hiring of boats. That last item was the one which interested me. As soon as we all spilled out of the bus I made for the nearest jetty. The fellow hiring out the dinghies advised me also to borrow a garment he held out to show me – a kind of waterproof half-sleeved poncho; and he suggested a pair of wellington boots with extra grip in the soles. I paid for the loan of all this, got into a dinghy and put out from shore.

The chattering thoughts in my head, like all the noises of land, grew faint as the shore receded, and I forgot everyone else, I even mostly forgot myself, as I pulled peacefully on the oars, welcoming the infinity of water and sky. Because my life stretched before me, I had all the time I could want to get to know the score, starting tomorrow; but today, just today, I was content to sponge off the universe, communing with its quiet immensity, and accepting the privilege of smallness, entitling me not to question and not to strive. Later would be full of bustle, finding a job, making friends, joining classes if need be, and cramming to speed up my assimilation to the culture of Savaluk. Today, none of that; today, right now, there was the lake, the sky and the slowly approaching Fountain.

I took my time, allowing other boats to outdistance mine. My boat was within a hundred yards of Fountain Island when I felt the damp spray and donned the waterproof to protect my clothes. I put on the boots as well, trusting they would be needed. A thin grey haze enveloped me; it did not prevent me from seeing that the island was a low, rocky, featureless cone maybe four or five acres in extent, with a summit a mere four yards or so above the level of the lake. The dinghy's keel scraped on hardness a few yards off shore; I got out and waded, pulling on the mooring rope, and made fast to a ring on a little post, next to some other boats, close to some steps cut into the rock.

Plenty of silent figures were shuffling about on the island. I recognized some of the tourists in my group. They were keeping apart from one another, and I, likewise, had no wish to speak. Slowly, carefully, I began to ascend, towards the centre, towards this utmost centre of all. The slippery steps, and all the rest of the ground, were covered with a film of water maybe a quarter of an inch deep pouring continually down towards the lake. Then I understood why I could not see any fountain up ahead. I was in it.

But what was causing the Fountain? I reached the summit of the cone and stood looking down into a bowl-shaped indentation in the rock. It was maybe six feet across, and in its very centre, under water, hovered a tiny sphere of radiance about the size of a ping-pong ball. It seemed to waver and bob about, but I knew that in reality, behind the turbulence and refraction, it was forever motionless while new matter in the form of water poured from it in all directions steadily, eternally.

That was it. I had seen it. I was content; I could leave, and let the next person take my place and have a look. Rich with inner peace, I turned and retraced my steps to the boat.

Having seen the real thing, I later went to look at the rather quaint display in the Visitors' Centre (and I was glad I had not seen this beforehand). As icing on the cake I also bought two guidebooks, "Nistoom" and "Life from Cosmic Law".

From the former booklet I learned something big, which I had not got round to noticing on my tour: the waters of Nistoom feed six rivers that flow out of it and divide and subdivide into the innumerable trickles which moisten Kroth all the way down. From the other book I gleaned a summary of the current theory of planet-formation:

VMAs, "virtual mega-particles", occasionally appear at isolated points in the Universe. Their special property is that they encourage the accretion of more normal matter at a continuous rate. Occasionally, so the experts say, there is a one-off bonanza in which case, bingo! all of a sudden you get a planet; more rarely still, if the planet possesses a "biogenic field", a little sun is formed at the same time, to orbit the planet, typically at a distance of about fifteen thousand miles, and warm it up. This allows life to evolve. As to whether all this is more or less believable than Earth cosmology, I refer you to my uncle Vic's overarching Theory of Excuses, which says that things are obliged to happen somehow, and any excuse will do.

*

There is no night, nor is there direct sunlight, in Topland, where the sun circles the world just out of sight below the horizon. People who want to see the sun, and experience the alternation of day and night, travel a few degrees south, then return, refreshed, to the polar realm and its gently diffuse illumination which, I am told, is all the stronger for some reason connected with the reflection of sunlight from the upper atmosphere. At any rate it is stronger than twilight, and the world seems full of colour; and when you get sleepy you just have to close the bedroom curtains.

Next "day" I awoke ready to get down to the business of sorting out how I was going to earn my living.

On Earth I had assumed that I would go to college, but here on Kroth I was not sure of my status or entitlements, and I wasn't even certain that college was what I wanted right now. An easy job, that gave me some breathing space to get used to being a citizen of Topland, would be ideal.

The doctor had suggested I might be employed as an experimental subject, paid a wage by scientists wishing to study my unusually clear Earth memories. That should bring in enough money for a while, during which time I could hunt for something with prospects. Then there'd be the task of finding lodgings, or perhaps renting a flat, and the question of whether I should, after all, get some further education....

My great hope was that I would not have to make all this adjustment alone. I still had some family – or so I hoped, as I looked forward to the hospital visiting hour.

The doctor was not the same one I had seen yesterday. Today I was referred to an ample lady in her forties, with a wise face and a kindly voice, who asked to have a word with me before I entered the ward.

"He's basically all right," she smiled. "Fully conscious, and looking forward to seeing you."

"That's great!"

She continued, "He's responded well to verbal and situational therapy. He can be quite incisive and articulate."

"That's a polite way of putting it," I grinned.

"But," she went on, "in his sleep he often calls out for someone named 'Reen'."

"That's his wife – my aunt Reen."

"Your uncle is unmarried."

"No. You must be talking about someone else...." My voice trailed off as she passed me a dossier. The photo on the medical record left me in no doubt that it referred to Vic. Near the top of the page was a box that said "Marital status: single".

"That's mad," I said, as I stared at the document. But some warning sense was trilling at me, telling me that I had better listen.

The doctor said softly, "It happens to lots of people. Their relationships in The Dream were different to what they are in this waking world. Sad, but it must be faced."

In a small voice I asked, "But he *is* my uncle? I do have that much family?"

“Yes, don't worry, you can depend on that. Also, you can rest assured that Reen exists, somewhere. But not married to Mr Chandler.”

“I don't get all this, doctor,” I said desperately, my voice rising. “I just don't get why I keep one relation and lose another – ”

“Think back,” she said. “Back to the Dream. Where was your aunt born?”

“Isle of Man.”

“And your uncle?”

“Er, like me, in Hertfordshire.”

“Interesting. We're not sure, but it seems often to be connected to Earthly geography – who remains linked with whom, when the Dream is over. The current theory is, the geography of Earth is in some sense the geography of our relationships here on Kroth, so that although, of course, there is no Isle of Man, and no Hertfordshire, in any literal sense, nevertheless these concepts do mean something.... and unfortunately for us, a good part of what they mean, when juxtaposed, is 'separation'....”

My face crumpled as her words buzzed in my head like wasps. I found myself quietly weeping for Reen and for all the pity of things. The doctor went on calmly, “The only consolation I can give you is that you're not the only ones having to endure this sense of loss. Millions of other people at the moment are in the same boat – and there I go, using the word 'boat', you see! Earth-ideas die hard. But for the especially unfortunate, the cases of fugue, it can be *exceptionally* hard. That's why I thought I'd warn you before you go in to talk to your uncle. He is a bit exceptional....”

I sighed, “I'm well aware of *that*.” I could just imagine Vic's cussed refusal to adjust; and then I brightened at the thought of his contrary personality, persisting from one universe to another.

He was sitting up, eyes alert, when I went in. He spoke to me as though he had last seen me only a few hours before. “Hi there, Duncan – just the fellow I want to see.”

“It's great that you've recovered, Uncle.”

“Recovered into what, though?”

“Into your old awkward self, I hope.” Indeed his face had that knowing look that always made me nervous – insofar as when he wore that expression it tended to mean he was about to shake up somebody's ideas, and at this moment I was the only target in range; but this was loads better than having him shuffle around like a zombie.

“Awkward? Me?” And he made a flicking gesture at a copy of the *Savaluk Times* that lay beside him. “It's life that's awkward,” he said.

“I'm certainly with you there,” I said with feeling.

“You reckon?”

“Eh? Yes, I'm saying, I agree with you!”

“Are you? Good. In that case, I just want your opinion about something,” he said. And then with studied casualness he blasted out the question: “What do you think of this dream so far?”

I found a chair and sat down hard. “Don't you start confusing me – what do you mean?”

“Relax,” he said, eyeing me a bit more affectionately; “let's get a learned opinion. Doctor!” he called out in a commanding tone that made me wince with embarrassment: “Doctor Rallod!”

The doctor at that moment passing through the ward was the young fellow I had seen yesterday. He altered course and came over and said, “Mr Chandler – how is it going?”

“Doctor, I haven't been given any drugs, have I?”

“No, you haven't.”

“No. Nor have I been operated on, have I?”

“Nothing's been done to you except that you've been given a bed to lie in.”

“That's just it,” said Vic triumphantly. “Dream logic: hospital – bed – sufficient symbolism for a slap-dash dream. No attempt to fill in the details.”

“Just a moment,” said the doctor. “I see you have your nephew with you. You need to bear in mind what *he's* got. Oneirogeocentricism. Exclusively Earth memories. And he's less than half your age; and yet *he's* not flying from reality. Maybe you should follow his example.”

“The young are resilient,” replied Vic, “whereas an old codger like me is far less adaptable, far more dependent upon props like rationality and plausibility.”

“Very well, I can dose you up with reason,” said the doctor. I could tell that he and Vic liked each other and enjoyed sparring with each other in this way. Just as well – for to me it was vitally important that my uncle should respect the doctor and come round to accepting the existence of the world as it was. Otherwise I did not know what I was going to do. Dr Rallod went on, “What you regard as omissions or discrepancies in the scene, are actually deliberate. Drugs or brain surgery would be irrelevant in your case. Instead, we had good reason to believe that the mere provision of a hospital bed would be enough to pull you out of your fugue, for that is how this particular cure is supposed to work: fugue is a mental problem that is best tackled by physical symbolism. Sure enough, it did work – otherwise you wouldn't be awake enough to deny it."

"You're a clever cuss, doc."

"Glad you noticed. Now, we were about to tell you, that if you really wish to leave today, you are free to do so. But ideally, we'd like to keep you in for another day or so, to do some tests on your memories."

"Oh, all right. I can stay if you want. Why should I object to being pampered for a bit longer? But as for accepting this peculiar world as real...." His voice dropped to a cantankerous mutter; Doc Rallod smiled, said he would see us later, and walked off, obviously satisfied that he had won this round.

Vic took a deep breath and blew out his cheeks and said to me, "Well, what did you think of all that?"

"I think," I said, "that they shouldn't have let you see that newspaper."

"Why? What makes you say that?"

"They should have broken it all to you more gently. It's too big a pill to swallow at one go. If they hadn't left evidence lying around, you'd have had time to adjust gradually to the fact that this isn't Earth...."

"Hang on just a flippin' minute!" he demanded. "Did you think I was like you? Just remembering Earth and nothing else? I'll have you know, I have a full set of Krothan memories too." And while I stared at him open-mouthed he launched into a tirade. "A full double set of two worlds in my head, contradicting each other! That's why I went into fugue. Did you think 'fugue' just meant a flight from reality? I'm not that kind of coward. What temporarily blew my mind was not just the change, it was the change combined with the retention of what I had before. Most people don't experience that full overlap. With most people, it's one or the other, and the rejected world goes faint and takes a minor role. But as I say, I have both in my mind at once: my memory of Earth is as good as yours, and my knowledge of Kroth is as good as the doctor's. I can compare the two worlds, the two universes, fairly with each other, and my conclusion is that Earth is a darn sight more plausible. 'Dream of Earth' – *bunkum.* Earth was real. *This* place is the dream. That's still my guess, despite what Doc Rallod said."

"Uncle, you scare me."

"Well, suppose the facts just *are* scary?"

Impatiently I replied, "I *know* I've got no choice but to face facts. That's not the point."

"Then what is the point? Is it the opposite problem – are you perhaps afraid of being caught out by wishful thinking? For I take it that you (like me) would *prefer* this ridiculous Kroth set-up to be a dream."

"No," I shook my head firmly, forcing my thoughts into line of battle. "Listen to me. This is dangerous. I am greatly afraid of what might happen if you refuse to believe in the reality of where we are. I fear that you will take it too lightly, even treat it as a joke of some kind, and then the first sticky situation you get into, you'll go and do something stupid...."

Once again, as had happened on other occasions in my dealings with Vic, I was pleasantly surprised at his ability to take criticism. He listened. He didn't mind being told off – he respected it, provided the point being made against him was worth considering.

"Tell you what," he said, "I'll ask for some books on science. The hospital has a library service. Physics, geophysics, cosmology...."

"Er – cosmology?"

"Yes, that'll be a laugh – unless the laugh's on me. Actually I already know quite a bit about this supposed universe; but if you really want me to take Krothan ideas more seriously, then, to keep you happy, I'll give it another go."

"That reminds me, Uncle. I have a brochure here, I think." I picked up my rucksack and the guide to the Fountain was still in it.

*

Next time I came to see him, his expression had markedly changed.

"You win," he admitted with tight-lipped amusement. He bent forward as a nurse plumped up his pillows for him. "I concede that this universe is real."

"You better had," said the nurse, downrightly, and went to slap the pillows on the next bed.

"First-rate mind, that Doris," murmured Vic.

I, meanwhile, sat down and said, "Phew! Thank goodness you've seen sense."

"Yes, well, I'm sorry if I gave you some anxious moments. I've been reading some quite advanced stuff – " he pointed to a small pile of books – "and combined with what you've been telling me, I can see that no mere dream would hold up to such detailed scrutiny. (Unless of course I'm just *dreaming* that it does. Sorry! Couldn't resist that.) Anyhow, I can reassure you, I'll be good, I'll play the game from now on. However, please let me tell you something else I learned from those books, something you won't have learned from your experience in Kroth so far. A piece of very good news."

"I'm all ears."

"*Earth wasn't a dream, either*. Both states of reality are true."

"Is that official?" I asked, experiencing a hot prickly sensation; not that I had any hope that I might get Earth back, but to be reassured that it *had* been real (actually, deep down, I suppose I had never doubted it) made my heart thump.

"They *call* it a dream," Vic explained, "because that is how they cope in ordinary language with a much more nuanced truth. Really, it just makes the point that for all practical purposes it *might as well be a dream*. If you want to find words to describe what it *actually* is, then you can only do it by analogy – like all ideas in advanced physics. In this case the analogy itself is taken from another branch of physics, namely, the theory of atomic structure. Take the hydrogen atom – hmm, are you following this?"

"Yes, yes. Go on!"

"Take the hydrogen atom.... er, well, to put it as simply as I can, its electron can rest in what we call its *ground state*. But then, wham, an influx of energy can instantly raise that electron to a 'higher orbit' – though it's nothing like an orbit really – from which it can again descend, after emitting a photon, back to the 'ground state'.

"Applying the analogy, we can say that the collective consciousness of humanity has its own 'higher orbit' – Earth. The energy for it is mental, because mind is the universe-maker, when there's enough of it. But when something happens to burst this energy bubble, our reality reverts to its 'ground state' – Kroth.... Of course, ideally, instead of putting it this way, it would be better to stick to symbols and equations, but apparently only about three people in the whole world understand the mathematics of it, so the rest of us might as well stick to analogies, or else talk of dreams." He sighed and added: "My marriage to Reen – now there was a nice dream."

I could not bear the sudden collapse in his tone, the bitterness and despair in that last sentence.

"She exists, somewhere," I said.

"So I'm told.... but what if she's married to someone else? As indeed she's likely to be.... Could I face that? I don't know what to do...."

"*You're* not married to someone else," I pointed out, "so why should she be?"

Bleakly he replied, "A woman has to be one in a million to put up with me; a man has to be one in a million *not* to want Reen."

*

I signed a 144-day contract drawn up by a consortium of medical scientists who wished to pump me dry of all my detailed memories of Earth. Then I got busy – pleasantly busy, despite my sorrow on Vic's behalf. I settled into a routine whereby every day I turned up at a special wing of the hospital where the medicos gathered to fire endless questions at me, and I had more talking to do than I had ever had in my life, but the pay was generous, the hours were easy, and it was, moreover, comforting to think that my Earthly experiences lived on, if only in the hospital archives at Savaluk.

The generosity of the Upland State extended further. I was given a flat, at a specially reduced rent. I was told that this arrangement could continue after my contract had expired, provided I found another post within the next 180 days. (By this time I was comfortable with what "Day" means in Topland, and could easily sense the main direction of the light, as the invisible Sun circled below the horizon like a clock-hand.)

In this secure position, treated in all respects as an adult citizen, I took a social step. I joined a hikers' club.

To make friends, possibly find myself a girlfriend: that was part of it. But there was more to the idea. Like a cat will stake out its territory, depositing its smells, I had to follow my own basic need which was to connect with the countryside of Topland, to kit myself out with that portable spiritual home which familiar countryside can provide. On Earth I had taken it for granted. Here, I had to bring it about, weld it to my imagination.

At first, on my days off, I went on half-day rambles from village to village on the periphery of Savaluk, dependent on the local bus-routes for transport to and from the starting points. You couldn't call it wild countryside, but it was outdoor freshness and an abundance of green, and a way of getting to know people.

On one of these hikes, as the group we were in was making its way over a stile, I happened to be at the back of the queue to climb over, and I found myself standing next to another newish member of the group, who was waiting beside me: a slim, olive-complexioned girl, whom I had noted to be a winsome, shy type. Now, however, I heard her mutter a word:

"Fraudulent!"

No one else had heard. I turned to her. "Pardon?"

"Cut-and-paste job."

"Explain?"

"Stiles, dry-stone walls, inn signs, lifted from your British countryside and plonked here on this crazy world – *fraudulent.*"

"No," I said.

I suppose she picked on me in the first place because there was something intense about me too; yet when I gave her my earnest "No", she looked at me in surprise.

When we had got over the stile I resumed:

"The 'cut-and-paste', as you call it, is just what I like about it. Just what reassures me that we're not on some 'other' world. We're on *our* world, and it's our job to get used to it."

"But *Earth* is our world!"

"Earth is – was – " I picked my words carefully – "a high-energy state of the collective conscious."

"Wow!" she laughed. "Where did you get that from?"

I told her what I had heard from Vic, the analogy with the energy states of the hydrogen atom, the ground state and the higher state. I added, "I'm Duncan, by the way."

"I'm Cora. Listen, I don't care what your uncle says, I say this Kroth place is *nuts*, it's *crap*."

I learned she was nineteen (two years older than I), and three-quarters Greek – I had guessed she wasn't British; her pronunciation was far too good, especially the posh way she pronounced swear words. Like me, she was a case of "oneirogeocentrism": her clearest memories were of Earth. She did not feel at home on Kroth, and what was more – this is where we differed seriously – she did not *want* to be at home on Kroth. She resented being here.

This was what gave me mixed feelings about Cora: I definitely did not want to be pulled away from my plan to integrate with this world. But she was certainly attractive, though moody and sullen.

On our second encounter she let slip that she had been engaged to a young man on Earth whom she had lost sight of since the Awakening. The same tragic story as with Vic and Reen. I said I was sorry to hear it; but I couldn't say anything useful, or at least, not directly. I was fairly sure of the strategy she needed to pursue, but did not feel qualified to talk strategy to a bereaved person.

Weeks passed, I went on with my life, I made other friends, and I saw little of Cora. Then, when I heard that the group was arranging a special long-weekend jaunt into the Mulkut Hills on the fringes of Topland – an area of woodland, moorland and fells, reaching to heights of between a thousand and thirteen hundred feet, which is high as "mountains" get on Kroth – my first thought was, great! this is just what I want; and my second thought was, why not tell Cora that this will do her good, too?

I said to her: "It's going to be a wonderful week-end, Cora! Have you ever been to Exmoor, or the Derbyshire Peaks?"

"Yes, I have seen them."

"Well then, in the Mulkuts we'll be in countryside which you can at least pretend is compensation for the world you have lost."

"What about the *man* I have lost?" she asked.

I was prepared for this point. "One sorrow feeds into another," I shrugged. "Grief for a person.... grief for a world...."

She absolutely staggered me then – she leaned forward and kissed me! A reward, I suppose, for showing some understanding. But I could sense that most of her bitterness remained. Still, she agreed to come along.

*

Our group leader, the man who knew all the paths, was a hale sixty-year-old called Pete Upton. I asked him before the start: when we got up into the hills, would we be able to detect the Slope? "By 'the Slope' I don't mean the hill slopes," I added.

He knew what I meant. "'Fraid we won't," he replied. "We'll still be only about fifty miles from the Pole, which is not far enough South to sense the beginning of the world's gradient...."

He thought I was disappointed. He didn't realize that he'd just rid me of my only worry. Now that I could trust that there would be no chance of sensing the dreaded world-tilt, I was raring to go, confident that nothing could mar the trip.

There were fifteen of us in the group that set off by bus for Twelgrem, the village at the foot of the Mulkuts. I was the youngest but not by much; we represented an assortment of ages and occupations, and this, together with the beautiful and varied scenery that passed the window, gave me what I had to have. Promise of a deep enough pool of ingredients for a satisfying, credible life. And I was going to get more. Something in me wanted to go further, to grasp all that there was of the patch of reliable goodness around me, though this would involve feeling my way to its borders. That vague risk was countered by an equally vague, pig-headed insistence that I knew what I was doing.

We got off at Twelgrem, shouldered our packs with their rolled-up sleeping-bags, and set off along the hill-path.

Now we were getting more into real wild countryside. Not absolutely untouched by humanity; but, like upland Britain, though affected by man's activities it was not cultivated, and by and large Nature still appeared to reign. The soil was thin, knobbly with protruding rock, suitable only for the sheep that grazed around us as we made our way up the lower slopes. The path became a track.

For a while I refrained from joining in to the conversation of my companions, because it concerned stuff that I did not wish to know about – stuff that had appeared in the papers during the past couple of days, of the sort that reminded me of the international tensions and crises which had afflicted Earth, only here it was "the Southern powers" getting restless and threatening. Some day I would have to get my head round all this dismal geopolitics but at the moment – *forget it!* South = Slope = Shudder! Not what I wanted on this trip.

Instead, I fell into step beside Cora. As we chatted, her mood seemed brighter than it had been. Encouraged, and wanting her to see the good side of things as much as possible, I brought the conversation round to my positive views about life on Kroth. But you know how it sometimes is, when you can't quite express the real good or bad point about something, you pick on a less important but more describable point instead; so I found myself making remarks about the economy! Not really what I wanted to talk about at all. (Yet, as things turned out, it led me towards what I did want to say.)

"Pete, over there," I nodded towards our leader, "is an accountant, but – imagine – Savaluk, the capital city of the entire world, needs so few accountants, that he only works part-time. What do you make of that?"

"Simpler tax laws, I suppose."

"But it's the attitude!" I said admiringly, in a tone that expressed my love and respect for the culture I was in. "I guess a world where accountants only have to work part-time can't be all that bad! I was fooled at first," I added.

"Fooled – how?"

"In thinking the economy here was like the one I was in on Earth. But this Krothan set-up is just a – a skeleton."

"Go on."

"Superficially it's similar to the economy of Earth's 'West'; the consumer goods most Westerners took for granted – like TVs and laptop computers – are equally well-known on Kroth. But – and here's the difference – they're not *amassed*. In Savaluk if you want to watch TV, you don't switch your own set on, because you don't have one; instead, you go out, don't you? You go to the local TV centre, like you would go to a cinema! Most people here don't have a TV in their homes. Same for the use of a computer: you hire the use of one, and use it more rarely. It is as though technology were rationed."

"You think that's good?"

"Wait – it's not actually rationing. It's natural rarity. It's the same for any kind of advanced machinery, including industrial plant: rarer here than on Earth because it's much more expensive to maintain, and that's because, for some reason, machinery is much less reliable here, so that it requires multiple redundancy and backup. Look at the way cars so often travel in pairs."

"And that pleases you."

"Well, look, you must have noticed yourself, the rareness of TV is a pretty great boon to the art of conversation! Here to my amazement is a world where, for people *my age*, the idea of a fun evening is to book a table somewhere and have a merry chinwag, rather than get boozed up and – "

I interrupted myself and glanced at her to see how I was doing. She seemed willing to listen. So far so good – and because I was coming out of my own shell and wanted to bring her out of hers, I dared to go ahead and say:

"To me the great thing about the Toplanders is that they aren't soaked in that yucky *tolerance* that amounts to a slobs' charter on Earth. For example: you don't get publicly drunk, or take forbidden drugs, in Savaluk. You just don't. If you did, you'd never live it down...."

She wasn't walking beside me any more. She had halted, scowling, as though she had decided not to go another step with me. Had my views angered her that much? But then I saw that the rest of the group had stopped too. Pete Upton up ahead was reading the small print on a notice posted at a fork in the path.

The large print said: NO ACCESS TO SUMMIT. Above the words a symbol showed an irregular black line, approximately an inverted "V", depicting, presumably, a mountain top. Above *that,* half a dozen dagger-points stabbed down towards the line.

Some of our group clustered round the notice and read the small print as Pete had done, but Pete meanwhile set off, obedient to the notice, keeping along the lower path, towards the pass between the summits. The rest of us soon followed him. We, likewise, were shunning the higher path.

Cora came stamping forward to catch up with me. "Now isn't that just typical. Meekly doing what we're told."

"But we weren't headed for the summit anyway. We want the pass to Strelk – "

"So what? Why aren't we at least discussing what that sign said?"

"Quite honestly, I don't want to know," I replied. "I'm new here, at least my conscious mind is new here, and I'm not about to question any keep-out signs, at least not right now. As far as I'm concerned – "

"All right," she snapped, "I get the picture."

I was as furious with her as she was with me, but maybe this is where I ought to have let her have the last word. After all, she was right in one respect: I had been a little disappointed that we had not made the easy detour up the higher path, to see the view from thirteen hundred feet, which is as high above ground as you can get on this world.

"No," I contradicted her, "you don't get the picture at all. You don't have to assume I'm a conformist 'square' just because I obey a signpost."

"Don't I?" she sneered.

*

Pete led us over the ridge of the pass, about nine hundred feet up amid grass, boulders, gorse and hawthorn that rustled in a cool wind. From this breezy point we scrambled down into a surprisingly steep valley, which became even steeper close to the bottom – it became a gorge, and the path became a flight of stone steps with a handrail financed and constructed by the Mulkuts Wilderness Trust. We clutched that rail as we felt our way down the last hundred yards while the shadow all around us deepened. By the time we reached the bottom we needed our torches.

Nowhere from Topland can you ever see the Sun, because it orbits only fifteen thousand miles from the equator of Kroth, so that the curve of the planet is bound to hide it at very high latitudes. But in general the polar daylight is still bright enough, like a minute after sunset on a clear summer evening on Earth, and therefore, normally, you can't see the stars either. On the floor of Strelk Gorge, however, conditions are exceptional.

By torchlight we unrolled our sleeping bags, unzipped them and spread them out as groundsheets, so we could lie down on them and look up at the sky: for this is the one place in Topland from which you can see stars. In that restricted crack of sky I counted about thirty stars at least as bright as Sirius.

One lanky, bearded young man in our group, named Rida Sholkov, was a physics student. (Somebody told me that he was Russian-Egyptian, whatever that may mean in Krothan terms; there must be cultures galore in the Krothan longitudes and latitudes which I have never visited, all of which, perhaps, have been reflected on Earth.) Now, pillowing his head on his backpack, he identified the individual stars for us by name.

"How far away are they, Rida?" I heard someone ask.

He answered, "Millions of miles."

"Is that all?" asked Cora's voice. "Only millions, not trillions? Rather small for a universe!" Her scornful remark fell flat; Rida did not respond; neither did any of the others. I, likewise, kept my thoughts to myself.

You're wrong, Cora, it's not small, because here when you look up, you really look up, and a million miles high is standing over you, towering over you, whereas a trillion miles away – well, the number might be bigger but the personal connection is absent: away is just away into nothing.

We explored a certain distance up and down the gorge, a small fraction of its entire length (it reaches most of the way through the Mulkuts); then we came back for a picnic and a rest preliminary to climbing back out. I heard a little voice behind me:

"Sorry I lost my temper."

I turned quickly and she went on, "Duncan, look, there's a space. Eat with me. I'll let you win the argument this time."

I grinned and said, "That is real sweet of you, Cora. Mustn't leave our quarrel unfinished."

Indeed, after we had finished our sandwiches, we did argue some more. Because we were the only two in the group whose memories were Earth-centred, it was natural for us to compare notes, but whenever we did so our opinions clashed. I accused her of hankering after the *grooviness* of Earth. To her, what she called the "social taboos" of Kroth were a sinister restriction on freedom. She sneered at "straightlaced" Krothan youngsters who went a-courting in old-fashioned style, and Krothan repression and "priggish condemnation" of anyone who abused himself with alcohol or drugs.

"Rubbish," I said, angry and fierce in the defence of my new world. "In this place, a jerk like my stepfather would never have been given the chance to harass my mother to her death."

"But I thought you said your stepfather was like he was due to an accident. Knocked his head in a car smash, didn't he?"

"So what? If I ever have an accident like that, I hope they snuff me."

That was too much for Cora. As soon as we had packed our picnic things she withdrew again, and I shrugged, perfectly well aware that to her my company was in any case only a fifth-rate substitute for the man she had lost.

We all climbed out of the gorge and went on further through the Mulkut Hills, hiking along ridges and down to pleasant villages on the other side of the range. Before we got too tired we took a vote as to where we should sleep: we could return to the gorge, where it would be dark, or circle round to a moorland plateau which would be less damp but daylit.

"The gorge, the starlit gorge!" said Cora, loudly. "So romantic!"

"But is it romantic to get wet?" asked Rida.

"Tcha," scoffed Cora. "You can't have everything." But she seemed more good-humoured than before.

I abstained in the vote. The outcome: we all slept on the plateau.

Next "day", circling round, we came back eventually to our former path, retracing it in the other direction. Soon in the distance I again saw that NO ACCESS TO SUMMIT signpost up ahead. It not only reminded me of my quarrel with Cora, it roused my curiosity, more than it had the previous time. As we approached it, I kept my eye on the forbidden path. The sign, with its upside-down "V" sketch of a mountain-top, and its halo of daggers stabbing down at it – what could it possibly mean? I thought of forbidden things on Earth: army firing ranges, electricity installations, nuclear test sites. Perhaps I should go and read the small print.

I broke away from the group and jogged up to the notice. I was about to examine it when my eye caught a moving glint of silver coming into view around the nearest curve of that forbidden higher path. Shock froze me as I found myself staring at what looked like men in spacesuits; half a dozen of them, carrying their helmets.

With my left hand I gripped the signpost while I summoned the defiant impudence, the refusal to budge, that allowed me to raise my right hand in greeting. If possible I would show a certain person that I wasn't as meekly conformist as she thought I was.

I half expected my fellow hikers to call out to me to retreat, and I more than half expected the men coming down the path to threaten me with the guns I saw belted around their suits. But when I raised my arm, one of them raised his, hailing me in response. This particular grim-faced man was one whom I hadn't seen for three weeks although he had been allotted a flat in the same block as mine, and he now seemed almost a stranger.

He and his companions reached our group and mingled with it, and I was aware of words being exchanged between their leader and Pete Upton, but I determined to 'buttonhole' (spacesuit notwithstanding) the man who had responded to my greeting:

"Have you been to the top, Uncle?"

"We have," said Vic heavily, swinging his helmet with one hand. He looked more grizzled, and his face more lined than I had ever noticed before.

"Isn't it forbidden?"

He grasped my elbow, steered me back close to the signpost where I could read the small print, and pointed to where it said: *The public must keep clear of the edge of the atmosphere....*

"Members of the public," he said, "don't have the right equipment."

"The edge of space...." I said, awed by the thought of being within walking distance of the shores of infinity. Just thirteen hundred feet up – the edge of space! And my uncle virtually a spaceman just for having climbed to the top of the Mulkuts! I had known that he had returned to his old job of science correspondent, but this, I now realized, could be a cover for just about anything.

Vic's leader, a stout bushy-bearded chap with glasses, looked like a scientist, but the rest of his group had a military feel to it – the way they stood and moved and spoke, quite apart from the fact that they were armed.

"Do guns fire in space?" I asked.

"You're not thinking, Duncan. Come on, or we'll get left behind." Vic and I strode after the enlarged group which had set off down the path towards Twelgrem. He went on, "Forget about 'space' – there isn't any."

"But the sign said 'the edge of the atmosphere'...."

"Which is where you need oxygen and body-armour to survive, yes. Because of what's beyond. But it's not space. What do you think keeps the air around Kroth from dropping away?"

Oh dear me, was this a rug-pulling episode? Was yet another of my preconceived ideas about to be tripped up? Evidently so; I recognized the signature voice-tone. I was in for some unwelcome education; a reminder of the Slope, or some other nasty consequence of this universe's absolute up and down.

"What keeps the air up? Er – humph! Well now," I retorted, "what keeps the world up, for that matter?" In my mood of irritation, I almost said *Gotcha.* "Yeah - if everything falls downward, why doesn't Kroth itself blinking well fall too, so that we're all in free fall? And what keeps the Sun up, circling round us? You can't have it both ways!" My voice became quite punchy.

"Is it all my fault, then?" grinned Vic.

"Not if your next speech makes everything as clear as crystal," I said shortly.

"I shall do my humble best."

We were still some yards behind the rest of the group, the men in silvery-armoured suits and my hiking companions all strung out together in a line down the path towards the village from which we had started out the previous day. In the middle distance I could now see the village green where our bus stop must be, and already a big vehicle was waiting there, but it was not our bus. It was an olive-green armoured car. Had we seen too much? Were we being politely shepherded towards military detention? My wayward mind began to construct all kinds of dramatic fantasies, concerning the secrets that Vic and his group might have uncovered.

He continued: "You asked for the reason why Kroth stays up. The experts explain it this way: Kroth's planetary mass brings it into the *unipositional* category of objects. You know, back on Earth, some organizations such as the big banks were 'too big to fail'? Well, here, planets are 'too big to fall'; they're not subject to the downward force."

"And the Sun?" I asked, trying to concentrate, trying to sound intelligent.

"No, not the Sun. Planets only – nothing else is unipositional. Everything else falls, or...."

"But the Sun doesn't fall."

"Let me finish. The Sun, far smaller here and far less massive than Earth's Sun, *would* fall but for Kroth's *biogenic field*, for which Kroth's Sun is the complementary particle. The biogenic field keeps it in orbit around Kroth's biosphere. Gosh, Duncan, you should see your face."

"No, actually, I believe what you're saying. My face looks skeptical only because I got the habit from you."

He laughed. "Good, but are you also going to believe me when I explain about the air? It's rather more important."

"Easy," I guessed: "'biogenic field', as you said before. Same way as it keeps the Sun orbiting, it keeps the air wrapped round us."

"No, that isn't the reason in this case."

While he spoke I saw a second armoured car pull up beside the first, and from it a figure emerged, a very tall man, who then went to the first car and put his head at the side-window, at the same time making an emphatic, arm-dropping gesture towards us. Then he went back to his own car, got in, sat and waited.

Seconds later, I heard a *beep* and one of Vic's silver-suited colleagues – the one I took to be the leader, the stout fellow with glasses – raised a mobile phone to his ear. It was the first time I had seen such a gadget on Kroth.

Then the silver-suited man turned and called up the path to Vic: "That was General Faraliew! Confirmation – time's run out!"

"Nice of him to tell us what we already knew!" Vic roared back.

"And he wants you to report to him!"

Vic, by way of answer, simply waved. Then, his voice reduced to normal level, he continued his talk with me as though nothing had happened.

"If the worlds of this cosmos floated in empty space, their atmospheres, because of the universal up-and-down, would drop off and fall away," he explained, "just as water runs down-slope, just like any other loose object can get tipped off Kroth's equator; but our atmosphere, luckily for us, is imprisoned, because in this cosmos *there is no empty space*."

"Imprisoned by what?"

I was being serious now, not "punchy" any more. I recalled the rumours, to which I had shut my ears before my departure for this weekend hike – the rumours of crisis in the South. And whatever my uncle was mixed up with, I could hardly avoid the belief that it implied some connection between the hostilities brewing in lower latitudes and the physical dangers of the upper air.

"The world's air is held in place by more air. But not by atmospheric, breathable air. It can't be."

"Why not?"

"Think!" he said, impatiently.

"I am doing," I replied. Maybe not successfully, but I was paying attention more intently than ever, determined not to miss anything of what he said, for I felt in my bones that this might be our last conversation for some time.

"All right – then do more than think – try realistically to imagine! Filled with atmosphere, wouldn't the universe be so hazy, that no one would be able to see the stars?"

"Ah," I nodded.

"Therefore, because at night (in Kroth's lower latitudes) one *can* see the stars, what's out there must be a kind of *invisible* air, utterly transparent – it has mass, but it is as un-breathable as empty space would be. You can use the old-fashioned term 'ether' if you like." His face grew ruddy with enthusiasm. "Fascinating stuff, but dangerous. Part of the danger lies in the fact that this – ether – doesn't always form a smooth boundary at the edge of our atmosphere; it can make jagged inroads into it, like icicles or splintered floes. And the analogy with ice comes even closer to the truth, for the ether tends to assume a crystalline form."

"You obviously know a heck of a lot about all this, Uncle."

"Well, at one time I was commissioned by the military to head a group for the investigation of the ether boundary, to chart it and to predict its patterns, with the aim of making air travel practical. And recently they recalled me...."

"Why?"

"The Awakening has weakened us – and our enemies are stirring. They're not going to miss this opportunity to attack."

The babyish part of me pleaded, *Too soon! I don't want this! Not yet!* In fairness to myself I will add that this was mixed into a larger fear, an aching concern for the land and culture I had fallen in love with.

A wider view of that love came upon me then, as a main reason for it flashed upon my understanding.

I had become immersed in a civilization in which popular culture *did not disgust me*. On Earth I had been so used to the disgust, that I had taken it for granted. Older men who feel it are allowed to express it in words; they belong to an accepted category, "grumpy old men". But what can a young man do? A young man is not supposed to have had enough time to notice that the world has gone to pot; so what can he do if (aided by the perspective of literature and classic movies) he *does* notice? Repress – that's all he can do; so that on the surface he continually pretends, even to himself, that the Britons he knows have merely "changed with the times", or that the clean heroes of olden times had not really been so clean anyway.... meanwhile he buries deep the obvious truth, which all the voices he admires are shouting at him – that the present is a disgrace to the past. But now I was in Topland, and Topland was *not* a disgrace. All right, there was quite a bit of crime, according to the newspapers, especially during the days of greatest disturbance just after the Awakening, but it was a good country, a paradise compared to yobland. I must not lose such a wonderful second chance! I must fight for this land if necessary! All this blazed through my mind like lightning while Vic's voice went on.

"This time," he explained, "we were hoping to get round the ether-boundary problem quickly enough so as to be able to build an air force.

Unfortunately, we're not going to be given enough time."

*

For months since the Awakening I had lived under the empty skies of Kroth, and yet I had not given a thought to the lack of aircraft. Now that the thought had come, I felt a tremendous attraction for the idea of flying – or floating, or hovering – immune to the Slope's downward pull. That should nicely beat the one fearful disadvantage of living on Kroth.

The snag, according to what I'd just heard, was that the air-force idea had come too late.

Then I thought of something else –

"This military job of yours, you talk as though you began it quite a while ago."

"Yes, a thousand days or more."

Perhaps some of my readers have been impatiently wondering for quite some time, about the status of Kroth before the Awakening. I belatedly considered this question now. When Earth occupied our consciousness, where in the scheme of things was Kroth? Was it empty? Of course not! As soon as I forced myself to think, the answer was blindingly obvious. All these roads and buildings and the entire culture of Kroth could not possibly have sprouted into existence in the second of the Awakening! It – we – our Krothan selves – must have lived here all along, simultaneously with our existence on Earth. Our two worlds, our two identities, had been running concurrently, so that, for instance, Vic-on-Kroth had been pursuing his researches on the Krothan atmosphere boundary even while Vic-on-Earth was writing articles for British and American journals.

Since this must have been true; since the two worlds could exist together; *could Earth still be in existence now?*

It wasn't that I particularly wanted to get back there, even if a way could be found. But I would like it to exist!

In a hurry I put this idea to Vic.

"No," he said sadly. "The ground state exists during the higher states, but not the other way round. That's what the boffins say, and I have to believe them. Yes, dual existence lasted *during* the Dream of Earth, so we lived our lives as Krothans even while we were also living at the higher mental energy state as Earth-people. But when Earth goes, it goes."

"But how do the boffins know?"

Vic didn't answer straightaway and I thought that was it, end of conversation. We had reached the village green and he was walking towards General Faraliew's car. I held back and said, "Good-bye then, Uncle."

"Not so fast," he said, retracing a step, catching my arm and hauling me forward. "I think it might be a smart idea for you to meet the General."

Ahead of us the door of the car opened and Faraliew extricated himself, uncoiling his great height – he must have been about six foot eight: a thin, leathery, unsmiling man in his seventies.

The giant spoke. "I want you on my staff, Chandler."

"We've been through this before, General. I won't accept any commission."

"Not even when the Gonomong come up *en masse*?"

"I'm not cut out – "

"Then be a civilian adviser, dammit!"

"Agreed."

"And is this the nephew?"

"Yes. General Faraliew, meet Duncan Wemyss, the Earth-mind with total recall."

"Interesting. He might do."

Vic recoiled visibly. "Now, General, I also am an Earth-mind. You don't need two of us – "

"Who says so?" retorted Faraliew. "Lots of wastage likely in this war! Besides, he may have something you haven't."

"What could that possibly be?" scoffed Vic.

"Ignorance!" Faraliew blared. "Or to put it another way – unbiased vision. I've known that sort to be useful on campaign."

"You're having me on, General."

Faraliew unexpectedly smiled, a kindly smile. "Yes, perhaps I am. I know, after all, why the purely Earth-minded are likely to crack up down South." He focussed his gaze on me and I noted a twinkle under his shaggy grey brows. "Are you petrified, Wemyss?"

"Yes, sir," I replied, fatalistically.

"But not by the thought of battle, eh? It's the Slope you can't face, eh?"

"You've read my mind, sir."

"Well," he said, "I might have been the same if Fate had dealt me that particular hand of cards. You can still contribute to the war effort although you have to stay up here in Topland. There is plenty for you to do."

Vic eagerly chipped in, "Exactly, General. He could become a boffin. He's got the brains. We were just talking about the asymmetric relationship between Earth and Kroth."

"Ah yes?" And to my utter amazement, the busy General stood there listening while Vic resumed where he had left off, prattling to me about cosmology. I could only conclude that I was being tested in some way.

"....I've heard the asymmetry has something to do with so-called cross-over phenomena. For example, Anaxagoras in the fifth century BC gave his idea of the size of the Sun by saying it was 'larger than the Peloponnese'. Well, the Peloponnese was, what, a hundred or so miles long? Something like that. And the Sun – the Sun here – is about a hundred and forty, hundred and fifty miles across. So we can assume that Anaxagoras' Krothan self was leaking the information to his Earth self, via the racial unconscious."

"Could just be coincidence," I remarked, playing along.

"Not when the Krothan Anaxagoras confessed to a dream of his Earth counterpart! And there are a lot more examples; think of all those writers and thinkers who have believed in the ether. But it doesn't happen the other way round; the line has gone dead." He paused. "It's unfortunate, because Kroth could do with some inspiration at the moment."

"What's up - at the moment?"

"The Gonomong."

Oh. That word again. That sad word.

The General then spoke, uttering a few sentences which sounded quite routine – and yet for me they tipped a balance: "Gentlemen, this conversation is of interest, but I must go and borrow Harrison's mobile, make some more appointments, go my rounds. See you at my HQ, Chandler. Good luck, boy." And he strode off.

So in one simultaneous breath I was "gentleman" and "boy". And *he* was a general who did not possess his own mobile phone but must *borrow* one from a scientist. Going his rounds, getting to know his human resources. In a society without yobs and without red tape. A culture which possessed the wizardry of advanced technology and science but which kept it as a delicacy to be savoured rather than a crutch to be leaned on. A civilization of honourable human beings that consoled me for the loss of Great Britain, the decent realm lost before I was born, lost as Atlantis.

Certainly a country to die for – but –

More than that: Topland was a country, I now knew, for whose sake I was willing at last to face the accelerating, downward curve of the far southern Slope. I would face it, haunted though it was by what lurked beyond. Not that

I yet knew how, but I peeked into the future and guessed that not even the terror of the ultimate clutching void would prevent me from joining up, becoming a soldier and fighting the Gonomong.

7: Southward

I confess, it may have been a close thing. Until my next sleep period I managed to stay on target, resolved to do what I had resolved to do, but when I lost consciousness I lost my courage as well, and slipped into the most unhelpful dream: I had fallen on my face; I scrabbled and clutched at a damp grass slope as I tried in vain not to begin the last slide, the endless fall.

I awoke; I forgot the nightmare. Reasonably determined to be a good brave boy and stick to my decision, I went off to work. But there, another backlash occurred.

It happened during the tea-break. While I and the rest of the staff on my floor were gathering round to pick our brews from the trolley, all of a sudden I turned clammy and sick: cowardice had pounced on me, a confused wave of love and need for my little niche in Topland broke over me; no kind of argument, just an inner shrieking that pleaded, cling, cling to this tea-trolley domain, rather than go and fight for it.

A single word bounced into my ear:

"When?"

It had come from one of the nurses' lips. A member of the admin staff replied: "As soon as I have cleared my desk."

"Any decade now, in other words," scoffed one of his colleagues.

Nobody laughed; and it was then that I understood that the clerk had stated his intention to enlist.

I broke into the conversation and asked where I might find the recruitment office. Nobody laughed at me either; my voice was steady, and I hadn't had the visible shakes, so they probably thought I was being cool about it. The clerk sketched a map for me.

The recruitment office was within walking distance, and I – glad that I had no desk that needed clearing; glad that my moral wobble was over – went off during my lunch break.

The office was just an office. The receptionist at this doorway to doom simply took down my name, looked in a diary and gave me an appointment for the next day. Naturally. To be expected. I had no reasonable cause for dissatisfaction; yet, keen to start my training immediately, to march south as soon as possible and get it all over, I felt jittery with impatience.

"You're crazy," I said to myself. "No I'm not," I retorted. "How long will my fit of courage last? I *would* be crazy if I didn't make full use of it before it fizzles out." Exactly how soon that fizzle would occur – that was the vital question. No telling when I might suffer another attack like the one at the tea-trolley, involving some other symbol of civilized comfort. The answer, I told myself, depends upon which is the stronger, fear of what I am letting myself in for, or love of what I'll be fighting for; and since fear and love cannot be weighed, I cannot foresee the outcome, so I must commit, fast! I could not trust myself even one minute ahead.

That evening, with these anxieties snaking around inside my skull, I took a gamble. The notion that my fears were of the kind that multiplied in darkness, and that I could dispel them simply by shining the light of knowledge upon them, prompted me, after work, to head for the local library. I was determined to read up on the risky topics. For example: the international situation; the Gonomong; and what conditions might await me on the lower, steep-sloped latitudes of Kroth. "Face your fears and get over them" – that was the idea.

Sound advice, no doubt; except that, in trying it, I almost scuppered my plans for good and all.

In the reference section I sat down with a heavy, one-volume, abridged *Encyclopaedia Universalis*. Intending to let myself into it cautiously, as if an oblique approach could help you across a tightrope, I decided to begin not with "Gonomong" but with "Armed Forces".

"So, here we go: ARMED FORCES.... hmm.... stuff about organization, ranks, equipment.... see FORTIFICATIONS.... so turn to FORTIFICATIONS...." I riffled on through the top-right corners of the pages and came to "FORT-" and heaved the wodge of pages over and they whammed down to display a full-page illustration which smote my understanding with such impact that as I heaved the volume shut again I almost fell out of the chair. No good, no good, I gasped in futile rejection of the fortress of Neydio, latitude 60 degrees, slope 30 degrees. Leave it alone, leave it alone, I muttered as I stumbled out of the reference room. Down the stairs I lurched, through the swing door and out of the library.

Perhaps if the picture had been described to me by someone else, instead of seen directly by my own eyes, terror would not have poked its bright eye over the parapet. I could then still have searched for knowledge by word of mouth; could have asked around, got chatting, joined a class to help myself adjust. But time was short and I wasn't taking any more chances. The only sure way for me to deal with the demon of fright was to *close the frontier of knowledge*, set up an Iron Curtain and post up "ignorance is bliss" along the barbed wire.

So there you go, Duncan my lad, your fact-finding efforts have left you in a worse state than before.

I stood sweating in the interview room at the recruitment office the next morning. A sharp-eyed man in his forties looked up from the papers that littered his desk. His was a kindly face, with that look of superior relaxation which is a sure sign of rank.

"Sit down, Wemyss. I'm Major Dittenden. I want to know your reason for joining the armed forces at this particular time."

"To fight for Topland, sir."

"To fight for Topland." He flicked at a document and then expressed himself with a mild Krothan expletive: "*Kerunk*, lad, according to these records you are oneirogeocentric, extremely so. Should you not confine yourself to some reserved occupation? Some task that you can carry out with honour to support the war effort from closer to home? As a soldier in the field I expect you'd be all right physically – it appears you passed the medical easily enough – but with your inevitable phobia about the Slope, you would be an encumbrance. You'd do us more harm than good. You must see that."

"I do, sir, but I also see that if things were as cut and dried as you say, you would be telling me, not asking me."

He smiled, "That's a little hit you've scored. Go on."

I have a trick, which sometimes works, when I need to say something effective. I de-focus my eyes. Then I can no longer see the person I am speaking to, and this helps me carry out a compensatory sharpening of *inner* focus, turning my ordinary verbal ability into something higher than average. I did this now, so that Major Dittenden's face became a blur to me as I replied:

"Sir, I heard General Faraliew say something positive about ignorance. Whatever he may have meant, I can tell you for sure that I have made a bargain, by which I am able to suppress fear provided that I suppress knowledge too. I can be a simple soldier – with the emphasis on *simple*. Yes, I want to live in Topland – I *need* Topland – and that means I must fight in defence of my home. I cannot endure *not* to. Even if I could do useful work at home, the idea of staying safe while others protect me – no, sir, I couldn't do it."

Major Dittenden thought for perhaps three seconds, then pushed a paper towards me. "Sign here." I signed; he countersigned. (*Kerunk!* thought I, my tactics sometimes work.) "Very well, soldier, you can report to barracks tomorrow afternoon," he continued, "provided you spend up the kit-list: just remember, you're not on Earth now." And that was that. Interview over. But what exactly – I wondered as I made my way out into the street – had he meant by his final sentence? Not wanting to seem dopey, I hadn't asked him. Never mind. I had said the right things. I was in.

I looked at the signed paper in my hand and saw that most of it, the kit-list part, was in the form of tear-off vouchers. So that was it. The idea evidently was that each recruit must equip himself, by going round the shops that sold the items for the kitbag. *Fair enough. Just a looser way of doing things here; admin less centralised, less spoon-feeding than in the dream of Earth. Only –*

I stared at the most disquieting voucher.

Weaponry: one pistol. Fight a war with pistols?

You're not on Earth now, that's for sure.

Oh, well, presumably the enemy, likewise, don't have anything more accurate or long-range than we do. There'd be no point in sending us south to be slaughtered, would there?

*

Dr Rallod, just before I left his employ, said to me: "You're following your conscience, Duncan. You're not being pushed, remember that. If you should change your mind and choose to stay, no women are going to hand you any white feathers."

"I know that," I said. "I know this is a good society."

"Better than Earth?" he smiled.

"Yes!" I gave back.

He lifted his brows at my defiant tone. "Well! A serious compliment! And I suppose it clinches the matter – but...."

His hesitation gave me the opportunity to interrupt respectfully.

"Please, no 'buts', Doctor. I realize I'm not trained, but...."

He, likewise, interrupted:

"That's just it, but but but! You won't ever get trained. There isn't time."

"Uh?" I didn't believe him. I could not have heard aright. Send *untrained* people to the front line? Was that the way things worked around here?

I opened my mouth to protest – and then I remembered that it was my plan to keep things simple, which meant, as far as possible, keeping my mouth shut. Anyhow, since I liked this world so much, I ought to trust it, too. Despite its apparent absurdities, it had been good to me so far. Life on Kroth was worth while.

I must just hope that I would live to enjoy it. I was seventeen; would I make eighteen? My thoughts focused on this, as I absent-mindedly thanked Dr Rallod and took my leave.

....Not that I would ever actually celebrate my eighteenth birthday here. Dream-words such as "year" and "decade" and "century" are still used, loosely remembered as they are from Earth, but there are no years officially measured on Kroth, only days. Hundreds of millions of numbered days of recorded history. For example, my Krothan birth certificate states that I was born on Day 935,305,651. The Change, or the Awakening from the Dream of Earth, occurred on 935,312,037, when I was 6,386 days old....

Dates on Kroth look more like bank account numbers. Or – credit card numbers!

I smiled at this whimsy. *Young though I am for a credit card, my minimum payment is already due.*

*

There were fewer men of military age in the streets than there had been the previous day; war-news had spread its influence like a suction pump through Savaluk. Drawing my cloak of ignorance about me, I averted my eyes from the placards and walked past them without buying any newspapers. "Since I'm headed for the real thing," I figured, "what need is there to read about it as well?"

The great blockish barracks building was magnificent in its heavy way, many-storied and fronted by columns. It stood well back from the street. This allowed space for an enormous square, which was crowded with soldiers and vehicles. As I neared the ENTRY sign several long jeeps carrying youngsters in sky-blue uniform rumbled past me on the other lane, on their way out.

I passed into the square and approached the building. Out of its front doors, like a lolling tongue, poked a queue of recruits. I unslung my kitbag and, carrying it by hand, joined the end of the queue. There were questions I was bursting to ask but the queue was shuffling forward, as fast as in an efficient post-office where all the counters are manned and none of the customers happen to want anything complicated; so there wasn't that stability which encourages conversation between strangers. Still, why not risk a word or two? I could tap the large youngster in front of me on his hulking shoulder and ask, for instance, *Are we really going to fight a war with pistols?* No, wait and you'll learn; so I told myself for the umpteenth time. On we shuffled, and the great doors drew closer, and I raised my eyes to the magnificent relief sculpture on the central frontage above them: it was an armoured man on horseback, three times life-size, with a wavy-lined cross blazoned on his shield. A phrase came into my head, that I must have heard somewhere: *the Ripply Cross.* A wavy line, in the iconography of Topland, was packed with connotations of heavenly peace, for the waves stood for the idyllic polar sea, Nistoom. And a *cross* composed of wavy lines combined this symbolism with the added quality of a Christian message. Love, peace, gentleness. On the other hand the man *was* in armour, astride a warhorse, and holding a long, strange, two-pronged lance. Curling above his shield were the words,

NOTHINGE DID HE DREAD

and below it:

BUT EUER WAS YDRAD

Underneath the sculptured hoofs was inscribed:

"General Necon Carredh, 935,120,419 – 935,147,904."

Others in the queue besides me were looking up at the impressive carving. The big lad in front of me said, "Uh – what does 'ydrad' mean?"

The youngster in front of him said, "Goof what do you think it means? Dreaded! Frightened! Means he weren't scared of nothing, others were scared of *him.*"

"Why is it spelt all funny, like?"

"I'm surprised you could tell! Fact is, no one knew how to spell in those days – bet you wish you lived then, eh, Archie?"

We passed through the doors. In the lobby, a close-mouthed official checked through the stuff I had bought with the vouchers, measured me and issued me with the one thing the Army did give out directly – a uniform, which I donned while they stored away my old clothes. Again I asked no questions; all of us were being processed with breathtaking speed (except for Archie; they had taken one look at him, and led him away to be measured for a special-sized uniform). Then, ordered to follow my predecessors, I was out again, in the open air. A voice told me to hurry and I – bewildered with the thought, *Is this it already?* – stepped up to fill the last space on a crowded jeep, which immediately roared off, swerving through the exit from the square and onto the avenue.

Including myself there were twenty men in blue, mostly young, in the back of the jeep as we rolled southwards. Pedestrians waved to us as we swept by, and we waved back, and then came the twinge, the moment of understanding, when there was no one left to wave to and no option but to take on board the fact that the streets of Savaluk were behind us and we had accelerated onto the Great Royal Road.

But can this really be it, already?

Better look intelligent; it might help.

We were on a section of the GRR that I had never seen – the part I had slept through on the way up, long ago it seemed, in Fabrizio's van. We were part of a strung-out procession, with similar vehicles some couple of hundred yards ahead of us and behind us.

Occasional hills varied the landscape, and where necessary the road curved around them, but for the most part this area of Topland was quite flat, allowing our stretch of road to run absolutely straight and our jeep to bullet along at motorway velocity, the wind roaring in our faces. I stole glances at faces and asked myself: was I the only one in the group who was flabbergasted at the speed with which this whole business had begun? Quite likely I was. The others, properly equipped with Krothan memories, must be more in tune with the unceremonious Krothan way of doing things. Nevertheless for them, as for me, it must be a solemn occasion. Some talked, but more were silent, and my own reticence did not seem unusual.

"Flat country" I call it, but of course nowhere on Kroth is it really flat, save at Nistoom, the actual pole. Already, therefore, we were descending the Slope, though, as yet, it was not detectable to the eye. I did sums in my head.... With roughly seventy miles to one degree of latitude, even at motorway speed it might be two or three hours before any gradient became noticeable.

Hurriedly amassing reasons to *look on the bright side*, my brain churned out a flow of morale-boosting thoughts:

I haven't chickened out, which is good. Some of the other lads look more worried than I am. Good, that means I am not the worst. On the other hand some look *less* worried than I am. Good, that means there's less to worry about than I think. Some look weedier and less fit than I do. Good, that means I am not the worst. Others look a lot tougher than I do. Good, they'll be stalwart when I have to fight beside them. Good, good, every way good. And the pistols: the ridiculous, footling pistols: could it be that the warring nations of Kroth have hit upon a set of habits and conventions designed to minimise battle casualties? Something like the Plains Indians with their "counting coup"? And whatever the range, we shall have the advantage of gradient. We're fighting from the North; the enemy has to climb up from the South. We can charge down on them. So all of that is good.

I did more sums in my head: we would make several hundred miles by nightfall.... and there would *be* a nightfall, for by that time we would have reached a point far enough south to enter the zone of day and night.... and wouldn't it be nice to experience sunset and sunrise again! So, again, good....

On the other hand –

(Stop that, I commanded as I found myself looking morbidly ahead to see if I could begin to discern the Slope.)

I had not yet spoken to any of my companions; I had, as the saying goes, retreated "into my shell". But most of the others were quiet too, perhaps for the same reason. They were, after all, Toplanders, who maybe had never set foot outside their fortunate level country; who might have even less experience of the Slope than I. I at least came from Guthtin, fifteen degrees of latitude lower down. This was a point that had not occurred to me before.

Approximately every half hour the jeep stopped for the sake of those of us who needed the loo. On the first such occasion, as we all clambered back on, I noted that the uniforms all appeared to be identical. Nobody wore extra stripes. We had no officers! Not even a lance-corporal was included among us. Yet the men seemed disciplined enough. Self-disciplined. That got me thinking: might I trust this lot? Trust them enough, for me to risk letting them know about my mental Earth-centredness? My lack of Krothan memories? I remembered the passage in Irwin Shaw's *The Young Lions* that vividly describes the "hazing" suffered by a recruit to the US Army during World War Two, ostensibly on account of his being a Jew, while in the same unit another recruit, likewise Jewish, is not bullied at all. As far as I could recall, the author gives no precise reason for the difference in treatment of the two men, but perhaps he was suggesting that Jewishness wasn't the main issue, it was more a case of one person giving out anxious vibes which aroused the bullying instinct in others, whereas another person didn't. In which case, all would depend on the manner in which I made my own admission of "differentness" – the "differentness" in my case being "Earthishness". The best way would be to emit a kind of *forthright* vibe. Abundant self-confidence plus zero sensitivity. That would be the style to adopt when taking the social plunge – which, sooner or later, I must do.

After about two and a half hours we passed a village sign which said: "Merebbon: 88 degrees North".

"Still can't see the tilt in the ground," I heard myself say to the soldier next to me.

The lad – he looked a couple of years older than I – answered with a bit of a Mancunian accent (although so far as I know there is no Manchester on Kroth): "Two degrees down not quite enough. Three, and you'll see it."

"Is that a fact?"

"So I'm told," he shrugged.

Seeing as my mouth appeared to have opened of its own accord to start this conversation, and since it seemed to be going all right, I had the confidence to continue: "It'll be almost a relief, you know, when the ground *does* start to tip. I've psyched myself up…."

Oh brother, that's torn it. Shouldn't have admitted that I need to "psych myself up". Fool to suggest that I have a problem with the Slope! Will anyone want to fight alongside a.... gradientophobe?

"Yeah, me too," came the reply. "Besides, I'm curious to see it. Must be one hell of a sight."

So – my mood swung to self-confidence again – I needn't have worried. This fellow had spent all his life in Topland, whereas my home village of Guthtin was way down at fifteen degrees of Slope, so (I made the point to myself again) I actually had the advantage of experience over him! My ego began one of its waves of expansion. It got to the point where, in making friends, I was ready to take the kind of risk that can sometimes cut corners.

"Have you ambitions," I asked him, "to become an officer?"

"Er – how did you guess?"

"You're trying to grow an air-force-officer-style moustache," I explained in cheeky mode, risking the use of humour to cut corners in making friends. Everyone remembered the dream of Earth; it was surely good enough ground, common and safe enough ground, for jokes.

My remark set off some snorts from others sitting nearby. "Colonel Prabbs – sounds good enough, Bernie?" "This guy's got you sussed out, Bernie!"

Bernie, the Mancunian, said loftily, "No he hasn't. He's got the 'air force' bit totally wrong."

"I should think so – seeing as there isn't one!"

Bernie said, "It's the Navy I'm interested in." He said it quite loudly, and I recognized his technique. Social chess, you might say. Occupy a key square to prevent your opponent doing so. For example, here he was defying them to make the obvious retort, "There's no Navy either!", and because it *was* so obvious, they couldn't say it, else they'd exhibit a weakness in repartee. Having won command of the centre squares he turned to me and went on: "What inspires me, is that I'm dead keen on the Hornblower books."

"So am I," I said delightedly. During the next few minutes a friendship was born, based on a shared admiration for those terrific yarns of the final war with France. In addition to the fun of discussing literature, I had further opportunity to gauge my own relation to the vast majority who did not share my Earth-centred mental world. The differences between us, but also the limits of those differences, became clearer. Bernie, like the others, like almost everybody, remembered Earth only as a faded illusion, an intermittent memory, subordinate to the real life he was living, rather than the full and vivid dream-set which I possessed; yet regarding literature *inside* that dream we were on equal terms. Neither of us had ever sailed in the Royal Navy in Nelson's time. (In fact I've never been on a real sailing ship at all.) It is only the magical skill of C S Forrester that can bring Hornblower's era alive for any of us; so in that topic I have no advantage over the people of Kroth.

A chance moment came when others had fallen silent and I could tell they were listening to Prabbs and me. Never would there be a better moment, thought I, to "let the cat out of the bag". With the help of literature – which is a dream in any case – I could make my confession harmless.

So I said: "The world of the seven seas is home to me."

He's an oneiro, the whispers went round.

"Well, not home exactly," I amended in haste, "because Kroth is what's real, and what's real has to be home. But Earth is what I remember, more than here. Earth is what I'm – er – centred on."

Silence stretched for a few ticks.

"Well, kid," one companion growled, shrugging his gorilla-sized shoulders, "you're an oneiro, but we're all *shonks* round here."

Not knowing what a *shonk* was, I didn't immediately reply. I was, moreover, becoming aware that no reply was needed just then: for the whispers and the comments were none of them hostile. They were just curious. I had got away with it.

"Speak for yourself, Jake," said another soldier; "I'm no *shonk.* I've been as far down as fifty-five. That's a Slope of thirty-five."

This drew immediate fire. "Be quiet, Terry, we know you can do arithmetic." "Yeah, Terry, we all know you're the globe-trotting type."

The driest response came from Jake: "I on the other hand am just a humble TV repairman." He sounded the opposite of humble as he said this – Krothan machinery being so prone to breakdown, repairmen are the elite of the workforce.

I interposed: "A *shonk*, I take it, is a Toplander."

"More or less," agreed Bernie Prabbs. "Or, more loosely, if you live on the Slope you can slap the label onto anyone who lives further north. That is, anyone who inhabits an easier gradient than you do, is a *shonk*, to you. So we Toplanders are the only ones who haven't got anyone to use it against, 'cause nobody lives to the north of us; we're the real, literal, ultimate *shonks* – the flatties – the softies – the lucky so-and-so's who live on easy-peasy level ground."

"And how serious an insult is it - *shonk*?"

The men looked at each other uncertainly. The much-travelled Terry offered an opinion, "Mild to moderately abusive, I'd say. Sort of on a par with *gringo*, maybe."

I confessed, "No matter how far south I lived on Kroth I'd be a *shonk* in memory, since my memory remains anchored on Earth, and, well, as you know, all over Earth there are – there were – slopes but no Slope with a capital S. As you all know," I repeated, "as well as I do."

"Yes, it doesn't do to underestimate us," said Terry dryly. "Our Earth memories, though no doubt fainter than yours, are equally informative as to details."

"So, *shonk* one way, *shonk* the other, what does it matter?" I continued to muse. "I've been slow on the uptake."

"How do you mean?" asked Terry.

"Oh, just that, for hours I'd been shy of opening my mouth just because I reckoned no one would believe I could – er – cope on the Slope as well as you lot."

"Hey, man, Cope on the Slope!" cried Jake. "Let's make a march out of it. Cope-on-the-Slope, ratta-ta-tum...."

I had "broken the ice"; I had admitted to my drawbacks and had suffered no social repercussions. As a bonus, in doing all this I had helped to enliven the group as a whole. No longer did I scan the horizon ahead with quite the same fearful attention as before, and in my elation I must have overlooked the first dread evidence of visible tilt. When I did notice it, I was amazed at my own lack of fear. *Careful! Remember, this is just the start. The steepening accelerates as you go down.* As I wobbled on the ridge between overconfidence and terror, I was, fortunately, jolted out of these musings.

"Looks like we're about to hit town," said Terry. "About time."

The jeep ahead of us swerved to the right, leaving the Great Royal Road, and we followed, onto a side-road that led us under a sign saying "WELCOME TO GHEEN" before widening abruptly. We debouched onto an asphalt arc that looked likely to form the wide rim of an enormous circle; along this rim we rolled past hundreds of parked jeeps, motorcycles, staff cars and supply vans, till our driver pulled to a stop in a section with space available. I guessed that the entire circle must be big enough to hold an army, and perhaps *was* holding one, in a scattered sort of way. Inward, the hub was a pedestrian zone with stalls, cafes, throngs of customers; and beyond that, beyond the circle altogether, rose some three-storied buildings with inn-signs upon their roofs, visible from afar: "The Tilt", "The Blue Yonder", "The Sagging Horizon", "The Slippery Slope". *Very funny*, I grimaced as I rose from my seat. On my original way North, I had probably stopped at this place, but I had slept through the experience. Like it or not, now was the time to catch up on what I had missed.

The others were pouring out of the jeep while the driver said, "Three hours liberty! Three hours, remember!" – just before he himself jumped off. He turned to me. "Come on, lad. Make the most of it."

I got down stiffly and followed. The pedestrian hub, positioned like a magnified island amid a traffic roundabout, diverted me and many other recruits who might otherwise have put too sudden a strain on the facilities of the inns beyond. I stepped onto the "island" alongside a notice which said:

Gheen – 87 degrees 30 minutes North

Where the Slope Begins!

Fair enough, I thought, as a poetic statement: this is the region where you start to *see* the Slope. But not on this precise spot: here, right here, you can actually forget it, for the vehicle park is banked up level. The stalls and the bustle and commotion would in any case mask a tilt of only two and a half degrees. Fear's creep is here concealed and easy to dismiss. I shall have to confront it later, but not now.

I pushed on among the stalls, benches, tables. Girls in white and yellow uniform were emerging from a pavilion carrying trays and handing them to anyone who wanted one; the smell of sausages wafted in my direction, nicely associated with the neat, welcoming, decorous sight of the girls; I wondered what they were being paid, to look so happy. No – that was a rubbish thought, an Earth thought.

"Thanks – er – Zory," I said, glimpsing her name badge.

"Not Zory – *Zorrie*," she simpered.

I set down my tray at the end of a table. "Zorry?" I said, cupping my ear; she almost doubled up at this witticism, and skipped off, leaving me with a plate of sausages and spring onions, a hunk of bread and a mug of beer, and a deep gratitude towards Life, Fate and the Army's catering department as I munched away. I paid no attention to the strangers at the other end of my table, nor did I try very hard to locate Bernie and the rest as I gazed around; I would see enough of them shortly.

Then when I had just about finished I did spot one of them: Jake, the ex-TV-repair-man. He was wearing the look of someone who has been given a job to do as he exchanged a few words with the diners on the next table; then as he lumbered over to my table I saw he was wearing a badge with letters on it.

"Hi, Jake – what does *CC* stand for? Commander in Chief?"

"Complaints Commission," he shrugged. "Any gripes so far?"

"Certainly not. This stuff's good," I replied, tapping the plate with my fork.

"Courtesy of the War Office."

"Well," I remarked, "if they're equally good at other aspects of the campaign, the enemy had better watch out...."

Jake merely nodded and said, "Anyhow, if you want to see the *gry pee*, he's over that way." He pointed, added, "See you," and left me for another table, where I saw him lean over and exchange a few words....

I wondered, uneasily: whoever heard of a *nice* army? A comfortable army, good at serving food, but providing no training. A clever army, scouting the opinions of its soldiers, to invite grumbling as a safety valve.... But what was the use of that if, militarily, we were a bunch of amateurs heading south to get slaughtered.... Jitters must be laid to rest, pronto. I jumped up and strode in the direction Jake had indicated, to locate the *gry pee*, the person to gripe to, the Complaints Commissioner, whose very existence abetted my suspicion that this army was far too soft to be at all convincing as a fighting force. Dare I point this out? Probably not, for not only did I lack confidence in the Service, I had no confidence in my own thought-processes either; I was aware that my assumptions about military life were coloured by having read

Starship Troopers and hence highly dubious.... Yet common sense did insist that *some* toughening ought to be involved.... I was soft, and to save my own life I wanted to be made hard.... Still, this was only the first day.... Ah, but already I had sensed an atmosphere far too peaceful....

On the far side of the pedestrian zone, a small audience – ten or so – was scattered around some semi-circles of mostly empty seats. I joined this gathering, a few other recruits drifting in with me. We all sat facing towards an officer, an upright sixtyish man, who was standing on a sort of podium at the central position, with what looked like four henchmen seated beside him on low three-legged stools.

"C'maaaan, roll up there!" roared the gry pee in the style of a desperate stall-holder. "Don't be shy! Let's have some serious complaint now."

A trooper in the audience stood up and said, "Sir, I reckon I have one."

"Good; spit it out! And you, jury, wake up, listen and record!" the gry pee added for the benefit of the four beside him, who had been hunched with their elbows on their knees, staring boredly at the ground. They reached for their clip-boards.

The trooper then proceeded at tedious length to voice his complaint. It concerned the lack of guidelines in the packing of equipment into vans. We listened to him make the point that not enough thought was being put into the order in which the items were packed. Serious delays at the other end would occur if the stuff could not be taken out again in practical sequence when the van had reached its destination.... It seemed a conscientious complaint, most likely self-interested insofar as the trooper foresaw his own involvement in the unpacking process and didn't want to get blamed when things went wrong, but none the less valid for that.

The gry pee said, "Jury! Is this a gripe worth listening to?"

The four glanced at each other, exchanged a few whispers and then bestirred themselves to nod. Their foreman said, "We'd give it a Cee-plus, sir."

"So! I am therefore obliged," the gry pee addressed us, "to provide an answer. And my answer is this: Doubtless the way the vans are packed *is* wasteful, but, in war, if you eliminate one waste, you create another, so that in this particular case, for instance, in order to spend less time at the unpacking end you would have to spend more time on organization at the packing end. So what the hell. We'll look into it, but don't expect too much. Jury! Have I answered? Yes? Thank you. Next!

I told myself that this was the moment, if only I could bring myself to stand up and voice my own gripe, but the trouble was, having heard his style, my mind raced ahead to guess what his answer would be: *yes, we could train you, but that would take time and resources, and so what you gain on the swings you'd lose on the roundabouts, as the enemy would be doing things during that time, employing his own resources...*

No one else volunteered anything either.

"Next!" roared the gry pee, peremptorily refusing to accept our silence. "Next!" His voice grated like a stalling engine, his disappointment coming through to me as real. A crazy spirit of helpfulness overcame me, as though I had nothing better to do than oil the wheels of this set-up. I rose to say my piece after all.

"Sir," I began, "most of us – I mean, sir, is it wise to send raw recruits like me southwards into battle with no training? I realize," I snatched at the clever thought that I might pre-empt the argument, "that if we start training, it might give the enemy ideas in the same direction, and *he* might get trained too, which you could say might lead to something as bad as an arms race – a skills race. But…."

Silence enfolded the scene. The gry pee was grinning at me.

"But, what?" he said. "Is the thought popping into your head, that maybe you have answered your own question?"

"Yessir, I s'pose so," I mumbled.

A loud laugh tipped the gry pee's head back and then he swung towards the "jury".

"An acceptable gripe nevertheless, wouldn't you agree? Keeps our show on the road, eh?"

"Yeah," they responsed to this heavy prompting. "Bee-minus," added the foreman.

He turned back to me and now his grin was gone.

"Your name," he demanded.

"Wemyss, sir."

"Private Wemyss, you have a fidgety brain."

"Yessir."

"Don't overdo it, and you may go far. And now to respond to your question – because your own answer doesn't *quite* fit the bill:

"A lot of people say we don't train our recruits, but this is true only if you are referring to *pre-combat* training. If you survive, you'll certainly get trained on the job. It has to be this way; do you see why it has to be this way, Wemyss?"

"No, sir."

"Come on, think. ALL OF YOU, THINK." He scowled round the rows of seats. "Let me make a comparison that ought to be familiar to everybody, since this point is likely to come up again and again, as we all remember what Earth was like. Cast your minds back to that old dream. Remember that Earth's universe is mostly a realm of weightless Space. Try to imagine the training problem *there*, if a space war was in the offing, you were going to have to fight weightless and yet your training had to be confined to the ground! You couldn't do it. There'd be no way of duplicating that Space environment. You could try underwater, but it wouldn't really be the same sort of thing because you'd be surrounded by the pressure and the inertia of the water instead of the true emptiness of Space. Now then. Our problem is not that we're going to have to fight weightless; on the contrary, *our* Space presents us with the terrifying alternative, since weight pervades this universe; but our case *is* similar insofar as we're going to face a thing for which we are not and cannot be prepared; a thing that cannot be imitated beforehand. What would you expect us to do? Build, in the flat terrain of Topland, mock-ups of the Slope? Use mere hill-slopes to fake a tilt in the very *world*? Actually it's been tried, and practice has shown that the so-called 'experience' gained is never any real good. It's never sufficiently convincing. Nothing prepares you for fighting on the Slope, except fighting on the Slope."

*

The physical task of transporting an army over two thousand miles southwards to the front line involved much wear and tear on Krothan machinery. Frequently a vehicle would break down and its complement of soldiers would be distributed among others; room for this had been allowed for, as none of the jeeps had started out full. We actually looked forward to breakdowns as a relief from hours and hours of monotonous riding and the inevitable stiffness and soreness. But for me, the *mental* business of enduring that journey was not much like any kind of ride at all.

Rather, it resembled crossing a dangerous torrent on foot. The "stepping stones" are the bright, optimistic moments. The gaps between them are the fears. To get across those gaps, you use the firmness and the lightness of heart which one good episode gives you, to jump you to the next. Jump a good jump and you don't fall in.

The tilt in the world had got to about five degrees when I heard the first engine switch off. One of the staff cars in our convoy, which happened to be running close to us, now ran silently, using the gradient alone, no longer needing to use fuel. It wasn't long before the driver of our jeep (a heavier vehicle, creating more friction with the road surface) was able to switch off likewise. The cessation of our motor, the awful sense of resigning all control, the surrender to the pull of gravity – that queasy moment might really have got to me if I had allowed it to conspire with something else, with the slight but increasingly ominous sag in the forward horizon.

Fortunately (and not a moment too soon) relief came. From here on downwards, the builders of the road had ensured that no straight stretch should last more than a couple of miles. So now, instead of hurtling directly South, we zig-zagged down. Let this be a lesson, I told myself, to trust the authorities; I might have guessed that they would not be so stupid as to allow us to get carried away by a lethal slide into continuous acceleration on an endless "free-fall" Slope.

That relief was my next "stepping stone".

During the following lunch-break we found, as we ambled back from the inn, that our jeep was gone. It had been driven back north. What? No more transportation? None of us could explain it.

"There's Murena. Ask *him*," suggested Bernie.

An officer was standing ten yards off, at a part of the depot where some other jeeps had been parked; those vehicles, like ours, were gone, and in their stead were some cheap and flimsy-looking metal carts, into some of which soldiers were already climbing. The officer, swarthy and imperturbable, supervised the embarkation with occasional languid gestures. When he noticed us he pointed to the cart assigned to us.

"Captain Murena, sir," said Terry Croale, "are we really supposed to ride in that thing?"

"Yep. Downhill all the way." His mouth quirked as he spoke those words, as happens when someone quotes a cliché. And that was the whole extent of the help we got from Murena. We got the message: *If I'm not worried, you ought not to be worried either.*

Well, the cart's brakes should work.... and the zig-zag road must in any case prevent uncontrolled increase in speed.... and if the authorities weren't worried.... it all seemed right in theory....

We got on, and our driver (a sergeant Paxton) released the brake. The cart began to roll. *Downhill all the way.* I tried my best not to be spooked by that appalling little moment of soundless release. *No motor. One-way. We're being poured down...* My thoughts backed off, like a snarling dog with hackles raised; only, I was snarling at the very laws of nature.... Really, you must take it easy, Duncan old ego, I whispered. Hang on, boy, hang on. Really, it isn't so bad. Only a few degrees as yet.

The fact that this army depot – Ullend was its name – was situated amid rich farming country, helped. It is hard to feel spooked when rolling past orderly hedgerows and fields dotted with cows. It all looked, from a certain angle, so familiar! However, this restful, reassuring effect had its limits. Strict limits. The place would have looked English in a photograph, but only in a photograph; in reality the overall Slope, slight though it was, wiped out any spiritual similarity to England, Earth.

At the stops, when the vehicles in our company halted for food or rest, Murena could be seen going from cart to cart, supervising our acclimatisation. He wasn't much help, in my opinion. I can't speak for the others, but I know that *my* fears could not be quietened by a sardonically amused look or phrase intended to belittle the creep towards geographical terror. It was all right for *him* – he'd been down to Neydio, sixty degrees, several times before – and so he paraded his unconcern, with a breezy "Downhill all the way!" or "It's a slippery slope – get used to it, men, it's here to stay!" I froze when I heard such phrases. He seemed to delight in needling us. In some ways he reminded me of my frequently cynical Uncle Vic, except that with Vic the needling was a device to provoke argument; whereas with Captain Murena, our superior officer, there was no answering back; we just had to sit and take the mockery. That was not the way to banish the ultimate vertigo that threatens you on a cart which rolls you down the tilting world.

I say all this, and yet – *was* he wrong? He gave us no guidelines at all, no rules, no tips. He ripped away our expectations of help and advice. He kicked each of us into our own individual void. At least we knew where we were with him – nowhere. Private Wemyss must fight his private battle. And what happens if he doesn't know how? Dare he strike out on his own?

Oh, go ahead, think your unreasonable thoughts; war is not a reasonable thing; you haven't even found out anything about the enemy, nor are you in any hurry to do so; you have your reasons to be unreasonable, to relax and swim in the ocean of events; let those who are paid to know it all, sort it all out. And talking of oceans, why not pretend that blue sky down there is not air but sea? Say: "One blue is like another." Say: "If the worst comes to the worst and you fall off the world and into the infinite sea of ether, what does it matter whether you freeze, starve or asphyxiate first? Dead is dead! It doesn't take forever! And the end result will be the same as if you had fallen into an Earth-type ocean."

But this kind of attempted trick, of trying to belittle my own fears, did not really work much more effectively than the belittling of them by Murena. Or at any rate, the benefit didn't last long. Worse terrors exist than those which simply threaten to *do*. The worst threats are the threats to *show*. Otherwise no one would ever be scared of entering a haunted house. No use trying to avoid *that* kind of fear by saying dismissively, "dead is dead".

A better idea was to get into a routine whereby I turned my head in accordance with the zig-zagging of the cart. Along a south-west stretch, turn to look north-east; along a south-east stretch, turn north-west. In this way I would keep my eyes averted from the South, as much as I could without making too great an exhibition of my cowardice. Many of my poor fellow-wimps, I covertly saw, were doing the same. Trying our best not to make it too obvious, trying to do it more with eye-movement than with head-movement, we could, however, look directly South *sometimes*, because in the game of hide-and-seek with Fear you can *sometimes* peek out at it, just as a mouse can emerge from its hole when the cat is not looking. And in my case, when Fear did cotton on to my presumption, and swerve to pounce, I did not merely have the option of turning my head away from the South; I could also, as an alternative, do my old trick of defocusing my eyes. Then the blue-haunted downward gulf became a blur which might have been simply a view over sea, rather than the outrageous cosmic tilt which it really was. I could do this, because the Slope was still relatively mild. Even so, I could not do it for long, because of the strain on the muscles around my cornea.

Hour by hour the Slope increased, as it must do, while every feature in the landscape, every growth or construction, maintained a vertical stance increasingly at odds with the ground. Trees, bushes, houses, pylons, even the long grass in the meadows shouted, look, the world really is tipping, it's not just a cockeyed view of your own, it's the real business, keeling over; we'll keep upright as long as we can but it's getting harder and harder and there'll come a time when we and you must topple!

The stupid part of me came to the rescue: *You're all right at the moment because you've been over this stretch before, when you went along it in the other direction, going up. Admittedly you were of course facing north on your way north, so you were spared the view south, but still, you were going over this very ground. You stood the strain then; you can stand it now, and in fact for a while yet, all the way down to the latitude of Guthtin, your home village with its Slope of fifteen degrees, you have proved that you can stand it.*

Sometimes you have to go for the stupid fix, like when you borrow more money to pay your debts: a temporary fix at the cost of making the underlying problem worse in the long run. Just what would I say to myself when I *passed* Guthtin? No answer, eh? Sometimes, you have to be stupid. You've no choice but to lurch onto a dead-end stepping stone, to buy time.

Is that not reasonable?

But in what condition were we going to be, by the time we had to fight? Fighting was bad enough on Earth –

The impulse to get my war-service over with, to get myself through the whole show with the minimum of fuss, I had illogically combined with the opposite worry, that we were taking it all far too lightly. We weren't doing nearly enough to get worked up about it. Now that old lack-of-training gripe presented itself again. This time it gave a clue to the next stepping stone:

If we couldn't be trained, could we not at least do some kind of equivalent of a war dance? Put effort into committing ourselves emotionally as well as physically? Perhaps I could try this idea out on Jake. Get him to snap out of his sullen acquiescence as the cart rolled us down the GRR towards our doom. I could suggest, tactfully, as a military comment, that the Henry-the-Fifth-before-Agincourt style might have some point to it. I would omit to mention the added hope that, in getting our blood up to fight, combat readiness might also blank out vertigo.

I spoke: "Hey, we're a quiet lot, aren't we?"

"Yeah," said Jake, brooding beside me.

"Yeah," I echoed loudly. "The tone is somewhat lacking in rage, hate, berserk fury, et cetera!"

"What must I do? Get rabies?"

"I don't fancy frothing at the mouth much myself, but aren't we going to need something in that line? Assuming, that is, that there is something ahead of us to rage about. And if not, why fight at all?"

"I dunno," said Jake.

Terry heard that; he laughed loud. "What a reaction! 'I dunno'. Don't bother with him, Dunc; you'd do better having another session with the gry pee. Mind you, I don't suppose he can do much else than tell you that it's early days yet…."

"Don't you think he's much good, then? The gry pee, I mean."

"You didn't recognize him? Jon Tsorego – the famous conductor? That's who he is in civilian life. Not bad practice, perhaps, for dealing with gripes. I'd say he's good."

"I must try to find him at the next stop."

It didn't work out that way – I lurched onto a different "stepping stone" instead. For the next stop turned out to be somewhere important in my life, none other than my Krothan birthplace.

The village of Guthtin.

*

A camp had been set up on the outskirts and the usual three hours' liberty was accorded us, long enough for me to walk into the village and re-visit the scenes that had met my eyes when I first awoke from the Earth-dream and found myself in the real world. I went into grumpy old Mrs Nott's corner shop and bought a carton of juice and a sandwich. She actually managed to grunt "hello" when she saw me. Then I walked past the house inhabited by sprightly old Miss Tyler and rejoiced to see her in the garden, busily planting a shrub. She straightened.

"Duncan! In uniform! How grand to see you!"

"I'm glad to see you, Miss Tyler; good thing they let us off here."

"How soon have you got to get back?"

"Oh, in a couple of hours."

"Well, you go and enjoy yourself! But wait – just tell me – how is it? Are you all right? You look fine, but, you know…."

"I know. It's confusing."

"Well, I'm sure you'll do fine. You go and confuse *them.*" And lifting her trowel, she pointed dramatically south, a jabbing gesture of future triumph. "'Bye now."

I went down the street to my empty home, sat and had my snack, and then went next door and knocked. *Would she be there?* I heard movement; footsteps approached across the hall; my mind built structures, framed conversations; but the steps sounded feeble, a bit blundering. By the time the door was fumbled open I was ready for disappointment. Sure enough, before me stooped the wan and tottering Mrs Swinton, instead of the tall, bland loveliness of her daughter. "You want Elaine. She's not here," and my disappointment deepened. But then the mother added: "She's enlisted as a nurse. She's gone to join your army now," and while I stood astonished, my quaint hope must have flashed in my face, for her manner became welcoming and she invited me in for tea. I looked at my watch and said yes, I could manage some tea. So I came in and sat down, my head whirling with vague plans, and presently I had the sense to take this opportunity to ask Mrs Swinton if she could tell me anything, from her own experience, about the lands to the south of Guthtin.

"Not a lot," she said. "You could ask around the village, but none of us travel much in the north-south direction. To save fuel, we do our commuting and holidaying mostly east-west. North-south's a bit impractical. After all, we slope fifteen degrees around here. Run down, plod up, as the saying goes." She vaguely added, "Elaine once went on a school trip down to eighteen degrees. Some biology thing. Come to think of it, I could show you her geography book...."

"No, no books," I replied hastily, remembering the shock I had received from the encyclopaedia in Savaluk, "I much prefer to hear things spoken. The human touch.... Hey, I'd better be off now. Thank you, Mrs Swinton," and I put my cup and saucer down. "I much appreciate the tea." And little did she know how true that was. As the porcelain clinked on the tray I took care to hoard it in the medicine-cupboard of my imagination, where my memory keeps its doses of normality.

*

That snippet of information about Elaine's school trip gave me some extra "breathing-space", some hours' extension to the bearable Slope: I could now say to myself not only "it must be all right as far as fifteen degrees, for I was born in Guthtin", but also "it must be all right for another three degrees down, as far as eighteen degrees, if school trips go there".

Not that I was really in much of a comfort zone even while still in Guthtin. I might, for a minute or two, tolerate the sight of the blue void gaping at me over the slumped Southern 'horizon', but then would come an attack of understanding in which I would not only realize but *really* realize what I was seeing, and that was no good at all. However, I had myself under sufficient control, so far. The task before me, as ever, was to maintain this control. One consolation: the all-demanding struggle against cosmic fear left little time for worry about the prospect of getting shot at, maimed or killed. *Those* nightmares were standard issue; I could have got them on Earth.

For some hours, both before and after Guthtin, the Road's zigzags got gradually wider and shorter, and the corner embankments more extreme, and thinking ahead I realized that we must eventually descend to a latitude where the gradient would have steepened so far as to make such a highway impractical. That would constitute the point at which the resources and expense needed to build the Road were too great for it to continue. Also, perhaps at about the same gradient, the vehicles' brakes would no longer endure the necessary strain.

I wondered if that was where we would find the border between our culture and that of the Gonomong. I suddenly pictured some situation like a frontier of the Roman Empire, the end of a road marking a boundary where civilization ended and barbarian peril began. I thought of asking Terry Croale whether this guess was good. It would be a risk to ask, because he might give me more information than I wanted; a conversation, once started, can be impossible to steer.... It would be a pity to spoil my record of not knowing, which had supported me up till now. I glanced at Terry's worldly-wise expression.

He caught my eye.

"Figuring it all out, Dunc?"

"Do I look it?" I countered.

"You looked as though you were about to ask something."

An interruption came as our cart lurched around the next bend.

"I was just wondering," I said as my stomach settled, "where's the next stop. I'm getting tired of this everlasting swivelling Road."

"Not everlasting," he said gently. "The next stop is *Dorington Dradett*."

To judge by his tone, the significance of the name was supposed to be self-evident. I must have looked blank. Terry's manners were impeccable; he could easily have showed up my ignorance but instead he left me to work out the obvious from the chatter which followed.

"Never been there," said one voice.

"It's meant to be good," said another.

"All right if you like skiing," said a third.

Skiing! I might have guessed.

*

For three days we stayed in the pleasant town of Dorington Dradett, famous at the present time because it marked the current southward limit of the Road's construction. During those three days most of us, including myself, had to train intensively, to learn to ski on grass.

This would not have been necessary had my earlier speculations been anywhere near the truth. I confessed this to Bernie Prabbs as we slipped and slid and made fools of ourselves under the eye of a weary instructor, along with hundreds of other novices on a wide damp tilted meadow outside the town.

"My idea," I panted, "was that the front line began where the Road ends. Stood to reason, I thought."

"Brilliant. You were only eight hundred miles out – ouch!" He landed on his wrist. "Aaargh!"

"Idiot Prabbs!" yelled the instructor, bearing down on us. "You too, Wemyss – cut the chit-chat! Concentrate! The name of the game is – balance! And what are the rest of you *krunkers* laughing at? At this rate you'll be a lot of *yemming* old-age pensioners before you're any good! Put some effort into these few days, for heaven's sake, 'cause you won't get another chance in this flipping war, I can tell you!"

We concentrated. To my glad surprise, by the third day's practice I had become proficient, having graduated from a beginner's zig-zag to the more advanced style whereby you keep your hips pointed down-slope while you do the swerving with your knees – though I knew I couldn't expect this to work when the gradient became severe. I think most of us enjoyed acquiring the skills of grass-skiing; I know I did. The practical necessity was obvious enough: the Road had come to an end; those extra eight hundred to eight hundred and fifty miles South which still separated us from the enemy had to be traversed somehow, and for a great army in a hurry the only practical option was to ski. A bunch of tourists with time to spare might have made some use of the haphazard local "cable-routes" which, we were told, basically amounted to rope-controlled slides, but I never saw them and did not like the idea of them. I wanted no more careening about in vehicles of whatever sort. I relished, I craved, direct contact with the ground. To be thus "grounded" was the only way I could imagine myself enduring a descent of the world's flank without going mad.

In a crazy sort of way, part of me was even looking forward to it.

The day of departure dawned with a blustering wind as our company of about one hundred and fifty men took its turn to assemble in one of the meadows south of Dorington Dradett. When I turned my head for a last look at the town, my view of it was blocked by the enormous oblong warehouse that housed the stockpile from which we had been equipped – the last such supply dump on our route. From this point on, the army must fan out over countryside, quartering in scattered villages, encountering no more big buildings or roads or prepared sites for the rest of the journey. We were going to be "spread thin". To make up for such diffusion, things were now more organized in a personal sense; I knew and recognized my superior officers, not only Captain Murena who faced us for inspection in these final minutes before our race to destiny, but also Colonel Reece who wished us luck as he passed through our ranks before disappearing into the next field to continue his review. I remember the Colonel's shiny buttons; how my imagination picked on them: "Relax! Things can't be *that* open-ended, if uniforms are *this* smart." All sorts of illogical senses of belonging, and of subservience to timetables, helped counteract the prospect of being thrown into infinity. And on the meadow's southern boundary a curved line of chestnut trees, lashed by the wind, suggested a cordon of friendly gesticulating giants barring us from the gulf. I knew of similar tree-lines beyond, planted out in a fish-scale pattern extending for many miles. It was the stately remnant of a much denser, thornier zone of defensive vegetation dating from days long gone when *this* used to be the frontier. Nowadays the action was far to the south.... My attention veered back to the voice of our captain.

"Now – sticks down and move forward!" Murena was saying. "Next, you in the second line...."

I looked down once at my stubby grass-skis, flicked my eyes to right and left, timed my push to coincide with that of my neighbours – and we were off. This – was – *it.* Murena saw us move, saw us come towards him in reasonably good formation. Satisfied, he turned his back to us; his face no longer a white blob at the end of the field, he became a brightly coloured helmet to follow. We wove our way through the first belt of trees. Then we were in another sloping meadow with a similar boundary, through which another company was just then disappearing. We reached and passed through that next tree-line – and, to my surprise, halted.

When I saw the reason for the interruption, I laughed out loud; and I wasn't the only one. "No!" I heard someone say, "they can't be serious!" It was so obviously too late!

Old Tsorego, the gry pee, was holding a session in that field. Very clever, the authorities. I saw their game now. How it's played: always hold the griping session too early (like the one at Gheen), or, like this one, too late. Because, of course, when we are already setting off on our skis, we've psyched ourselves to advance and we don't *want* to have to rev up our courage all over again, don't *want* to voice complaints. Very clever it is, to give out the appearance of willingness to listen, without any danger of actually having to listen to anything substantial.

We were told we could break ranks; we were given an allowance of ten minutes for questions. Since none of us felt up to framing any questions, we mutely gathered round the wooden dais on which the gry pee stood surrounded by his jury – who had nothing to do on this occasion – and listened to Jon Tsorego.

The elderly conductor wasn't embarrassed at all by our silence; he *invented* gripes, to supply our deficiency. He voiced them and then he refuted them himself, in a manner which flaunted the self-confidence of the government. A weaker regime would not have dared the risk of putting ideas into our heads. The message was clear: *Our trust in your loyalty and maturity is so complete, that we can afford to discuss the causes of this war in an objective, judicial spirit, considering all sides of the question, even while we are sending you out to fight...*

"I have heard the view," Tsorego was saying, "that the peoples of the South are bound to be oppressed; that we Northerners hog the best land, the nicest, lowest gradients, and that all our wars are therefore unjust. I have also heard the opposite view, that it is the peoples of the South who are the natural oppressors, because it's so easy to fight down-slope that, over centuries, waves of aggressive types move South and their habits take root there, while the meek – that's we Toplanders – stay North and enjoy our more gentle lives.... until times come, like now, when the bellicose Southerners turn envious eyes back in our direction.... If they recapture the North, the entire process may repeat itself over millennia, a kind of cyclic class-struggle. Remember that old nursery-rhyme about the two hemispheres of Kroth?

Yeyld doth Hudgung
Overlie;
Yet Hudgung conquereth
By and by...."

The words, to me, were just words, though around me I sensed some trembling at the rhyme's sweetly sinister lines. But then Tsorego continued the lecture in a kind of sub-Marxist sub-Darwinian style until we got bored and the ten minutes seemed too long. And that, of course, was the idea. I admired the entire skilled arrangement, and what was more, I came to the conclusion that it was all fair enough: designed, wisely, to show us that griping is *always* too late. The message: we're here not to complain about the idiocies and futilities of the campaign but to get on with it.

Fatalism gripped me as we set off once more; *really* set off, this time. All complaints on campaign boil down to one thing: the ultimate and only gripe: war itself, the sheer wastefulness of war. But then life itself from beginning to end is all one long squirt of waste. Nature is "by nature" inefficient, slapdash, incompetent to an appalling degree, matter and energy blown to the winds... This being so – on we go!

The last line of trees approached. This was a vital test. Beyond must stretch open country and the obviousness of the Slope, pointing us at twenty degrees down into the endless gulf. And now I would be skiing directly towards the sagging blue. The solemn ethical stuff about war and peace – how much had it diverted my attention? Distracted me, while a crust of stability formed over the molten terrors of vertigo? And when the crust got too brittle and thin, what then? Already, war and duty had become insufficient to prevent my thoughts spilling beyond them, and within seconds I was about to find out how far I had progressed in my ability to play good mind-saving tricks on myself.

The moment came, we were through the trees and click! I knew I'd got it. I had somehow taken on the posture of mind and body which could get me through another chunk of downward distance.

Take note – this is what you must do:

Hunched on your skis, being tilted yourself, you re-interpret the Slope *as a level stretch* with your movement as a magnetic pull *along* rather than a gravitational pull down. You can do this provided you refrain from looking too closely at trees and houses and anything else that is too plainly not at right angles to the ground. Of course it's just a trick. And the trouble with this kind of dodge is that you can't rely on it for long; sooner or later the cloak of protection it provides is snatched away by a sudden jolt of reality, and when that happens you'd better have a replacement ready to wrap round you, because it's rather late to search for your next illusion when you're thrashing about in panic.

In my case, the next "replacement dodge" turned out to be easy to find; in fact it could hardly even be called a trick, for it grew naturally prominent in my awareness. It was the great consolation of being on foot (skis count as footwear); of no longer being wheeled helplessly down-slope in some hurtling wheel or cart. No longer having to feel that I was being tipped into infinity without any control over my fate, now I was doing my own hurtling;

I could stop if I wanted to – though if I did stop deliberately and without orders, I'd get into trouble. I suspected that some of the "accidental" falls I witnessed were of people who suffered an outbreak of fear and *had* to stop while they pulled themselves together. For me, it was enough that I *could* do the same if I had to. Enough that I could feel the steady ground underneath me, tilted though it was. Enough that I could exercise some vital degree of control in my direct contact with the world.

Beyond this particular reassurance, a larger comfort grew. The physical experience of days of continual skiing gave me a sense of the sheer solid bulk of the world. "All right, it slopes, but it's so huge it seems endless; and there is consolation in that." With such illogical trust did my spirits lean on Kroth's massive planetary shoulder as I voyaged microscopically downwards, so that, on a journey which might otherwise have blown my mind, the simple *size* of it saved me.

Yet of course you can't fool the intellect all the time. Truth has a nasty habit of crouching in wait. The Slope isn't really an endless inclined plane, it's a downward curve; its gradient must increase in an accelerating trend from which there is no escape, the trend which makes a certain four-letter word increasingly taboo among all Krothan societies to be found along the route, until, after thousands of miles – supposing you somehow got that far – you would meet the vertical outrage denoted by that four-letter word, DROP....

I say, then, that the planet's comforting size is but a treacherous friend to one's peace of mind; its consolation false.

Consolation nonetheless, because the acceleration of tilt is slow, imperceptibly slow, to a skier. Its gradualness gave me a chance to acclimatize my Earth-oriented soul to the unthinkable doom that lay ahead.

Already in accomplishment I was way beyond what had been my capacity during the first days after I had awoken on Kroth. Back then, I could not have remotely imagined daring a ski run into the face of the south's gaping blue. My personal frontier was certainly advancing; what was I turning into? "A survivor," answered my quiet inner voice. "Just another survivor." Without realizing it at the time, without knowing its name, I was preparing to acquire my version of *The Slant*. My equally quiet companions, likewise, must have been concocting their own recipes for survival.

Because we were on foot, and because we and the rest of the army were fanning out from the zero meridian path (which had been the Great Royal Road before Dorington Dradett; now it was just called the Wayline), we learned a lot more about the country we went through. I noticed a tendency among my companions to heed those of us who were amateur naturalists and bird-watchers, as they pointed out different species, and the slight changes in the colour of the grass we skied over, the turquoise tinge of the shellgrass, the richer and darker green of the shovelgrass. I noticed also that the grass became generally drier, more pleasant to sit upon when we stopped to rest or to camp out; the root system getting more efficient and sophisticated the more we went south, retaining a higher proportion of the moisture that trickled down from the Pole. Increased surface dryness might have made skiing more difficult, except that, of course, this effect was offset by its cause, namely, the steepening gradient.

We appreciated the evidence of contentment we found in the populations of the villages and the little towns where we halted for our food and drink. They treated us generously, as well they might, since we were headed south to defend them, but even more important than this, they provided us with an inspiring example of successful adaptation. We chatted with them about their homes and their lives, and derived reassurance from how ordinary they were; all we had to be careful of – our officers warned us – was never to use the word *drop*, which was considered very bad language, more seriously bad the further one went South. I only boobed once, in this regard. A group of us, resting in a village, had been stood lunch by a charming old couple who were keen to support the war effort by showing kindness to soldiers. We were at a round table, in an idyllic outdoor restaurant. At the end of the meal we thanked them and I lightly said something about "dropping in to see you on our way back". Silence fell. The villages winced. "We don't use that word," said the gentleman.

"Oops. So we don't. Sorry, sorry."

"Having said that," said the lady, "we would like to add: *do* please d – r – o – p in on your way back!"

"Lisa, you're awful," said her husband. "Now look what you've done," he grinned at me. And so I was let off with a good-humoured warning.

In these village scenes, I often found it possible to narrow my sight and pretend I was looking at a street scene on a steep hill on Earth, though of course as the days passed, and we met more constant reminders of change, such cosy moments became rarer. From Latitude 65° onwards, that is to say after the Slope had increased to twenty-five degrees, we observed much more terracing than before, in the fields and gardens we passed. It meant more frequent interruptions of our ski runs, on the approach to each settlement, and we had to make more effort to seek the long stretches of common land where the Slope continued unimpeded. And of course as the gradient increased we had to zig-zag more widely with our skiing, so that the narrow runs ceased to be acceptable to us and we had to walk further across country to find a useable stretch.

I have mentioned "terracing". In a larger sense, not all of it was artificial. Imagine a hilly landscape on Earth, and then imagine it all tilted. It will then happen that the up-and-down hill-slopes will look more like steps. I mention this in case I have given the mistaken impression that we were always descending a smooth slope. The Slope had its corrugations, which would have been hills and valleys on Earth but which on Kroth seemed increasingly like a series of giant steps leading down – naturally, for while northern faces were tilted towards the horizontal, the southern were tilted away; tending towards ridges and scarps, respectively. All this applied in "hilly" country. Elsewhere the Slope *was* flat and smooth, and especially good for skiing; yet on average our progress South underwent a gradual deceleration as we had to pick our way with increasing care.

I must stress that this change was very gradual, hardly noticeable from one day to the next, though becoming obvious if you compared any one day with a week before. The slow-down was fortunate because after about three weeks of skiing, as the Slope approached a gradient of thirty degrees, my mental defences against the terror of the void were threatening to crumble. They had got me this far but they could not be expected to last much longer. It was as if I were dreaming on the edge of a precipice and an unwelcome hand were shaking me, an unwelcome voice saying, wake up you fool, look where you are.

Social pressures worked on me also. I become quite a regimental mascot, a butt of friendly jokes and of some that were not so friendly, though there was no actual bullying. Much in demand for my anecdotes of Earth, I seemed to have become a never-ending source of amused fascination on account of the vividness of my memories, which, to many of the men, made the old dream-planet seem almost real; but the tension in some quarters got channelled into a kind of envious contempt, either of me, or of the picture I evoked: Earth where the ground was always flat; Earth where life was soft.

Juldwin Ronth and Jason Kerallg were two who liked to tease me about Earth.

Juldwin Ronth was a "black" guy, that is to say, African in features though grey-skinned like all Krothans. French was his first language, but he also was fluent in English. I met him through his sister Aswen, who was one of the nurses on the expedition; I had asked her if she knew where I could find Elaine Swinton, and though she hadn't been able to give me any information, the sweet-natured girl not only promised to let me know if she found out anything, but also invited me to dine with her and her brother. His pal Jason Kerallg, a ginger-haired "white", was a self-confessed Wild West buff; which is to say, his hobby was that particular aspect of the dream of Earth. Kerallg and Ronth more than once dragged me into their arguments about Earth history. At first I responded with approval of their thirst for knowledge, but their jokey indirectness, their frequent laughter, their habit of ignoring my opinion after having asked for it, put me off – even before I realized that they were using my ego as a punch-bag.

"Have another beer, negro!" suggested Kerallg to Ronth.

"It's my round, blanco!" offered Ronth. "Hey, Dunc, what do these words mean, anyway? I keep forgetting."

Desperate things can happen in dreams, which would have no importance in the waking world, and vice versa. I wasn't up to explaining Earthly verbal taboos about race.

"I told you enough times," I snapped. "Negro means black, blanco means white. They're just the Spanish words."

"But why call people by different colours?"

"Because people *do* have different colours on Earth! Come on, you must remember that much! They're not all grey there!"

"Ah," broke in Kerallg, "but there's more to it than that. Blanco never got used in English. Negro got used, then forbidden. Forbidden in English anyway. You had to say 'black', instead."

"Really?" said Ronth. "The Spanish word is bad, the English word good?"

"Yep, I guess so. It's called political correctness. Isn't it, Dunc?"

I said sullenly, "We've been through this before. Historical pressures…."

"But what about the Spanish?" insisted Ronth. "*I'm* interested in the *logic* of this. What do politically correct Spanish people say? Are they not allowed to use their *own* world for 'black'?"

"Well, you got me there," replied Kerallg, giving his head a solemn shake. "My guess – mind you, it's only a guess – is that the letters n-e-g-r-o must give off some evil vibration when spoken inside an English sentence but the vibration fails to get triggered if the accompanying words are in Spanish. What do you think of my theory, Duncan?"

"I think…." I relaxed my features. "I think both of you have succeeded quite well in establishing that the people of Earth were a pack of idiots. The topic is therefore exhausted, and we can proceed to talk about something else."

"I might ask Captain Murena," mused Ronth, "about whether there's such a thing as Spanish political correctness."

"Don't blame me if you get shot," remarked Kerallg. "That guy looks like General Santa Anna about to give the order to storm the Alamo…." From here, to my relief, the conversation took a new turn, diverted into whimsical physical comparisons between various famous people and our officers.

The next time they invited me for a drink, the eerie "where am I?" feeling nudged me in a big way. By this time we had journeyed so far south, we were actually in sight of the official boundary of Upland, or "Greater Topland". That is to say, we were coming at last to the border beyond which the government's writ did not run. We sat in a tea-shop (that's what they called it, though it sold beer as well), in a village called Volost, latitude sixty degrees North. I could hardly refuse the invitation; Ronth's sister Aswen was still my best hope of finding Elaine.

"That's right, Dunc, sit with your back to the wall," said Kerallg light-heartedly as I took my place at one of the tables. "You take your lesson from Hickok."

"I take it," said Ronth, "this Hickok personage was shot in the back?"

"Uh?" Kerallg gaped at the other's ignorance. "Sure was! Sat with his back to a door – the last mistake he ever made. Best-known fact ever came from South Dakota. Man, it's part of the general human racial subconscious by now…. Wassat, Dunc?"

"I said," I said, "I just wondered if the Krothan Hickok met a similar end."

"Aw, never mind about that. I don't suppose there ever was a Krothan Hickok of any importance. Say, you're looking a bit green, you know."

In truth, queasiness had swamped my innards. *It's not the door*, my thoughts slurred; *not anything to do with the door*. It was the window that was at my back. *And I wanted it to stay that way.* Unlike the ill-fated Wild Bill Hickok I was likely most of all to be shot *in the eyes.* If I turned my head. If I did that, I'd see through the tea-room window, and I'd be afflicted by what I saw.

Of course, I had already seen. Had already realized. Our company had been halted here in Volost for a couple of days now, waiting, presumably, for the leadership to decide which ski run to go for next. But to see a thing need not mean much. It's only when you can add the word "really", that's to say when you *really* see it, when you *really realize* it, that the crumbling begins.

Searching for the next ski run? Rubbish. That couldn't be why the army was waiting here. At a Slope of thirty degrees it was time to admit that it was getting too steep for skiing. This was the end of the line for us Toplanders. This was where we were going to have to stand and fight. And this explained what I would see if I turned and looked out of the window; what I had once glimpsed weeks ago in the encyclopaedia back in that library in Savaluk.

The fortress of Neydio had affected me badly then, as a mere diagram on a page. It oppressed my awareness now, yet I won't say that I felt as horror-stricken, in sight-range of the real thing, as I did when it was just a picture. A silent revolution was taking place as I sat in that tea-room: some mighty wrenching process was going on inside me. The sick feeling was positive, a sign of something good. My mind needed to be churned, as a tin of paint can need a stir with a brush. Speedy re-arrangements of thought were accompanied by an understanding of the many good-byes I had heard during the past couple of days. Over a dozen members of my company, and similar numbers from other companies, had turned to plod back up-Slope. These departures signified that not everyone had been able to make The Adjustment. The Thirty-Degree Adjustment. The special slant you had to acquire if you were going to have what it took to live in these parts. For practice seemed to show that a Slope of thirty degrees was a kind of psychological turning point: the world now tipped so much, that there was a mass-extinction of those pretences and mental subterfuges which had kept us going so far. *You gotta get the Slant, else it's no good.* You adjust fundamentally, or you go back. *And those who remain, such as I – what have we become?* When next I stepped out the door, I might gaze unflinchingly down into the sagging blue sky, but would I look forward to crawling down the side of Kroth all the way to unspeakable Hudgung if need be?

"The line's gone dead. Hey, Dreamy, you all right?" came the voice of Juldwin Ronth.

"Sorry. Fine," said I, straightening. A moment's effort was enough to bring me to a state of concentration and of clarity of mind. I actually felt good.

"We want your advice, man," said Kerallg. "We hear you met the General."

"Faraliew? I met him once," I admitted.

"You know his tea-habit?" asked Ronth.

"No. His *what* habit?"

"Any one of us, any time, may get summoned socially. Along with the colonels and majors in his tent, we may find ourselves sipping tea and discussing strategy; yes, it happens, some poor sap like one of us gets chosen to attend, dragged into the conversation…."

"Socially, heck!" I snorted. "If he is doing that kind of sampling, it must be he's sounding us out, wanting to know how well the army will fight."

"Well, then: suppose it is that. We still have to say something. Any ideas?"

Before I could think of an answer, Kerallg broke in: "Hey, how about this: we could tell him how eager we are, how much we're looking forward to battle; then he'll conclude we're mentally ill and send us home."

I smiled, wondering how likely it was that his sort would remember stuff from Earth literature, or whether he had thought up *Catch-22* independently. Either way, it was all right as a joke, but that was all. "It's maybe not so crazy, to want to stay and fight," I suggested.

Ronth stared at me. "What? You – a fire-eater?"

"No, but think a moment. Are we really in such a hurry to start off for home? *It's a long plod back.*"

After a moment's silence the faces of the other two lit up, and, for once, they gave that kind of laugh which made me feel I'd struck just the right note. At that point we were interrupted – everyone in the room was interrupted – as the door was thrown open and an officer on the threshold shouted for quiet. "The Gonomong!" he cried. "The Gonomong Fingers have been sighted! All men under arms: report to your units – we are going to have to be ready to fight in a few hours. Locals: continue your normal activities, except when requested otherwise. That's all." The officer disappeared. I and my companions shouldered our way out as the hubbub began.

8: The Battle of Neydio

A new man, wiped free of fear, I stepped out of the tea-room, in that strange condition known as readiness for battle.

Of course, as usual, I distrusted the mood, was convinced there must be a catch to it, a price that in the long run would have to be paid for it. On the other hand I was also willing to try out my calmness in the open. I would be a fool not to test how it performed; a fool not to reap what advantage I could from it, while it lasted.

But (came the thought) – but suppose it lasted forever? Perhaps my nature had changed permanently!

Perhaps, in adapting me to the Slope, the Slant had turned me into a warrior.

Hell – I would have preferred to have been asked.

Fine, yes, to become brave, but what about the accompaniment to this change: a certain blanked-out feeling, an odd hesitation in recognizing myself? Courage at the cost of identity – must life bring such package deals?

One sensible precaution I could take: *look, now, at the running crowds in front of me, and at nothing else.* Maintaining the narrow focus of attention, the guarded motions of my eyes, which I had learned during the descent to Latitude Sixty, I joined the throng of regular soldiers, local militiamen and civilians who were rushing down-Slope, and as I allowed myself to be thus swept along, I clung to the motto, *one thing at a time.*

We jogged over the east-west railway nicknamed the Spoing, which connects Volost with the other villages strung along Latitude Sixty; we passed through a dramatic line of boulders poised on its southern edge, and continued down towards the far greater landmark which drew us, the great defensive embankment parallel to the railway but a couple of thousand yards further south.

It was called the Vallum, that artificial ridge; but no ancient Roman army ever built an earth-wall that size. It looked like a magnified Offa's Dyke with a Great Wall of China running along the top of it. During the past couple of days I had found out something about it. Its immemorial prehistory was intertwined with folklore; its construction and maintenance had for ages been a kind of national hobby for the folks in these parts. Time had not crumbled it; had, instead, made it stronger, since through millions of days it had become pervaded by the tough root system of shovelgrass.

Within minutes the vanguard of the crowd reached the base of the embankment and began swarming up its close-cropped north-facing slope. I, and those with me, each followed at our own speed, knowing that there would be space for all of us at the top; we had an easy climb, with plenty of footholds on the exposed shovelgrass roots, much easier than what the enemy would have to face on the Vallum's southern side, which we had left covered by the broad dark green blades, cultivated to be slippery.

I reached the stone topping, which was marked on the near side by a line of low pillars rather like hitching posts for horses; and I stepped onto the crenellated summit. Many of those who had got there before me were already opening the storage bins, containers the size of skips which rested along the wall's outer edge, one of them every ten yards or so, and taking out various hand-weapons, mostly a variety of spears, eighteen feet long, which they then stood against the battlements' notches, ready to be seized. (I call them "spears": you could more literally refer to them as forks, since they were double-pointed, with two barbed prongs at the end, ten or twelve inches apart.) But most of us were given no job to do as yet. There, among thousands of men (and some women and children) along a line that reached for tens of miles, I saw with new eyes, and learned new things.

I had crept up here before, during the past few days of being quartered in Volost village, because the view from such a landmark, the line where Upland officially ended, was a "must" for tourists; but I had not been able to look around properly until now. Now I was able to gaze directly into the blue southern gulf, the *sagorizon*, coldly and unafraid. The old psychological bias towards flatness, towards assuming that flatness was normal, was – *click!* – gone. Horizontality no longer formed a part of my nature. From now on it was the permanent tilt, the forward foot lower than the other, which would seem normal. What one of the modern poets of Kroth has called the "expectation of roll and slide and angled consequence" meant that my inner mountain goat had come alive. In other words I had *got the Slant.* The Slant can be defined, simply, as the attitude you have to have, if you're to cope below latitude 60 without going nuts. And I had "got it good". *I've changed, it's done,* the news kept blaring in my head. The immediate result was that I could stand on a viewpoint and stare freely – stare down the slope of the world without flinching in the slightest – and so in a relaxed manner I could satisfy my eager curiosity concerning the landscape south of the great frontier wall: the northern edge of the immensity of Slantland, which must steepen all the way down to the vertical Equator.

The tilted plain, dotted with groves, fuzzily receding into an apple-green haze under the plunging sagorizon, seemed quite peaceful and still; the Gonomong had been sighted, but not from here.

Their approach must therefore have been noted from higher up, and this is where I must mention the second thing I learned.

I turned and looked to the right, westwards, to where, a few miles off, stood the fortress of Neydio. At such a moment I could have done with a twin brother, a second self to confide in and to compare impressions with. Though the enormity of the fortress no longer scared me, as it had done at that horrible moment I saw it illustrated in the encyclopaedia in the library in Savaluk, nevertheless a grimness remained in my heart where fear used to be.

Because I had done my homework, I had been informed of the thing's scale; therefore I knew it was no good pretending to disbelieve my eyes as they gawped at that artificial crag: its horizontal summit really did jut forth for two miles, coming to an end with a vertical drop of about a mile. Of course I knew better than to suppose that such a mass had been built up entirely by human hands. It must have been fashioned from an already existing scarp slope, engineered into the regular, indecently huge shape I now saw. Grudgingly, my mind could admit that it was possible, borderline possible, to sculpt a geological feature in that way. But it *set an unfortunate tone*. By this I mean that Neydio's flouting of the Slope, far from doing anything to blot the Slope out, *accentuated* it. You will grasp what I'm trying to express if you ever get to see the thing; you too may be driven to conclude that one extreme abets another, that Neydio's outrageous bulk threatens to unbalance an already wonky stage. You've just laboriously achieved some acceptance of what is going on, you've just "got the Slant", and then along comes *this*, and you're left with a skin-prickling sense of unreality.

I suppose that if I had grown up in Volost or one of the other villages round about, I would have taken the thing for granted. As things were, I would forever be too much of a stranger here to get as used to it as that; nevertheless, *I was able to look at it.* That was the important point I now learned. I was a different person from the Duncan Wemyss who had cowered in the tea-shop with his back turned from the uncanny sight of the fortress.

Here, then, was another confirmation of the change in me. What might earlier have been a dagger of terror that ripped into my mind, here and now was nothing much worse than a pinprick. It took a bit of an effort – but my recent acclimatization was preserved. I had indeed "got the Slant" for good.

"Wemyss," said a level voice.

I turned. It was Captain Murena, wearing the slightly pitying look I had often seen on his face.

"Sir," I said.

Murena's tone was quite mild: "The General wants to see you. Come on. I'll take you to the car."

The General? I swallowed some bitter saliva. Suddenly I was afraid I knew what this might be about.

It was popularly supposed to be random, the way in which Faraliew sampled the morale of the ranks. Certainly there was no known pattern in his choices. But had my number really come up just like a raffle ticket pulled out of a bag? Unfortunately for my peace of mind, I could immediately think of an obvious reason why I might be chosen today of all days. A very unflattering reason, which made me feel sick. *"If a mere oneiro like Wemyss can stand and fight, the rest of the army should do quite well."*

The injustice of it! I, the sensitive, stress-avoiding Duncan Wemyss had, after all, made sufficient progress that I could now stand calmly scanning the scene while many of my friends and companions, whom I might never see again, had been turned back days ago and were at this moment far to the north, retreating up-Slope back towards an easier life. For not everybody could function down here; not everybody could click into tilt-mode as I had managed to do; and thc army did not want people who could not adapt. I, for some reason, *had* adapted, *had* got The Slant, and that fact, in my view, should outweigh the blemish on my record, my dubious status as an "oneirogeocentric" Earth-dreamy. If they just gave me a *chance*, I could show them I could blend in, I needn't stick out in any way at all….

I growled helplessly under my breath as I kept up with Murena's eastward stride along the summit of the Vallum. His habitual expression of faint, ironic mockery did not help my mood, but at least he made no further remark, and I made an effort to rise above personal resentment, to take the opportunity to observe, especially whenever he stopped and I likewise had to stop and wait while he spoke to people. Sometimes he held brief conference with other officers; sometimes he would take a moment to borrow a spyglass that was held out to him by an important civilian, to assure the owner that he, Murena, could not yet see “the twinkling” on the sagorizon which would betoken the enemy advance. As far as all that was concerned, I asked no questions, and so the gap in my knowledge remained as huge as ever. I did not seek to know more. The approach of battle, I told myself, is too late to change one's approach to life. For me it was enough that the people in charge seemed confident that they knew what they were doing. I gathered the impression that when the officers spoke they were calming exuberant militiamen, persuading civilians to go home, and assigning regular troops to various stations along the wall, but whatever the case, I would just obey orders like a good cog in the military machine, so long as I was allowed to remain a part of it. We had time; the Gonomong were still some hours away. Just then (silly though this sounds) I was more perturbed by the thought of seeing the General than by the thought of fighting the Gonomong.

Finally we reached a blocky metal housing which marked the lower end of one of the cable-car lines that link the Vallum with the Spoing. An empty car, ready to go, hung at rest beside it. Murena motioned me to get in. It held room for four, but I was the only one to be using it this time. “Sit there; press that lever,” the captain said. I obeyed without a word.

A wobbly jolt, and the dangling car swung away, carrying me off the summit of the Vallum. Skimming upwards back over the ground I had run in my recent descent, I was as pleased as a little boy who had been given a treat, having all to myself a conveyance normally reserved for officers. Not bad, this, not bad at all! Stupid to get touchy a few hours before I might get dead! The delightful ride, enjoyed for its own sake, put me in a much better mood, and that sensible attitude persisted as my eye-level finally rose to the ominous line of boulders, parallel with the Spoing railway; a zone of silent preparedness, solemn enough to dampen any ego: the Marraspang, *the Dislodgeables.* Each boulder was now attended by its squad. Each boulder-squad, I guessed, included one man whose job it was to be ready to handle the release lever, and another man whose job it was to ensure that the order to do this – when it came – was obeyed.

No doubt these men, like those who waited in nuclear bunkers on Earth, had good hope that the order would never come; but though it was thought unlikely that an enemy could ever take the Vallum, yet if one did, the Marraspang were the next, the final, line of defence. Great weights rolling under gravity must constitute the ultimate weapon on Kroth. The unrestricted use of such weapons on an endless gradient was contrary to the principles of civilized warfare, and banned by the Savaluk Convention, but the presence of the Vallum less than a mile further south meant that here they could be used in a restricted sense; for the Vallum would be bulky enough to stop the boulders from continuing their irresponsible roll down the entire slope of the world; from crushing their way across neutral and enemy countries alike; from killing and destroying all in their path, right the way down to the vertical jungles of the Equator, through which they would smash and finally plunge into the endless void.

In other words, the Vallum thus permitted the Toplanders to use the principle of the avalanche without flouting international law.

It would of course be very bad news for anyone, friend or foe, caught in the boulders' legally permitted limited path....

I was glad I was not a general!

Then, looking east, I beheld a railway carriage moving in my direction along the tracks of the Spoing, at hardly more than human running speed; a deliberately slow, observational speed. I waited with my arms at my sides. I forbade myself to shuffle or fidget. I did not try to talk to anyone in the nearest boulder crew.

Faraliew's inspection coach drew to a stop about twenty yards away from me; I remained standing still.

I had sorted myself out. The not-very-flattering idea, that "if a mere oneiro like D.W. can face battle, the rest are likely to stand firm too", no longer offended me. I now thought: if Faraliew wants me as the barometer of his army, he can use me that way.

There seemed no reason to doubt that the authorities, contemptuous though they might be, would at least allow me to fight in the battle. Therefore, let that content me! Physical battleground under my boots; orders from my superiors; the chance to cope.... a crack at the glittering prize of self-respect, of afterwards knowing *I was there*.... Given the situation, it was not too bad a deal.

The coach door opened; Faraliew's tall form stooped in the doorway. He exchanged some words with the sergeant of the nearby boulder-crew, went back in, and some more minutes passed; then the sergeant, after looking at his watch, came towards me. When he had got half way he called curtly, "Wemyss?"

"Yessir."

"In there." He jerked his head; I came forward, telling myself to be a good, credit-worthy sample; and I stepped into the coach.

After one glimpse at the General and his side-kick I defocused my eyes and retreated into a semi-dreamlike internal cringe, in which I remained vaguely aware of where I was standing, Faraliew seated in half-profile, and the side-kick standing some way beyond and behind him, silhouetted at the far window of the carriage.

The General was saying, “Face it, we may have to. The balloon-scouts know what they are about. Since they confirm that we have to deal with an entire Rip-Mig of Gonomong....”

“I still maintain,” said the other man, “that a water-dam would have been better than these boulders. We could even have placed a line of dams south of the Vallum. Because any flood unleashed would get re-absorbed by the ground after a certain distance, water-defences are not forbidden by the Savaluk Convention....”

“Quite the strategist, Chandler!” Turning to me, Faraliew said: “Ah, Wemyss. You already know my Civilian Advisor, of course.”

“Yessir, I do.” Thank heavens I had the sense not to add anything stupid like “Hello, Uncle.” My suspended mind could hum along with its “pause” button depressed for quite a while, if necessary.

Faraliew continued, “Yes, of course you do, I was forgetting....” He turned back to Vic. “We've been through this water idea before, Chandler. Let me point out that whereas a flood would sweep away foot-soldiers, the Gonomong are mounted men; the Fingers would cling to the turf with their claws. Besides, dams would require further expense, further engineering. We must work with what we have.”

“It may not be too late, General, to divert some of the pipes....”

“No, I won't hear of it! Enough now!” Faraliew turned to me with a whimsical smile. “What about you, Wemyss? Do *you* have any thoughts on strategy?”

The kind Providence that looks after these things took care of me again and prevented me from uttering some stupid sycophantic laugh. Instead I responded seriously enough to give the General the minor amusement he was doubtless looking for.

“Neydio seems a pretty useless fortress, sir.”

“Really? Do go on.”

“Of course it's impregnable from the South, sir, but it's no more than ordinarily defensible from the North, at the point where it juts from the Slope; so what's the use of its enormous size? Just a colossal, expensive, tempting target - sir.”

Faraliew chuckled. “Hey, Chandler, what do you think of that? Shall we tell His Excellency Governor Fodnam what this lad thinks of his fortress-city? Neydio the Great, Neydio the Impregnable – what word would *you* use to describe it?"

"Preposterous," said Vic.

"Hm." Faraliew looked sharply at both of us in turn. I kept my face straight and indeed my amusement was short-lived, quietening to a solemn appreciation of the perfect word my uncle had chosen. *Neydio the Preposterous.* That sure said it all.

Then the General let out a short sigh.

"Your remarks were well put, lad. But since the thing's there, we have to defend it. Always we have to defend whatever we have, using what we have. Thank you, you may go now. Return to your unit." Silent and blank of face, I saluted, turned and went out, full of surprise that he did not mind my suggestion of the futility of the great fortress.

Rumour had been wrong in one respect. There had been no offer of tea.

The sergeant took me back to the cable car.

*

Captain Murena received me with the words, "Come on, we'll jam you in somewhere."

The scene on the Vallum had developed quickly during my absence. The civilians had all departed. Along the miles of wall, thousands of soldiers, serried and waiting, in alternate companies of militia and regulars, now leaned in readiness beside their spears, concentrating their gaze upon a sight that had not been visible half an hour ago: the dreadful crawling light on the sagorizon.

One thing at a time, I told myself as Murena escorted me to one of the few spaces left in the line: the small gap between the left-most man in our unit and the right-most man in the unit to the left of it. I took my place. An extra spear from one of the bins was propped against the parapet in front of me, ready for me to seize when the time came.

To my immediate right was Jason Kerallg, the gingery Wild West buff whom I was acquainted with from the march south. Appropriately, he had been issued with what looked to me like a Colt .45; and I had noticed other museum pieces on my walk down the line. I myself had been issued with a Browning automatic. Long ago I had ceased to trouble myself with these inconsistencies, and by now I accepted the terms of existence as passively as an ocean floor receives the down-floating remains of a jumble of past ages. Why chew on it? Neither machines nor logic worked well on Kroth; they functioned intermittently, spasmodically, but what did any of this matter, in the face of death?

"Seen the General?" asked Jason.

"Yep."

"Well, what did you think of him?"

"It's a bit late for thinking."

"Yeah, that's the spirit; welcome to the *Ploing*."

The dry tone in which he spoke that local slang term for the Vallum, caused me to glance at the militiaman on my left, to see how he took the jibe.

I saw a mop-haired fellow scowling southwards, his right arm curled round his spear.

"That's Shaz," continued Jason loudly; "whether it's his first, last or only name, I haven't discovered. Shaz, this is Duncan Wemyss."

Shaz briefly turned his head and grunted a surly greeting which I would have found off-putting in normal circumstances. In these moments, however, it did not matter at all. In fact I viewed his unsociability in a positive light. For he, I guessed, was taking the only attitude which might get us out of this pickle alive: diving into rage-mode. Sullen rather than berserk rage; nevertherless I could sense that something which I had been complaining about for weeks, namely the army's lack of serious emotional commitment, was at last being remedied, better late than never, in sight of the enemy. Yes, that's what had done it: the actual sight of the Gonomong. For I could see them at last: the little winking lights that meant so much pain and suffering headed our way. And so as I settled, hunched forward between battlements, spear-shaft at my elbow, I felt at last that I was part of a long projected wave of hate and defiance on collision course with the now visible horror creeping up from the South.

My eyes smarted with staring during the hours that followed. "One thing at a time", I had often muttered, and now the enemy *was* that one thing. Steadily the milky mass of winking reflections down South very gradually brightened and broadened as their vanguard merged with the other ranks of Gonomong, mid-afternoon sunlight glancing off innumerable shields. The horror lay in the slithering vastness of this mass of mounted men. And – mounted on what? I did not yet know. I heard comments: "Damn *Mongees,* what do they think they are, a row of silver trophies?" "They ain't gonna win any trophies today." I ought to have joined in with my companions' stoical expressions of contempt and their good-humoured, laconic repartee, but instead I suddenly asked myself: *What the hell am I doing here?* That devastating question – that treacherous stab of moral confusion – Every decision, every attitude, every slide and drift that had brought me to this point now clamoured for review, until (thank goodness) into my floundering mind there popped the most telling point of that old classic film *High Noon*; namely that *you can't be expected to remember* the arguments to fight, when the time comes. You must simply hope that they are good, for it's too late to draw back. Never mind that film's lack of historical realism; the main thing is, it captured the great truth, by showing how moments came for Marshal Kane when he was too tired to think, too tired to understand why he was taking the course he was taking. He could no longer prove, even to himself, that he was doing the right thing, yet he went on with it, trusting that *what he had once understood* was still valid though he could no longer grasp it. In other words it wasn't so much his courage as his *obstinacy* that saved the day. Well, I wasn't too hot when it came to courage but I could – just – manage the obstinacy. Big deal, you may say. Absurd to compare myself with the Marshall, considering he was left alone to face his enemies, whereas I had an army around me! Nevertheless there is a sense in which all of us are always alone against our *internal* enemies, and, for each lonely one of us, "going through with it" is an essential statement of who we are. End of question. I re-focused my attention upon the enemy.

With the endless Slope against them the horde nevertheless were advancing tirelessly, as they must have done for months, perhaps years. Originating in a land where the Slope was far more extreme, their steeds, unfortunately for us, must now be finding it comparatively easy to climb a gradient of merely thirty degrees. There seemed to be no end to the oncoming enemy tide.

"Keep yer strength up, I would," advised Shaz, munching a ration bar.

I knew I could not eat a bite; I was so keyed up I feared to be sick. "Binoculars," I said, "are what I need."

He lent me his (the militia seemed better equipped in that respect) and with their aid I could start to make out individual Gonomong "Fingers", at first not clearly enough to give me more than a confusing glimpse of their odd shapes and motion, but enough to reinforce my impression of their awe-inspiring numbers. Hundreds of thousands, at least. And why were they coming this way; why didn't they detour round the wall, which surely did not encircle the entire globe? Well, there was no end to whys. So numerous did the questions become that they shrank to particles of drizzle, continually sinking into the ooze of passive acceptance – my brain once more in ocean-floor mode. What else could I expect? I was just a spearman. Generalship, fortunately, was no business of mine. Besides, there was one question which shockingly answered itself. "Why do we call them Fingers?" I muttered as I squinted through the binoculars, but no sooner had I said this than my mind grasped what I was seeing – the humping "inchworms" twice the size of horses, with armoured head-shields the shape of fingernails. Yes, the creatures could resemble giant crooking fingers if you looked at them that way.

I continued to stare, frozen and wide-eyed, while the occasional jutting elbow or peeping head revealed the riders behind the "Fingernail" shields. Riders astride exaggerated caterpillars? - should I laugh or should I have guessed long before, that the extreme gradient far down South must produce a monstrous divergence of life? The question answered itself. Way down there, evolution must favour creatures that could claw and cling.

I saw the disgust on the faces of my companions. They, naturally, had known. *They* had not had a policy of keeping themselves in ignorance.

Now that I saw what we were up against, I felt a vast puzzlement. This whole business seemed ridiculous. *High Noon* was all very well, but what chance did we have against these monsters?

I muttered to Jason, "You'd think we would have lined this wall with cannon, or something…."

"What, and try to blast holes in *that?*" he asked. "Like shooting at a plague of locusts."

More hopeless than that, I thought. *Like shooting at an advancing tide.*

"Well then, why haven't *we* captured and bred those decapod things…." I spoke without thinking. If I had thought, I'd have realized it was ridiculous to suppose that any gimmick I might dream up had not already been considered by our High Command.

My bright suggestion caused Jason to snort, "Ugh! You're crazy! We leave that sort of thing to the Mongees." He sounded really put off, really sickened by what I had said.

"Sorry, sorry. Forget my stupid remark."

But although his aversion to the idea was so strong that I back-pedalled immediately, I did wonder if maybe I wasn't so stupid. After all, why *hadn't* we bred and trained decapods or other Slope-adapted steeds of our own? Deadly indeed they looked, but (to me) not disgusting.

Perhaps my Earth-mind allowed me a certain immunity to Krothan phobias. Sure, the Gonomong were out to kill us and seize our country, but their weird steeds did not unsettle me any more than well-trained war-horses or war-elephants would have done. And so, while the monsters did dismay me in a practical sense, I was spared the aversion which – I learned by and by – they seemed to inspire in each and every one of my companions.

Anyhow, all creatures must fit perfectly well into their *own* environment, else they would never have evolved in the first place, so what were that lot doing encroaching on ours? What was this invasion all about? There must have been some big historical or ecological cause, big enough to be known, to be studied, and a way found round it; whereas to neglect the question, to let it boil over like this, and then "solve" the problem by large-scale bloodshed – it just wasn't good enough! We should refuse to take part! We should force our leaders to think again! And so on, and so on; this was me being seized by my second bout of moral confusion. It took the form of an atrocious squeamishness, a one-sided nausea about killing. Never had I believed in pacifism before, and now I was about to become a pacifist on the very verge of battle! To do me justice, I did know that if I acted on these feelings (supposing I was in a position to act on them), I would be letting everybody down. I saw that much.

But then a more intelligent whisper attempted to seduce me from the path of duty and loyalty. *All right, it does seem outright cowardice to become, as you call it, " a pacifist on the verge of battle". But supposing pacifism is not only true but also the kind of truth which you can only expect to learn when battle looms? What do you do then? Go through with the killing just out of pride and shame, these emotions which so often have let humanity down? In other words, "let people down so as not to let them down"? Come off it! The only way to start better habits is to say, blow this, I want no part of it. Go home, and never mind what people think!*

Of course there was absolutely no chance, wedged in as I was, that I could simply turn for home. But there was the danger that the whisper might sap my will to fight, might make me useless to my own side and an easier prey to the enemy. So it must be rebutted.

The rebuttal came.

You whisper that I'm doing wrong, and indeed I know that it is obscene to kill. But why is it obscene to kill? Because, ultimately, it is a desecration of the spirit. In which case we must care most about spiritual things. Which means caring about more than just the flesh. Loyalty is a spiritual thing.

Loyalty, honesty, reliability are more important than life or death, and so the thought returns full circle: we kill when we must, else we lose life in another way.

As for the point that wars should be prevented at an earlier stage –

That, too, was dealt with. The answer came quick as a spear-thrust. Indeed you could say that inside my head the battle had already started, insofar as the strife between attitudes must affect my performance against the Gonomong. Imagine the following paragraphs condensed into one flash of thought:

Of course it would be good if everyone were to cultivate a general awareness of the pressures on humanity which lead to war; if everyone could then pay his tax of personal attention, of allowance, to alleviate those pressures before they resulted in conflict. If those "attention taxes" were paid by the great majority, no warmonger would ever find excuse, or ever rise to a position in which he might give orders.

But we're individuals, not group minds. We have the limited attention-span of individuals. Most of us aren't rich enough in awareness, to pay the attention-tax! That is the true cause of war. It is not badness. Badness gets as far as causing crime, but war is another matter. In war we are paying the penalty, not so much of our plentiful badness, as of our lack of concentration. Nobody, except maybe for a few professors and philosophers, has an attention-span stretched far enough to maintain deliberately those complex conditions of economic, social and environmental equilibrium which are necessary for universal peace.

And even if you, Duncan Wemyss, happen to be one of those philosophers, it's too late to skive off now, so shut up, stay put and do your bit.

Whew! I shook my head to clear it. Nothing like waiting for battle, if you've got a fidgety mind! You find yourself arguing with yourself rapidly, intensely, and then all of a sudden the bout is over. It was obvious that here was a case of kill or be killed; obvious that the Gonomong must be repelled at all costs.

The only problem was, I could not see how we were going to win this battle. If cannon were no good (and no doubt it was against the Savaluk Convention to fire projectiles down-Slope anyway), just precisely *how* were we supposed to defend ourselves and our land? One thing seemed certain: my remarks were a waste of time, my "common sense" (as usual) a waste of time; so I subsided further into that ocean-floor mood of quiet acceptance. My muscles tightened on the haft of the spear at my right. If I had to play the part of some medieval infantryman at Bannockburn or Agincourt, so be it. Panic was the killer; salvation lay in discipline. And the experts must know best.

An awareness of some methodical activity at my back prompted me to turn my head and I saw that another line had formed, not of spearmen but of men who were lifting coils of rope from the bins. In the minutes that followed, members of this rear line quietly threaded our spears like needles, putting a rope through a hole in the back end of each spear and tying the other ends to that line of "hitching posts" along the north edge of the wall's summit. Good, thought I; I liked that idea. A spear that had been let go of in the heat of battle, and had fallen southwards, could be retrieved by means of hauling on the rope. As for why the ropes were being added now, rather than earlier – *Not my problem!* From somewhere on the crag-like summit of Neydio our high command must have telescopes trained on the enemy, and must make decisions on deployment according to what they saw. Which meant that the "preposterous" fortress was doubtless some use after all, if only as an observation post.

"Look tough," Shaz broke into my thoughts.

"Eh? What?"

"That's Captain Fadron," he warned, out of the corner of his mouth.

Sure enough, the militia company commander was approaching from our left. He strolled alongside Captain Murena as they inspected their units together. I saw something that chilled me. Every so often Fadron would tap a soldier with his cane, whereupon the man would abandon his spear and retreat into the rear line, his place being taken by someone from there. *If he does that to me....*

I hunched ferociously forward. To all appearances, I stared south at the enemy, but in reality during those moments I hardly saw the Gonomong, which were now only about a quarter of a mile off, almost dazzling us all with their polished "Fingernail" shields; instead I thought daggers at the object of my greater hatred, Captain Fadron, who suddenly represented to me a threat I could not accept. Rejection. Demotion. *Don't you dare touch me with that cane....*

I had slipped again into one of my phases of being more alarmed by some aspect of my own side than by the enemy. Of course I had no real reason to assume that the rope-haulers' line was any less honourable a position than the spear-line in front of it; nevertheless the skin crawled on my back as I waited for the dreaded nudge.

My ears told me that Fadron and Murena had stopped somewhere close behind me. They were discussing something, I couldn't hear what, but it wasn't hard to guess, that decisions regarding the deployment of personnel in this part of the line were equally the business of both commanders, since any weakness in either company would affect the position of the other. After a minute or so the voices receded, and I was again able to draw breath. A theory constructed itself in my head: Fadron had wanted to swap me over, but Murena had dissuaded him. In my relief at the outcome, my resentment still flared at Fadron on account of what, I was convinced, he had *wanted* to do. Demote me, would he? Pull me back to the rear line? The rat, the *krunk!* Hot resentment, not a very nice emotion in normal circumstances, had its uses just then, putting a certain fizz in my blood as the Gonomong drew ever closer. Just as Tarzan, swinging rapidly through the jungle, will use whatever branch or creeper comes to hand, so the untrained soldier, living on his nerves, must swing from dodge to dodge, from one emotional tactic to the next, the object always being to cross the next gulf, survive the next challenge. My terror of the Slope had been evaded in this way; the next test must be the violence of battle.

A quarter of an hour before the clash, our captain walked to and fro, repeating final instructions. "Don't waste energy in thrusts; aim to lodge the spear-points in chinks between the decapods' scales; you gotta push, gotta *repel;* fire your pistols in spare moments, but otherwise leave that business to your support; remember, that's part of the rear line's job, to aim past you at any vulnerable spot that presents itself – but meanwhile *you* are the backbone of the army, *you* must not break. Hear that, men? Don't break before those misshapen *krunks!* All right, the Mongees outnumber us grossly, but they're just a horde, just a mindless horde…."

I wished I had been issued with dark glasses; the reflections off the "Fingernail" shields were by this time a serious irritation, wetting my face with tears. Through narrowed lids I could see that the Gonomong ranks were maybe about fifty deep. Far, far too many, but it was no good complaining, this was our task and we had to face it; if we failed, if our line broke, the enemy's killing spree would really begin.

Captain Murena had fallen silent. Our adversaries were four hundred yards away. Unhappily for us, the riders didn't present much of a target; their heads were hidden behind the "Fingernail" crests, through which eye-holes (I now noticed) had been pierced; their legs, astride their mounts, were completely protected by a kind of flared scaly ruff around where the decapods' necks would have been if they had had definable necks. However, now and then I caught a glimpse of the riders' long, over-muscled arms that seemed to have the mass and musculature of legs. (A voice muttered, "Man, just look at those Mongee apes.") A minority of the Gonomong held pistols, confiscated (so I had been told) from the native population through which the horde had passed on their long climb northwards. But most of them had swords gleaming in their right hands. Their left hands held long hooked poles. If our eighteen-foot spears did their stuff, we'd never be in reach of the swords, but what about the hooks? With my foreshortened view, I couldn't be sure of their length. My nerves knotted as I considered that life-or-death question: the precise reach of those hooked poles.

Then, to my right and left and in the line behind me, some snatches of conversation stirred my spirit with their last defiant chorus of decent ordinary life.

"Glad I stayed. It's a long plod back."

"Won't matter if we win. Take our time, then."

"Yeah, but meanwhile, here's our excuse to stop awhile...."

And again and again, *It's a long plod back*; as if my phrase, which back in the teashop had made Jason and Juldwin laugh, had now become a kind of verbal mascot for the whole army.

The enemy wave reached the foot of the Vallum. Daft jumbled thoughts tripped over one another in my mind as we leaned over the parapet: we were each holding our spears as though we were about to fish with them, though of course you could never actually fish with a thing that size; I was gladder than ever to know that a rope held my spear, for the weight of it meant I wasn't sure I could brandish it downwards for long; but anyhow I wouldn't have to, since, the rate things were going, the enemy would be exerting his upward pressure in the next few seconds, because the decapods' front claws were already tearing handfuls of turf from the Vallum slope, creating crude steps by which to scramble up –

Pistol-cracks from friend and foe made me jerk my head wildly for a second or two; none of my companions seemed to be hit, nor could I see any sign that our own firing was effective. Even if guns had worked as efficiently as they did on Earth, the Gonomong were shielded by their mounts' naturally-armoured scaly fronts and "Fingernail" heads; we, on our side, had the parapet and battlements of the Vallum, though this still left me feeling terribly exposed from the chest upwards. And now, inexorably, the enemy wave began to flow up the embankment. O God, I pleaded, make me the right sort of person for this. I thought of the Vikings and their berserk joy of battle. I had often thought how stupendously thick that sort of person must have been; this moment made me admit, "I could use some of that thickness right now."

Appalling as the ground coming up to meet a parachutist on his first jump, the humping line of Gonomong Fingers reared at our spearpoints and to my amazement as the clashes began, the Toplander army shouted as a war-cry, IT'S A LONG – PLOD - *BACK!*

My own spear-points hit a "Fingernail", glanced off this invulnerable head and onto the decapod's chest, lodging between chest- and shoulder-scales. I held. I leaned, as far as I dared adding my weight to that of the spear. I was glancingly aware that to either side of me other roped spears, the entire Topland line, formed itself during those seconds into a bristling, anchored but semi-flexible, united weapons system. I felt, rather than saw, this unity; mostly I didn't dare peer around, for I had to put all my effort into focussing upon my pair of lodged spear-points and hoping that the arrangement would not slip. I pressed, I held, I yielded a bit as the decapod scrabbled to rise further, I held, I pressed it down. To either side of me my companions likewise strove to hold the line, while the decapods pushed forward and upward both by their own efforts and with the pressure of those behind them. More than once I believed it was all up with me when a decapod shook off the pressure from the points of my spear by means of a twisting dodge followed by a forward lunge, to dart upwards through the gap between my spear and that of my neighbour. I couldn't draw back and re-aim in time; I didn't have the strength – but the support fellow behind me saved the situation: he had been watching, he pulled on the rope, my spear drew back up to a position from which I *could* re-aim, and I caught the Gonomong steed again before it could finish its climb. Our line held, though the enemy individual facing me had, by his manoeuvre, gained a higher foothold on the south face of the Vallum. And now that Gonomong rider, who had been hardly visible so far, concealed as he had been behind the upper half of the "Fingernail" crest of his mount, leaned a bit sideways as he jabbed, so that I glimpsed his face – the only feature of which I remember is that it was the face of *my* enemy, the man who was trying to kill me personally; he tried to reach me with his hook, but he still couldn't get me and after a couple of seconds, probably at the sound of a pistol shot, he jerked his head back behind the shelter of his steed, so that little round was one to me; but a yelp and a choked-off cry from some yards to my right told me that one of my company had been less fortunate in his fight, and out of the corner of my eye I saw a man's body being dragged by the neck over the battlement and down. This sight must either harden or unnerve me; I must mark it "lesson": *So, one of ours has made his last mistake, perhaps because he was simply not strong enough, or had not been supported quickly enough.* I concentrated harder than ever on managing my spear, but aware, now, of what a fool I had been to suppose that the rear line was less prestigious than the spear-line. At any moment my life might again depend on the man behind me handling the rope. Also, the same man was more free to use his pistol than I was to use mine, and in fact he did have a go at trying to hit my opponent every time the Gonomong's head or arm was exposed in an attempt to use the hook. Bullets spat past me in both directions, and in my opinion it was just as well that so many shots were duds; quite likely I owe my life to the tendency of Krothan guns to misfire. Occasionally someone got hit; and I, cringing inwardly as I awaited my turn, tried telling myself that my own screams when they came would be nothing special. Mercifully my sense of time got lost somewhere among the stretched minutes that seemed to crawl in circular repetition, the great mindless animal minutes of pounding blood and darting reflex, which were most of what happened. Lost amid that pulsing desperation, the thoughts and speculations which fill so much of my narrative were mere jabs of awareness.

The enemy's gradual climb towards the parapet confronted us with the unpleasant choice, either to stand further back, or to shorten our grip on the spears and thus put us in reach of their hooks; and some ghastly individual results taught us to stand back. So the tendency was for our line to retreat. Gonomong voices began to impinge on my ears; shouts of triumphant encouragement in a lingo full of "eengs" and "ungs". Answering shouts came from our people: *"It's a long plod back!" "C'est un long retour!" "Rückgang lang!" "¡Regreso – paso pesado!"* The rearing Fingers were almost on a level with us now, and our spears were almost horizontally levelled at them. At this stage, fortunately for us, it became evident that the point where Vallum slope met vertical battlements was too much of a challenge for the humping decapods. Their front ends reared again and again and had to fall back without getting a proper hold on the actual summit. Jason on my right yelled at his support (whose own gun seemed to have had a high proportion of dud firings) to snatch his Colt .45 and re-load it and pepper the joints of a decapod whose paws were clutching at the parapet right in front of him. The creatures seemed un-killable, but just as you or I might flinch from a stinging nettle, so did that particular decapod draw back from the heavy lead slugs of the .45. Meanwhile I had some success also, as I lunged and actually toppled my opponent – to my own surprise just as much as his. In no time his place was taken by another, but I minded this little; I had become curiously immune to disheartening logic; curiously undismayed by the overwhelming numbers which opposed us; for at some point in these nightmare minutes I had become a person I had never been before, so that all the garbage I had read about the "joy of battle" turned out to possess some truth, this much truth: never had I felt so alive. If the next trick, which was to get out of this in one piece so as to profit from the experience, could somehow be managed, how nice that would be – but in the meantime I must be like those sensible Vikings, aware of the sound practical point that mad, berserk rage was the antidote to fear and pain, and so I must value the dazing quality of this horrendous boiling mess, for it would be fatal to cool down. Somewhere there *was* a person whose job it was to stay cool, namely, General Faraliew, whose duty it was to implement whatever battle plan had been decided; he must have a plan; after all he had not sounded too surprised that we were to face an entire Rip-Mig of Gonomong, whatever a Rip-Mig might be. Alternatively, if events had ruined his plan, why then, he must adapt! And yet when – as happened at odd moments amid the hot-blooded din and the stretched emotion demanded by courage – my brain allowed itself an honest thought, then I had to ask, was I really able to believe that Faraliew, or anyone, could improvise a victory out of *this?* I could imagine no way. But so what? Faraliew, no doubt, could see the whole picture, like those marvellous football-professionals who have that mysterious spatial awareness that tells them where to pass the ball, as though they're watching themselves on TV, looking down on the pitch from above. He must have that skill. Trust the experts.

What was that bit of relief I sensed just then? In what small way did things seem to be better? Pistol cracks were now sounding only from our side! The enemy must have run out of ammunition; whereas we still had bins stacked full of cases of the stuff, as much as we could ever use. So that was an advantage. But I couldn't see what good it could do us, given the decapods' apparent immunity to bullets, and the fact that their riders were so difficult to target, sheltered as they mostly were behind their steeds except when they made astonishingly skilful lunges with their hooks-on-poles. The swaying, rearing motions of the decapods confused our aim; the creatures, now that they were almost level with us, gripped with their four back limbs the highest bit of turf on their side of the Vallum, and with their six front limbs in the air weaved their bodies about like a line of outsize cobras above the parapet – yet surely if we could just hold our position, they could not break it, else they would already have done so. No, thank goodness, they just weren't managing to get over that last bit of wall. And as the dusty, sweaty hours dragged on, while the sun to our right slunk towards its setting close to the foot of the fortress of Neydio, and the most nerve-jabbing moments became dulled with frequency, another hopeful thought came to me: no matter if their ranks were to double, or treble, no matter if the entire land down to the sagorizon became carpeted with Gonomong, only a certain number of them could fit along the Vallum at one time, only so many of them could come at us at the same time, so, in that sense, our position was a kind of Thermopylae, impregnable so long as it could not be turned. That raised a question I'd wondered about before. *Could* we be outflanked? Were they already trying it, somewhere out of my range of vision? Hard to believe that Faraliew had not made provision against such an obvious manoeuvre. Perhaps, indeed, all was well; for all my ignorant mind knew, the Vallum might extend around the whole world, or (since every time I wondered about that, I found it rather hard to believe) perhaps it stretched so far east and west of the Wayline, that the Gonomong would run out of supplies and maybe starve in desert wastes if they tried to go round. Which would explain why they had thrown their entire strength directly up this central route. Yes, that must be it: their only possible strategy was to meet us head on and force their way over the wall, and although our strength was stretched to the limit, we weren't letting them do it, we weren't letting them past us, so that was all right, that must mean they could not win! The time must come when the force of their attack was spent, they must fall back and that would be our cue to counter-attack. For when their formation broke, we could get at the riders. So – *that* must be how we were going to win.

Oh yeah? whispered something. *Who says we must win?*

More than a voice, it was a sly ingredient in the scene, which I could not at first identify, that replied to my optimism as if with the shake of a hidden head. Ah, there – down in the blue, in the void above the sagorizon: it must be those spots, yes, a little cloud of spots, rising in the air since a while back, that now gave me my presentiment of disaster.

Quick glances to either side confirmed to me that others besides myself had caught the same whiff of foreboding, intensifying into dismay, so that before long a slump of despair aged the faces and flattened the voices of the men around me. But perhaps I was not so astonished as they; all along, in a dark corner of my mind, though I knew far less of this world than they, I must have been more than half expecting something to turn the tide against us.

The spots grew into blobs. Continuing to rise from the depths of the South, in another minute or two they were high enough in the sky to be level with us. Still they rose, so that it became hard to keep them in view because all our concentration was still needed immediately in front of us, leaving us hardly a moment in which to crane our necks. Nor could I spare the attention to discuss the matter with anybody, and so I wasn't sure what the others thought; no one expressed any firm idea as to what the things were. I only wished I had not thought of Thermopylae: I sadly guessed, that whatever it was which was flapping towards us was about to do for us what the outflanking Persians' secret pass did for the end of *that* story.

When the objects came in sight again, they were revealed as several hundred Gonomong, each man borne in harness slung underneath four great birds larger than eagles, rapidly dropping in unison towards a part of the Vallum summit some few hundred yards to our right. Their descent was silhouetted against the setting sun, so that only with odd blinks snatched against the dazzle could my eyes follow the manoeuvre – but its significance was obvious. We had been outflanked in the third dimension, the dimension of the air. Pistol shots met the descending enemy but my sinking heart told me, *Faraliew hasn't foreseen this. Faraliew is Leonidas, and we're his doomed Spartans.* A breakthrough on any part of the Vallum must blow our entire defence apart like a punctured balloon. I and my companions had no choice but to fight on as hard as ever, but now we fought with our senses attuned to the developing disaster on our right, somewhere between our position and Neydio; though it was almost impossible to see anything of what was happening at the spot where the birdman task force had landed, rumour spread quickly down the line, confirming that that position had been seized. I could picture it all with complete clarity. Spearmen and their supports reeling as the birdmen came down on their heads; the decapods exploiting the chaos to prance over the parapet and onto the Vallum summit at last. Now, nothing could stop them.

A cry, "Untie! Untie!" came from behind us. The ropes were unthreaded, flung away. It was an essential move, but also it was an admission of imminent defeat. Our spears must be freed for that moment when the enemy, expanding the breach they had made in our defences, rolled up our line far enough to reach this part of it. For then we'd have them coming at us from our right as well as in front and we'd have to fall back eastwards.

"This," panted Jason, "is not looking good." "We ain't dead yet," muttered someone else. *A mere technicality,* thought I.

For the Gonomong had the game in their hands. All they had to do, to finish off our whole army, was, firstly, to overrun the entire Vallum summit – which now could only be a matter of time – and then, by means of another attack by their bird-men, do a similar job a bit further north, capturing our last defence, the Marraspang, the line of boulders. And it was no use trying to forestall this move by an early use of the Marraspang. For us to set off an avalanche while the enemy stayed up on the Vallum summit would do us no good; it would only be of use if they were stupid enough to swarm off the ridge and into the avalanche's path, and no general has any right to rely on his opponents being that stupid.

The overwhelming truth burst upon me, that the Topland strategy had been fatally flawed from the start. We had staked everything on the strength of a fixed line. Didn't history suggest that such fixity was a bad idea? Earth history, anyhow. And no matter what universe you inhabit, if your Maginot Line breaks or is outflanked, you've had your chips. "Oh, well." You can't expect to beat a principle like that. Big blanket principle, covering one's deathbed. *Defeats happen. One side or other has to lose. This time, we're elected. You take it when your turn comes.*

My world narrowed down to my own little share of the fighting, and for several more minutes I gave every ounce of my concentration to the maintenance of a steady grip on the spear-shaft, to the perpetual task of making sure that the point did not slide off the armoured scales of the decapod which faced me from the other side of the parapet.

A strange, seemingly useless fact came to my notice. This particular decapod had a pair of mauve stripes down its front. Decoration of some kind, presumably. It reminded me, in some ways, of a caparisoned horse. Maybe its rider was someone specially important. My brain had just revolved around to this conclusion, when, *crack!* a lucky shot of ours smote the said rider from the side, I saw him topple off, and his mount reared back. I gave an extra push with my spear and encouraged the thing to retreat a step or so further. That was the last miniature success I can remember, before – a few dozen heartbeats later – everything went haywire.

First came shouts from Captain Murena, ordering the regulars some way at my right to wheel to *their* right and form a line across the way, so as to form a barrier against what was coming at us from that direction. The men obeyed as fast as they could, but hardly had they done so than the flanking Gonomong were upon them like the wave-crest of a tsunami, causing the new line to buckle inward almost as soon as it was formed. What made the momentum of the attack irresistible, was that here we had no advantage of slope; this lot were pushing at us along the flat summit instead of up the embankment's side, which made all the difference. Murena's men were forced back, back, eastwards along the top, their retreat rolling up our front until the wave of chaos reached me and buffeted me out of position: I was forced sideways, fearing to stumble and be trampled by both friend and foe, while Captain Fadron shouted futile orders as he urged his militiamen to shore up Murena's crumbling line. I utterly ceased to think, which was fortunate in one way, as else I would have known that I was by this time physically exhausted, each jerk of muscle borrowing energy from heaven knows where. Now we were being squeezed towards the northern edge of the Vallum ridge; the Gonomong to the immediate south of us had vaulted over the parapet and were joining with their fellows in a co-ordinated assault on what remained of our position; and if my ears did not deceive me I heard another tumultuous blend of thuds and cries which told me that yet another large body of the enemy were coming at us *from the north*, behind us; they had overflowed that way and were flowing back now to surround us.

Our company's best attempt to break out of the trap was led by the amiable lout named Archie, known amongst us as Archie the Speller because of his dim hesitations when signing his own name. Built like a tank, he had a good go at forcing his way into the briefest of gaps which chanced to open in the wall of foes, so as to wedge it further open, with the help of some dozen supporting spears. I watched him try it, I saw him fail and go down as the gap closed upon him; *this is what you get, Archie, for making one wrong decision; I've made several, and my big one was to enlist. It just goes to show, Archie, that if you had learned to spell, if I had learned to think, each of us might have found a better job than this. My turn will follow shortly in the mincemeat queue.*

I could no longer spot Shaz, or Jason, or my other former neighbours in the line that had ceased to be. I was part of a jostling mass of spearmen being edged towards the northern slope of the embankment, and once we were forced over that edge we must lose our footing and be trampled. Or so I thought. When the moment came and I went over, I found we were wedged so tight, we remained upright; this was thanks to pressure from below, the new enemy pressure from the north, less than that from the south, but enough to keep us on our feet. I felt relief at still being able to stand; but our numbers were rapidly diminishing; we still bristled in defensive formation but only because we were caught in it, and our spears were being gradually wrenched out of position, leaving us to be reached and cut down one by one by the enemy's tearing hooks and slashing swords, until only a few of us were left, and although I glimpsed other such pockets of resistance nearby, we had no hope that we could co-ordinate, and so, silently, I said my remote good-byes. Be a good boy, Duncan, replied my mother; make sure you've got all you need for the journey. You haven't packed that suitcase very well, have you? Sorry, Mother. This, added Uncle Vic, is an unpromising situation. I wouldn't start from here if I were you. Sorry, Uncle.

The inner voices, the garbled memories, were drowned out by a new, real sound.

Not merely a noise but also a tremor and a smell of shaken dust and new panic rising into a hubbub of many screams and a terrible growth of understanding – and then a collective shift, a retreat before a power that threatened every living thing in its path. Wedged like a tinned sardine, I let myself be pushed back up to the Vallum summit. There I was safe from the avalanche, but I was not able to stop there, for those who were not yet safe were still applying pressure to the packed mass of bodies and so I was swept on, I was forced to plunge over a battlement on the *south* side, and I rolled over and over and down and down, until my head hit hard and my light went out.

*

I opened my left eye.

My gaze met sky: it had become duskier, but not by much; I sensed without raising my head to look, that the sun had disappeared behind the Slope only shortly before.

My eye followed the line of my out-flung left arm which lolled southward; beyond my hand I saw grassland, interspersed with small patches of forest, extending down the slope of the world to the deepening blue of the sagorizon. Maybe half a mile off, some moving figures were visible: Gonomong, on their mounts.

I stared, awake but hardly knowing it.

Those figures –

Retreating?

Yes, retreating they were, retreating into the distance, a dim multitude of decapods carrying, or in some cases dragging, their fallen masters....

Stickiness smeared my right cheek, which rested on my shoulder; coming from behind me, groans and whimpers penetrated my woozy consciousness. As I listened, screams broke out, and just as suddenly were cut short.

Next thing I knew, my wrist was held, then released. "This one's all right, I reckon," said a voice. I opened my eye again. A youngish man squatted beside me. The twilight had dimmed somewhat; real night had not yet fallen. I must have passed out again but not for more than a few minutes.

"You're all right, mate, aren't you?" the man said, sounding fairly sure about it. I also saw the boots and trousers of a companion standing to his right, one knee bent in the typical slope stance. A bulky satchel rested on the ground between them.

"Yaaagh," I said, or words to that effect.

"Flung out this far, yet no bones broken; I'd call it a krunking miracle." The squatting man shook his head in wry admiration of my good fortune. "You were born lucky, I guess." As he stood up and reached for the satchel, I suddenly heard some more screams, from a different direction than the first lot. In a tired voice the man said to his companion, "That one next."

"Urrgh?" I called.

He looked back.

"Just get up when you can; there's no hurry. We've got more urgent cases than headache to deal with!" He and his companion, who was carrying a folded stretcher, walked past my head.

"Wait – " I was able to croak. "We won?"

It was the other man who spoke this time. "Of course we won, ye daft bat! D'ye think the doctor and I'd be picking up the pieces otherwise? I tell ye, if we'd lost *this* scrap, we'd ken nothing about it."

"Sorry," I mumbled.

"Don't be sorry; be proud. You laddies have done yer job well. Sent the Rip-Mig reeling for a generation, in my opinion. Things can only get better from now on."

Propped up on one elbow I twisted to look where they went and I saw maybe a dozen or more other medical teams picking their way among strewn bodies. I sat up, while waves of dull pain sloshed in my head, and got my right eye open, there being nothing wrong with it except for some blood stuck around the lid. I felt terrible and lucky and guilty and joyful at being alive. I tried to shut my ears to the agonies of the wounded. I had to look, though, because my nervous system was still half keyed up to battle, a situation in which you *have* to see what's coming.

The base of the embankment was about six or seven yards from where I lay. Most of the bodies lay along it, like snowdrifts against a wall, though a sizeable minority, like myself, had been flung further a-field by the force of the rout. Hundreds of bodies, all in the blue uniform of the regular army or the brown jackets of the militia. We had won only at a fearful cost. But why could I not see any dead or injured Gonomong?

Well, it would have taken more than this rout down the embankment's south side to kill those mounted men; their steeds would have retained their footing. The dead Gonomong were the ones who had been trapped instead on the Vallum's north side. The triumphant, the exuberant Gonomong, who'd streamed through the gap they had punched in our line, and fanned out in their drive to surround us completely – they were the ones who must now be lying dead, mangled and pulped in the avalanche that crushed them. We had won because as it turned out they *had* been stupid enough – forgetful enough, in their elation – to put themselves in the path of the Marraspang.

As for the rest, the survivors....

I remembered what I had seen southward. Turned once more in that direction, I peered in fascination through the deepening twilight and saw, very obscurely, that the defeated survivors were still visible, silent and dim, now too far away to distinguish as individuals as they receded into the dim depths of Slantland. It appeared that no attempt was being made by our side to pursue or harry them. We had given them a beating and we were letting them go.

Perhaps we lacked the strength to prevent their escape, but I guessed, also, that their escape might suit our policy. Tales told by the surviving Gonomong would serve our purpose. The terrible surprise that had turned the tide of the battle, as it gained in the telling, would inspire such dread of Topland's ingenuity, it might well earn us a generation of peace.

From this, another overwhelming truth burst upon me, namely that the previous overwhelming truth that had burst upon me was actually a load of rubbish.

Topland's strategy, far from being fatally flawed, had been vindicated, and our general actually did know what he was doing.

*

One curious minor exception to the enemy's retreat, a riderless decapod was crouched about twenty yards from me.

Its four back limbs and its six front limbs lay flat on the ground; between them, the central length of body arched like the curve of a capital Omega. Its head-shield lay tilted back which allowed me to glimpse a blunt face somewhat like that of a tortoise. At that moment, as if suddenly aware of my gaze, it moved its head slightly round, whereupon I hastily looked elsewhere, purely as a reflex, to avoid eye contact – I didn't know why. I felt no aversion for the creature, nor could I see any reason to fear it.

Meanwhile, lights came on as technicians strung up lamps on aluminium poles, the closest of them not many yards from where I lay. Soldiers, medicos and nurses were moving around, setting up a field hospital with equipment lowered on ropes from the Vallum. Everything was placed on platforms which in turn were set up using standardized wedges, or "chocks" as they were called, bevelled to compensate for a 30-degree Slope. I admired the way in which, with practised rapidity, the chocks were placed to serve as foundations for planks on which, in turn, plastic bricks were laid, building up to the larger platforms for beds and tables.

Amid all this activity, no one tried to approach the decapod, or, alternatively, to shoo it away. People ignored it. They wanted nothing to do with it. If someone unthinkingly approached within a few yards of it and then became suddenly aware of the thing's proximity, he or she would shrink away.

I thought, *that creature is staring at me.* Just on the edge of the illuminated zone, it sat waiting. Was this a melodramatic way of putting it? For a human, a "wait" implies purpose, and I must remember that the thing was only an animal. Yet the fact remained, that while far off in the gathering night its defeated brethren were retreating southwards, *this* one lingered.... Of course, I repeated, it was only a beast. Should I let myself get jumpy at being stared at by a decapod? No, and yet –

A nebulous suspicion came into my head, that in some way or other the battle was not yet over for me. Part of my problem, no doubt, was a stupid sort of guilt at having got through it all intact when so many had been killed or maimed. A kind of embarrassment at being a favourite of Providence. I found it did not help to say, "accidents will happen, including accidents of survival"; I could not accept pot luck so easily.

This perhaps made me more receptive to the fuzzy idea, that *I was alive because I had a debt still to pay.*

I eventually scrambled upright. A nurse saw my swaying step, hurried towards me, grabbed to steady me and said, "Come on, I'll clean you up."

She escorted me towards a zone marked out by folding chairs and a wash-stand, an area for those like myself, the dazed but not too serious cases, the lucky ones. I allowed myself to be led, and while the nurse removed the caked blood from my face, I encouraged myself to relax, to quieten the core of horror which still quaked deep inside me. Silly to be jumpier *after* the battle than while it raged....

"Wemyss," said a weak voice.

I did an eyes-right and saw a man with a bandage round his head, resting in one of the chairs. He said, "Glad you survived."

I recognized Murena. "Captain – great to see you, sir." And it *was* great, even though I had never particularly cottoned to him. For he was doing something which deserved an affectionate hurrah: he was continuing *in existence,* he was *alive.*

"Seen any of the others?" he asked. "Our company, I mean."

"No sir, none yet."

"Don't reckon we will. Not many."

"But, sir, we did it: we won the victory." A pause.

"Yes," he murmured. "We had to win. It was that or *kerunk.*"

"No chance they might, er, mount a counter-attack?" I inquired. I was glad he hadn't said anything cynical, but I wanted at the same time to rouse the old Murena disdain.

He replied in a rambling style which wasn't much like him.

"Gonomong counter-attack *now?* If there were any chance of that, our look-outs on Neydio would tell us. Infrared scopes they have up there; turn night into day."

"I hope so, sir."

"You 'hope so'. Breathe again, Wemyss - the war's over!" The curt Murena, the one I knew, was back again. He added, with a dry husk of a laugh, "We put such a scare into the Mongees...."

"For another generation," I nodded.

He chuckled again. "That'll do me," he remarked. "One whole generation of peace? I'll be satisfied with that."

I, on the other hand, was not at peace. No matter how much I wanted to sit back and enjoy the miracle of life after the prospect of death, I could not yet relax. Conscience was a needle between my shoulder blades. Get up, it said. Get up and see to one last job. You will then be allowed to enjoy your luck.

But I've already done my bit! I fought all through the horror and came out the other side!

Yes, with the aid of that extra allowance of luck, an item for which the bill has now arrived, and you must pay.

Pay with what? You don't mean –

Yes. Turn around.

You may theorize, if you like, that the transition from battle to quietness, from dire peril and the expectation of death to sudden safety, is likely to be as unhinging as the opposite change. You may think you understand that it might make an unstable fellow begin to hear voices. You may decide, that the only thing wrong with me was my inability to unwind, to cope with my own relief. I won't argue the point. The reasons for my action are debatable, though there's no doubt that the action itself formed a turning-point in my life.

The nurse had finished with me; no one, except possibly Murena, was watching me. I swivelled in my chair. The voices around me grew faint, while pesky Conscience grew louder. I found myself staring once more at the placid decapod, which sat isolated, shunned by all, as it munched grass in the half-light on the edge of the hospital area. *See? You cannot refuse the opportunity.*

Opportunity?

To ensure that today's horror will not happen again.

I could, I must, rise out of my chair. All right, Conscience, I know, I know, I will confront the creature....

Though drained of most of my energy, I felt basically sound and whole. Ready for a final gasp or two of effort, I was nerved by a spirit of resolve that seemed to blow into me from the night breeze. It was a surge of trust: a conviction that honesty in the long run really does pay: a decision to face the truth, the real reason why I was alive and unhurt.

It was not at the very foot of the Vallum, not on the heap of the fallen, that I had recovered consciousness after the battle. It was at some distance from there that I opened my eyes. If chance really did fling me so many yards away from the rest, then no bodies can have broken my fall, so I ought to have been seriously injured, probably killed.

So it didn't happen that way. I did fall with the majority. But then that thing picked me out, dragged me from the heap, dragged me several yards until, to avoid discovery, it withdrew to wait.

Now I was walking towards it. One ruby eye fixed on me, it was tearing up some grass when it saw me approach. Its jaws ceased to work. Then its head and front paws and the whole front third of its body subsided, lay extra flat and still, and waited for its new rider.

Confidence came to me from I knew not where. I was convinced I was about to do the right thing; the basis of this conviction was an unidentifiable cotton-wool blur of assurance, floating without logical support. Sharper reasons did exist, but they weren't what made me dare. My motives remained fuzzy until – as my strides brought me closer – details came into focus and I became overwhelmed by the creature's *fitness* for its role of steed. In place of arrangements such as saddle or stirrup, the shape of its body was adapted in detail for conveying humans: its hide was stepped and flapped where the rider's feet must go; its ruff provided protection for one's legs; the holes in the head-shield were positioned for one's eyes to see through....

If war is to be avoided in the future, or at least made less costly, we Toplanders need to beat the enemy at their own game – learn to be properly mobile in Southern latitudes – meet the Southern powers on equal terms, instead of cowering behind walls or relying upon avalanches.

I, the dreamer of Earth, free from Krothan phobias, free from Topland terrors, free from any Northern antipathy for the worms of the South – I shall be the first "shonk" to master the steed of the Gonomong.

All this was true, but it wasn't enough to explain how I dared, or how I succeeded.

What did make me do it? The pull of destiny? Not a nice idea, really – being pulled by a force. You don't know where it's been.

"Hey! Look what that feller's doing!" cried a startled voice.

"Quiet!" said Captain Murena. "You – fetch the Colonel. You – find me a camera."

The decapod had reared, revealing the mauve stripes down its front, whereupon I remembered that I had seen this particular beast during the battle. Now its front paws waved close to my face. Then it lowered itself again and fawned on me, rubbing the edge of its head-shield against my side, gently nudging me round to where it wanted me to step up. In another moment I was astride it.

"Great krunking *gadrop*," called another voice. "Will you look at that?"

"Quiet!" repeated Murena. "Do not interfere. *Nobody interfere.*"

I wanted the creature to rise to its feet, and no sooner had I formulated the thought, than it rose; I wanted it to take a step forward, and immediately it did so. The fuzzy blur in my brain, the cotton-wool presence, was, it seemed, one end of a psychic conducting rod, the other end of which extended into the decapod's brain. *Krunking gadrop,* indeed. And yet swear-words seemed inappropriate. It was all happening as smoothly as a lullaby.

With effortless skill, borrowed free of charge I knew not how, I took the decapod through its first paces under my command. You have seen an inchworm move: the front end goes up, quests for a moment or two, goes forward and down, and then the rear end likewise goes up and forward and down. Imagine you're sitting near the front end of a giant version, just behind a kind of prow that is formed by a head and two front limbs raised on a neck that extends beyond the central arch. You might think that the up-down, up-down motion would make you, the rider, sick. But actually it does not feel that way. A fuzzy blur in your head, a rapport and command link, provides constant and instantaneous feedback, so that you experience the thing's movements as properly yours, as quite natural and expected. You don't in the least mind the up, down, up, down. I'll put it more strongly: you hardly even *think* of it. When, in an everyday situation, a man wants (for example) to raise his arm, his inner command and the act he performs are, so far as he can tell, simultaneous. To my amazement, my control of the decapod was just like that. No sooner did I think to wish it to move than it moved in obedience to my thought. It might as well have been a part of me.

"He makes it look easy," commented Murena.

"Too easy," came the clipped response of Colonel Reece. He arrived with a look of glum disbelief on his thin face. "Meanwhile, captain, I note that everyone else round here has seen fit to stop work to watch this curvetting."

"Perhaps they need.... need to witness...."

"But what, may I ask, are we witnessing?"

"History, sir," said Murena.

Indeed the crowd continued to swell and it was not long before my little area of grassy Slope was surrounded by men who evidently were not quite exhausted by the hours they'd spent fighting for their lives, men who still had the energy to come and gawp at something new. They must, I thought, be as crazy as I am. But then after all why should I be the only one who had sensed unfinished business at the end of the near-death experience which we had all undergone today? Why shouldn't I be given moral support? That, no doubt, was why I sensed no actual hostility, despite the distaste I could see in the drawn faces around me: they saw the point of my efforts, they understood, or at least they intuited, that I was trying to see to it that the war *was* properly finished off, that the whole nasty episode could be filed "closed".

Of course there was bound to be a lot of argument. I could hear the murmurs, and the lamplight revealed to me the faces on which fascination, even admiration, contended with disgust and loathing. Colonel Reece's expression of wincing amazement was no different from the crowd's average. While he conferred with Murena, I went on with the demonstration, I turned in various manoeuvres, meeting the stares on every side with a stare of my own in which I packed as much confident reassurance as I could. Finally the Colonel called out to me:

"Wemyss! How *can* you control that thing?"

I could tell by his tone, his question really required I prove to him that it was not controlling me.

I shouted back: "It responds to thought control, sir."

"Tell it to turn three times clockwise."

I did so and it happened.

Reece nodded, "I'd rather believe your explanation, than believe that it heard me and knows English. Now listen carefully, Wemyss. This business could be big, but we've got to make sure we finish it properly. Suppose you want to get down, what will - No! No! Don't actually do it; just tell me. I see, I see." For I had ordered the decapod to let me off and it had begun to descend into its crouch.

Reece seemed satisfied. "Don't get off yet," he emphasized. He spoke to someone by radio. Then he said: "We can make a start. Clear a way, you people…." and he began to snap out orders for an escort of spears to form around us. "Now then, Wemyss, start moving. I've found some secure quarters for you and your mount." Further orders – by radio, these – must, I guessed, concern what was to happen at the other end of the rapidly organized procession.

"Am I under arrest, sir?" I hazarded.

"You're not a prisoner, but your mount is. As for you, you're a hero. So shut up and co-operate."

Not wishing to receive another blast of what I took to be irony, I obediently refrained from asking any more questions. I had done what I could. My task was over; for me the day was done, really done, at last, and I hardly cared whether they took away my liberty or not, so long as they put me in a room with shower and clean bedding. The exhaustion which I had so far kept at bay now took possession of me so that I could hardly move a muscle, and only the fact that I rode by means of mental command enabled me to continue. Follow orders, I told myself, and don't try to think ahead.

We approached a space at the foot of the Vallum that was now cleared of corpses. Boards had been placed over the bloodied ground, wide enough for us to tramp over.

Up the Vallum's south slope, we progressed; going home now, I thought, groggily. The escort carried torches, whose beams swung this way and that. In addition, little blue-white glares, from ground-lamps shining up into our faces, began to line the path we took, as the Army's technicians went to further trouble to light the way: not so much a torch-light procession, as a cats'-eyes procession, I thought in sleepy wonder. The effect flowed up to the top of the embankment, to the battlements. My decapod then stepped, my escort clambered, over onto the Vallum summit, where I averted my eyes from the havoc revealed by the torch-beams. Switch off, I wanted to shout: I don't wish to see. Yet the veil of night in any case couldn't cover the horror, couldn't abolish – rather, worsened – the smells and the stumbling. Despite all this, peace crept into me; the tired-out sense of a part played, disgrace avoided, approval earned.... all rewarded with permission to surrender to weariness.

We crossed over, to the north edge of the embankment; here the line of lights continued over the planks of a bridge which must have been thrown together with impressive speed, to reach horizontally from the Vallum to a point on the Slope beyond. Why had such a bridge been built? No need to ask: this was where the great mess lay, the gruesome mash where the boulders had come down. Some of my escort played their torch-beams over horrid fragmentary sights which my eyes skidded to avoid. I thanked the new bridge for saving us from having to clamber over the great rocks and wade through the crushed remains amongst them.

Faraliew, I reflected, must take responsibility for this. He it was who composed this scene; he must have given the actual order, whereupon the rocks rolled and rebounded to their rest amid the splashed and pounded meat. He – none other – spoke and it was done.

What a way to earn a mention in the history books.

I did not try to be fair, to weigh points for and against his military decision; my mind simply gave way to revulsion. My hatred of what had happened flowed up to the general in command, and, past him, flowed higher still. The sheer ghastliness of it all shocked my entire belief system into a new shape.

An "Act of God" – that was how an insurance company would refer to a naturally occurring avalanche. But if Nature's acts are God's, and if Man is a part of Nature, it follows that all manifestations of human wickedness, including wars and battles, are also Acts of God. In the beginning God created the heavens and the earth.... and in so doing He unleashed an avalanche of cause and effect which had evidently escaped from His control. "God," thought I, "You have acted irresponsibly." In my present black mood I told Him that He ought not to create any universe which was liable to lead to something like this; it just wasn't worth it.

I had meant well, I had wanted to do my bit, to fulfil my sense of obligation to the society of Topland, the wonderful yob-free civilization to which I was proud to belong.... but I hadn't joined up in order to play a part in a massacre.

Admittedly – so I conceded – He has earned high marks for having created all that is splendid and loveable. But what's the point doing that and then *smashing it up?* Or rather, letting it be smashed up (for I was now convinced that He had lost control).

So my view shifted. I thought to see God's career on Earth in a new light. My religious background (my mother had brought me up as a Congregationalist) turned out to be insufficiently strong to stand up to the test of battle, or rather, of the aftermath of battle, and so a host of new perspectives came crowding in on me all at once. Christ's ministry, instead of a triumphant turning point to put mankind on the path of salvation, now seemed a desperate rescue attempt, or even less, a mere morale-boosting exercise like dropping Allied propaganda leaflets into Nazi-occupied Europe to reassure the oppressed that they had not been forgotten. Well, maybe a bit more. (I struggled to be fair.) All right, it was a new voice in history, a new kind of voice. Nevertheless, the status of the One who uttered that voice was reduced in my eyes to that of a mere hero, a basically good guy who was out of his depth, a beloved leader but (this was most unfortunate) definitely not a sure-fire winner. The odds against Him were too great; by which I really meant, that my former belief in God's omnipotence was a position I must retreat from if I was to continue to believe in His goodness – and without *that* belief there isn't any point in bothering with religion at all.

And because I could no longer believe in an all-powerful benevolent God, the field was left open, unfortunately, to belief in another sort of power. Not that I believed that a Satan existed; not yet. But conditions seemed right for fragments of a potential Satan to develop. Light-headed thoughts, dark imaginings assailed me with ideas of *emergent* evil. "Bits of Satan must assemble," I slurred, "unless we do something.... do something...."

Well, it had been a tiring day.

*

The procession came off the bridge, away from the scene of carnage, and proceeded up-Slope towards Volost. In a few minutes I saw that we were headed for the illuminated front of the Volost Hotel.

The building's main east-west front and its two north-south wings all formed three sides of a square; now the fourth side was also walled, by a hastily constructed fifteen-foot fence, the centre of which swung aside on hinges as we approached.

The escort stayed behind me; I rode into the corral, and carefully and silently ordered the decapod to crouch down. It sank, it aligned its snout with the ground and I dismounted without a hitch. I turned, saw the line of spears, all of them held tensely, in the hands of men who were not sure, even now, what to believe; as the decapod lazily tore up some mouthfuls of lawn and began munching, I walked towards the exit and the spears parted and made way for me. Colonel Reece said: "Well done, Wemyss. It seems you really were in control." He turned his head and spoke formally to an aide: "Halton, see that a watch is kept on our new prize. Topland has waited a long time for this." To me once more he spoke: "Congratulations, man!"

I looked back as they closed the gate. The creature now appeared to be dozing like a contented sheep; I wished to do the same. Dulled by fatigue, I was slow to respond to the Colonel's congratulations. Reece stepped forward, grabbed my arm and put on a smile. "Wemyss," he hissed, staring into my eyes, "don't go all absent-minded on me! Snap out of it."

"Yessir, sorry sir."

Rapidly he continued to bite out the words: "Do you know, I am quite happy to have risked my career by allowing you onto our territory with that thing, because I am trusting that you really are a hero. *So be one!*"

"Of course. Of course," I repeated dreamily.

Reece let go my arm and muttered to Murena, "He's like a damned zombie. He'd better not let me down."

"Put him to bed quick, that's what I suggest, sir, then go see the General."

"Yes – this is one issue I won't be sorry to dump on Faraliew."

A gentle push at my back, pressure at my elbow, and I was coaxed into a walk, round the front path towards the main entrance of the hotel. I was not inclined to speak. I understood what was bothering Reece, but I could not feel any concern. A couple of times he addressed me, muttering hesitantly, “How's the brain, Wemyss?....Feel anything funny in your mind?” *I feel fine, sir,* I could have said, but I was too worn out to bother. Too exhausted to give him the reassurance he yearned for, reassurance that he had done the right thing. Let him fear; it was just too bad. *I* knew that my thoughts were my own, my mind was still my own, not some alien-influenced cuckoo in the nest of Topland. I *had* changed my religion rather rapidly, but no one need know about that. One day I might tell Uncle Vic, if I ever saw him again....

These thoughts passed across the dim backdrop of my fading awareness as I was led through a lobby and up some stairs till we stopped just outside an open bedroom door. The number of beds that were squeezed into that room, and their wheels and frames, reminded me of what I had heard, that the hotel had been requisitioned for use as a military hospital for long-term cases; was I a long-term case? No, if only I could have a good night's sleep, I'd show them, I'd be bright as a button tomorrow morning.... Other patients were being wheeled out. Then, in I went. Nurses came and washed me, dressed me in clean pyjamas, enveloped me in the fresh crinkle of crisp bedclothes and left me to sink into oblivion.

*

Morning light slanted through the window. A well-built blonde nurse was bending over me. The name badge on her bosom read “Belinda Brown”, which, I thought, had a nice ring to it.

“And how are we today?”

“Fine,” I replied, and meant it: I had awoken warm and relaxed, full of well-being.

“You've had a touch of fever. But,” she felt my forehead, “it's better than it was.”

Fever? Yes, come to think of it, I did sense it, lingering but not enough to spoil my appetite; I felt ravenous, and grinned ecstatically when Belinda said, “Ready for some breakfast?”

She slid one hand behind my back, lifted the upper half of me with no more effort than if I had been a three-year-old, and slid more pillows behind me. Then she handed me a breakfast list and asked what options I wanted. “All of it, please,” I requested – ready to find out how much I could get away with, but also ready to pretend that I was joking if need be. Belinda put me in mind of a feminine ju-jitsu expert I'd seen in some film, and my instinct told me to stay on the right side of a girl like that.

She took back the list and ticked every item for me. “I like a man who knows what he wants,” she remarked in a cheerfully saucy tone, and departed.

“Wow,” I said when she returned with a loaded tray, and I did full justice to the fullest English breakfast ever. Afterwards, the nurse helped me up. I was surprisingly weak on my legs, though after she had got me to the bathroom door I was able to persuade her that I could manage thereafter on my own. When I came out, she pointed back to the bed and I meekly obeyed, but I began to wonder. What exactly was supposed to be wrong with me? Battle fatigue? Did that really explain the pampering?

I had no objection to being coddled, up to a point, but the government surely lacked the resources to give this VIP treatment to *all* the able-bodied survivors, so some explanation was wanted.

Either I must be weedier than most, or I must have been singled out for the special treatment for another reason. That I was being rewarded for my taming of the decapod, was an explanation which rang false. You don't (or at any rate, you shouldn't) reward a man by isolating him, or embarrassing him.

I watched Belinda as she pottered about, tidying this and that. Nurses must be much in demand right now, yet this one seemed to be hanging around, spending rather a lot of time in sight of me. My growing suspicions were becoming clamorous; I wondered how to quiet them. Well, one good rule is, pick a person you like the look of, and start a friendly argument with that person.

“Nurse, can you tell me where my clothes are?”

“You can't get dressed just yet.”

“Am I allowed to know why not?”

She straightened, arms akimbo, and looked at me squarely. “Take my word for it,” she said, “you're biting off more than you can chew.”

I felt a bit light-headed as I retorted, “Better than lying here chewing more than I've bitten off.”

She went a bit red. “I was told not to let you have your clothes just yet, but.... well, they said nothing about not letting you take a little walk in your pyjamas. As far as the rear garden, anyhow. Let me check.” She went out into the corridor.

A minute dragged by, then another, and I simply had to get up. I went to the door, looked to the right and saw Belinda under the transparent cowl of a telephone nook. She turned and saw me, spoke a further few hurried words, put the receiver down and strode towards me. I held my ground, hoping she was not annoyed with me; to my relief, she wasn't, but she was brisk.

"We can make a move. Let's get going."

If she was on my side, the last thing I ought to do was distract her or make any kind of trouble; that would be really stupid; so I did not ask, *Whom are we going to meet?* I gambled on putting all my trust in Belinda. I was feeling stronger every minute but I continued to play the part she appeared to wish me to play. With my right arm round her shoulders she took some of my weight, more than she needed to take, as we went out into the corridor and commenced our voyage towards the back entrance.

Fortunately the corridors were busy and I was not the only patient being escorted while clad in pyjamas and slippers. I noticed that Belinda steered me away from full-face encounters with anyone in a white coat. "Dr Alldred is all right," she muttered, "despite his name, but we don't want to run into my immediate boss, Dr Stearne."

"Is *he* well-named?" I muttered back.

She giggled, "In more ways than one! Anyhow, my excuse is, I don't think there's anything wrong with just giving you a breath or two of fresh air."

I made no immediate comment. I was staring at a wall calendar with the red-circled date showing that today was *two* days after the battle. My need for that gulp of fresh air sharply increased. I peered wistfully ahead down the corridor. "How long can I stay out?"

"We'll see how it goes. Don't push it; I'm doing my best." She sounded edgy too.

Reckless gratitude surged through me, and I blurted out, "I think you're wonderful."

"I've known that for a long time. Now: here we are. It's a nice warm day so you should be all right as you are." We went through two sets of double doors and emerged into the hotel's rear garden.

The lawn was cut into the Slope to form a level area that ended a hundred yards or so ahead of us in a wall of rock. It wasn't crowded; a few people were out strolling or sitting on benches among the flowers. Closer to us was an area scattered with round tables, each with central pole and sunshade, each surrounded by four or five chairs. None were in use at the moment – except one table where a man I recognized sat waiting for us: one of the older members of my company, who seemed to have survived unscathed.

I sat, the nurse on my left, the veteran on my right.

"Glad to see you're one of the lucky fifth, Terry."

Terry Croale nodded solemnly. “Glad to see you likewise, Duncan. You're right: about eighty per cent of us bought it. See any of the rest?”

“Murena.”

“So…. he's now a captain without a company.”

I gazed around the peaceful garden. “I expect we're going to spend the rest of our lives saying to ourselves, 'Why me?'”

“Maybe some of us need to say it more than most.”

Belinda reached across me and put her hand on his. “Now please, Terry,” she began, while he gave me a speculative, calculating look.

“All right, love,” he said.

I guessed that Terry, who had a certain way with him, had influenced the nurse to arrange this meeting. They were in it together; but I also guessed that she had more to lose than he, if they were found out.

I asked him: “Were you by any chance a reporter, in civilian life?”

“If I were – if I am – don't worry that I'll quote you,” he smiled. “See – no pen in hand – not writing anything down – my notes are in my head; besides, visiting isn't forbidden and we can surely chat a bit. You're rather famous now, you know.” Again that calculating look. He went on: “So it's natural that I'm interested in how you feel about it all. This decapod business, I mean.” He paused again, and I kept my lip buttoned, and now he got to the point:

“Funny that you were able to do something no one else has ever managed to do.”

I scowled.

“Maybe that's not the only funny thing.” I glanced at the nurse as I spoke. “Maybe it's also funny how I develop a fever after having come through the battle with negligible injury. Funny how I woke up to find I'd missed a whole day.”

Belinda and Terry exchanged looks, so nonplussed by my remarks that I don't think they heard what my ears picked up just then: a voice some way off saying, *there they are.*

“Yeah,” mused Terry, “a fever and a missing day – maybe it all is a tiny bit strange.”

“Listen, you two: I follow orders,” Belinda declared. “I give the injections Dr Stearne tells me to give. I don't necessarily have to like it.”

Terry's eyes avoided hers. “Hm, well, I don't want to land you in the soup. Better go back – ” He broke off and froze.

My reaction was different: I gave a sudden start which must have looked comical to General Faraliew, who grinned as he sat down at our table.

His first words, however, were not addressed to me but to Terry and Belinda.

"Don't get up. Relax. I know what you two have been up to. And it doesn't matter."

The four of us sat eyeing each other, the general's eyes twinkling, celebrating his control over the situation. In addition to his rank and his natural presence – he was a very tall, imposing man – he was now cloaked in the aura of victory, of prestige which I could sense fairly oozing from him. He was going to announce our fates – and Terry Croale, by contrast, would henceforth sit back, silent and stiff, his little initiative over. Terry's audacity had its limits. He wasn't going to tangle with Faraliew.

Which left me to carry the can; not that I even knew what "can" it was.

"Wemyss," said the general, "I want your motive. Tell me what possessed you to have a go at taming that decapod monstrosity."

"Er – well, sir – I just followed a mad train of thought. A string of hunches.... which suggested that I could make a contribution to the future defence of Topland."

"Creditable," said Faraliew, poker-faced. "Go on. I want to know why *you*, and not another, did it."

"Among the entire Topland army I might well be the only man without a phobia against them.... the only man who could establish a rapport with one of them.... bring it back for study.... that's how my thinking went, sir."

"Anything else?"

"Instinct told me that here was a specially intelligent mount, trained to carry officers."

"The stripes on it?"

"Yes, sir, those mauve stripes. And it seemed already to have decided that I was suitable rider material. If I turned my back on it, rejected it, the opportunity might never recur."

"So you went and tamed a Gonomong Finger. I shall now tell you, Wemyss, what *I* have done. When the report came to me from Colonel Reece, I understood that I had a hero on my hands, a tricky hero whose deed might inspire a wave of horror as well as admiration. You can imagine, can't you?" (I nodded. He nodded in synch, smiling.) "Yes. So, for your own good, and for my Army's peace of mind, I – er – used some influence on Dr Stearne."

"Ah."

"Ah. Feel any resentment? Tell me honestly."

I thought of the "fever" and the day subtracted from my life. But then I also thought of all the kinds of trouble he might be trying to avoid, and that I also might have an interest in avoiding them.

"Honestly, sir, I suppose not – "

"Cagey one, aren't you?" Faraliew leaned back and chuckled, in complete control. "Anyhow that extra day, with you k.o.'d, was just enough. I used the hero theme, and my publicity contacts, to circumvent the public phobia. Articles slanted just right – eh, Croale? – have appeared in the *Bugle*, the *Neydian Times* and so on, yesterday evening and this morning. Your status is now safely fixed." He grinned once more. "You're looking twitchy again, Wemyss. What's the matter now?"

"Sir, if I had any chance of getting away with it, I'd have no objection to being built up as a hero. But.... sir, it's *the* problem for any impostor: what to do when the real one turns up? In my case, it's like this: real heroes do exist, and when I meet any I'll want to be able to look them in the eye."

"Yes, it's hard, isn't it?" Faraliew was full of amused sympathy. "And the worst of it is, the status grows on you, and you grow into it, so that before too long you are expected to be a hero *again*.... Don't groan, Wemyss. Somebody has to do it." Then he lifted his right hand to a chest pocket and undid the flap and extracted a grey metal object and placed it on the table in front of me. "Take that. It's yours, to wear in this afternoon's victory parade. Keep it switched on."

It was a mobile phone. *Cell* phone, I named it American-style, with an uncanny pun on *cell*, as I touched it with a forefinger and experienced a little jolt of apprehension, in which I half expected ghostly prison bars to rise around me. I felt really spooked, but it was merely one of those overwhelming insights of mine which turn out to be a lot of rubbish. The only conclusion I obtained from it was that sometimes it can be a disadvantage to have read too much science fiction, especially the spooky bit in Philip K Dick's *Ubik* where the guy learns he's dead when he sees a message scrawled on the wall of a urinal.... I had thought, for a shocking instant, that the mobile phone was an equally disconcerting message for me.

For to see one at close quarters at this late stage – after I had lived on this world for twelve weeks or more – seemed weird.

Faraliew, admittedly, had used one the day I first saw him. And in parks in Savaluk, during lunch breaks, I had seen a few executives with hand close to ear, though they might have been scratching their heads or adjusting their hats....

"Pick it up, Wemyss! It's not a grenade!"

"Sorry, sir." I gave a weak laugh; my fingers closed round the thing. "The sight of it gave me the jim-jams for a moment," I added as I tucked it into my shirt pocket.

"Why, may I ask?"

"Because, sir, I'm just a daft, maladjusted oneiro."

"I see. Well, in my opinion you have the virtues of your defects. And on that jolly note – " He stood up; we rose likewise. "Captain Murena will give you the schedule for this afternoon."

I could picture, at least vaguely, what was going to happen. Some kind of procession, lots of cheering; me no doubt receiving instructions over the mobile phone, as to what to do and when, just so it could all pan out nicely, and the people have their show, and it all reflect to the credit of the powers that be. And why not? A battle had been won. A vital, generation-saving battle. A victory parade would be a natural sequel to it, surely.

As a parting shot Faraliew added, "You'd better get properly dressed, for a start! You need to look good, sauntering on Ydrad."

"'Ydrad', sir?"

Faraliew quoted, "'*Nothing did he dread, but ever was ydrad.*'"

"Ah," I said. It came back to me: the inscription below the sculpted form of General Necon Carredh....

"I see you got it, boy. Just to help you in your role as hero, I decided your decapod ought to have a powerful name." In great good humour the General departed.

*

The nucleus of a crowd began to form as I rode Ydrad out of the hotel "corral", and scores more people gathered to watch me direct my strange mount westwards along the main street of Volost. Following the captain's instructions I veered north-west to head for the main gate of the fortress city. The crowd drifted along with me, growing from scores to hundreds. Gesticulations and open mouths met my every glance, a multiform pressure that squeezed me into the role *celebrity*, while privately I pictured myself as a plodding fish-thing, fins partly evolved into legs, crawling up an underwater incline way back in Earth's Devonian period. According to this dreamy quirk I was headed for a shock on my first crawl towards the big surprise called *shore*, a drastic horizontal revelation which promised to burst upon me when a certain altitude had been reached – even though I told myself not to be silly, told myself that the only "surface" I was about to break was the jutting ledge of Neydio, a mere city-sized interruption in the natural Slope of Kroth. The ledge was bound to *remind* me of the out-of-date bias towards flatness, from which my soul had weaned itself.

I continued my oblique ascent, into an uninhabited zone, currently sunlit but over which, every afternoon, the crag of Neydio must cast a tremendous eastward shadow. No one would ever choose to build here. This bare region gave me a simplified view ahead. It was as though I were now merely climbing a grassy ramp towards the top of a cliff-like wall; meanwhile multitudes on foot streamed ahead of me, eager to get good places for the show.

Reaching the Spoing (the east-west railway that runs on a level with the join between City and Slope), I gave the silent order for Ydrad to turn due west. Now all I had to do was to follow the line, with the city's ordinary "built" wall, its modest-sized north wall, soon on my left – follow it till I came to the entrance station and the main gate.

The gate's double doors were wide open. I turned smartly left and rode through, and in doing so I rode off the Slope and onto the great platform city. At last I had entered Neydio, and for the first time in what seemed like ages I could see a horizon of sorts – a couple of miles away.

The entrance square, overlooked by the gate towers, was flanked by lines of three-storey stone buildings, baroque style. The southern side of the square was open to the avenue that stretched away to that horizon, that edge, that drop. I reminded myself, it was only a drop, and as I got closer to it I would have to view it less and less as a horizon and more and more as a mere precipice. But here at the eastern end of Neydio, I could just about pretend I was back among the vistas of Savaluk, or even of Earth; an innocent pretence, not likely to undo my recent acclimatization to the natural sloping order of things. Sufficient merely to evoke a nostalgic smile.

The square had not yet filled up and there was room for me to let Ydrad lope around a bit as I admired the splendid sights of this end of the city. Some of the assembled burgers flinched as we sprang about and curvetted; others waved at me and I waved back. I heard shouts of encouragement and simple expressions of exhuberant optimism, on the theme of "Now we can show 'em!"

At the start of the avenue itself a more disciplined body of figures was taking shape. The first few hundred soldiers were forming into companies.

More were coming in through the gate; I had got here none too early. I looked around for Murena, in case there were orders for me. *Bzzzzzzz...* The mobile! I slapped my pockets, found the phone, fumbled with it.

"Wemyss, this is General Faraliew. How are you doing – have you reached the city?"

"Yessir, I'm in the entrance square."

"Payne from the Globe is waiting by the foot of the West Tower to have a word with you. Give the hack something to bite on, will you?"

"Right," I said, unsure whether he had said "Payne" or "a pain" was waiting for me. I rode over to the Tower's steps and a woman with a bouffant platinum hair-do detached herself from the onlookers.

She approached to within a couple of yards and looked up at me. "Duncan the Fingerman!" she called out. "I'm Lucinda Payne from the Neydio *Globe*. Ever been here before?"

"Never."

"What do you think of our city?"

"It was *cruel* of the builders to build it so big!"

She laughed appreciatively. "Does something to you, eh?

"Yep – nothing like it on Earth, that's for sure." I mopped my brow. What had inclined me to use *cruel*? Corner-cutting, epigrammatic smart talk. Clever, also, to finish with the oneiro-style comment, "nothing like it on Earth". The readership of the *Globe* would want an oneiro to sound like an oneiro.... must stay in character.... Quite suddenly I was mortally sick of being clever. Stabbed by a childish yearning, my inmost self wailed, *I want to go home,* but it was only a brief wail; my more adult self amended: *Go home when you're finished, not before. Remember that sentence from The Lord of The Rings. 'The way back, if there is one, lies past the Mountain.' And what's my own Mount Doom? Probably upside-down.*

Lucinda stepped back and waved her hand. "I'll catch up with you!" she called, while my phone went *bzzzzzzzz-bzzzzzzz* again.

"Murena's waiting to show you your place. There by the north-west plinth."

"Right, sir," I acknowledged, and turned my steed towards the captain some fifty yards away. *I'll hang on* – I promised myself in a moment of optimism – *hang on and finish this parade, and then I can reasonably claim the reward of service: to leave the army, go home and lead a normal life.*

For it was mighty obvious that I was weary of living by my wits, and that this weariness had good sense behind it. I simply wasn't cut out for continual cleverness. I might sparkle for a while but the longer I stuck my neck out the more catastrophic the eventual let-down; just as for the grand avenue of Neydio the further the protuberance, the bigger the end drop must be.

Faraliew's voice crackled in my ear again:

"Remember to keep your phone switched on. And keep that reporter woman happy; I'd rather she followed you around... get me?"

"Understood, sir." Now there, thought I, is a man who will never "go home". Good luck to him, but *I*, having let him move me around like a piece on a chessboard, shall deserve some private life when the show's over....

I rode up to Murena. He stood in a courtyard, beside one of the groups of soldiers to be fed into the procession; I recognized a few faces, not many, in the group. Other groups had already begun their march down the avenue and Murena was keeping an eye on his watch for the right moment to tell us to join. I obeyed his instructions, positioning Ydrad on the indicated spot, and then had to wait a minute or so, facing into the late morning sunlight, a warm breeze buffeting my cheek. Forget about going home, whispered a sudden, unwelcome thought. The battle isn't really over.

Come off it, replied my intellect. The fighting is finished.

Don't you believe it, twitched my nerves.

"You next," said Murena to me. "Off you go...."

I "wheeled" onto the avenue, entering my place in line. I, and those next to me, and the group of which we formed a part, became blended into the slow parade that stretched way ahead already half way to the finish; crowds on either side waved and cheered all along our route down the great avenue of Neydio. Cheering with real enthusiasm: but of course I understood perfectly well that they were cheering an image, not the real me; they didn't know the real me, any more than I knew the real them; so it wasn't really personal. It was the skill of a propaganda department which, lucky for me, had managed to put a positive spin on what I had done – representing me in newspapers and in Army despatches as a hero. I strongly suspected that public opinion might have swung violently against me if left to itself; if people's minds had connected "Decapods – yuck – rider – yuck", instead of "Decapod conquered, ridden, subjugated, hooray!"

Faraliew, bless him or curse him, had brought this about. And because he'd confessed his manipulation quite openly, even to the extent of naming the doctor whom he had somehow suborned into keeping me in hospital for an extra day for political reasons, he'd be all the harder to oppose. He was as good as saying to me, "Go ahead, try to make trouble for me if you want; I don't care a bit; I shall always be one step ahead of you." Not that I wished to make trouble for him. It was just rather hard to accept all the cheers. They were well-meant and yet at the same time they were a pack of mysteries snapping at my heels and propelling me down an alley towards some destiny waiting to gulp me at the far end. To counter this sinister fancy, I straightened my back; I rode tall. Battle not over? Silly idea! Silly, at any rate, to fear a surprise attack. Faraliew must have seen to it that only a fraction of the Topland army, units chosen by lot, had been withdrawn to participate in this carnival of victory. The rest of the troops, plus reinforcements to make up for losses in the battle, guarded the Vallum as before, while the boulders of the Marraspang, winched back into start position, could if necessary be used again.... I took all this for granted as though I had read the General's mind. And all accounts agreed that the Gonomong, once beaten, stayed beaten for a long time. Even if, this time round, they happened to possess a turner of tables, a Lee or a Rommel, such genius would have nothing to work on. There was no scope for them to effect a sudden military reversal. So what was I worried about? Our territory was saved. Yet inside *me*, along the pathways of my nervous system, obstinate doubts insisted upon waging guerrilla warfare against the occupying forces of common sense. Anxieties, beaten by the rules of logic, just as the Boers in 1900 had been beaten according to the ordinary rules of war, refused to lie down and surrender. So could I perhaps do a mental Kitchener and set up some kind of concentration camp system to starve out rebellious thoughts and give my head some peace? Trouble was, I couldn't get rid of the notion that links of some sort connected all the various mysteries swirling around me, threatening to unite into a grin that jeered, "Too late! You spotted me too late!"

Very well, we'll see about that, I decided. Broad daylight, and the applause and good wishes of a friendly crowd, and my incredible good fortune in being uninjured and alive, easily pumped me with more moral energy than any bizarre fancy could suck away. I actually felt pretty good – unsettled, yes, but not depressed; no matter what skull-shaped doubts pestered my imagination. It was hardly surprising that I should find it difficult to relax after what I had gone through. So, find that lurking skull and *sock it*. If you can't rise to an occasion while a whole crowd is cheering you, it's "a poor do", as my Aunt Reen would have said.

I was impressed by the behaviour of that crowd. Whereas, on Earth, any similarly large and enthusiastic gathering would require a police presence, on Kroth it was not so. But if I were to state the reason for this difference –

namely that Krothan people are sufficiently mature and self-controlled to express their good humour without any degeneration into yobdom – I would sound like a prig; so I won't say it. I'll merely point out that the reporter, Lucinda Payne, was able to run alongside the procession, in a gap between it and the crowd, a gap maintained by no fence or line of police but kept in being solely by the restraint of the crowd; and while she ran to catch me up, I noted other reporters running beside other selected marchers in front of me, and in no case did elements in the crowd follow their example. In other words there was no "if they're doing it, why shouldn't we?"

Lucinda jogged at my side and turned her face up eagerly towards me. "Duncan!" she panted, "what's it like to triumph on Carredh Avenue?"

So that was what it was called. Not surprisingly, the road down the middle of Neydio had been named after the ancient hero of Topland. I sensed the tremendous civic pride in the reporter's voice. "I feel a kind of inevitability," I shouted back.

She liked my answer. "It had to happen here, eh?"

"That's it! I'm alive, so I have to end up here!" Of course that couldn't apply to everybody. For one thing it would be madness, while the enemy still lay within range of detection, to withdraw every man from the defences to throw a party. And in any case there couldn't have been room to parade the entire army; participants must have been chosen by lot from the survivors.

Except, of course, that *my* presence had not been left to chance.

Lucinda Payne was quick to point this out. "You tamed that Finger – you had to be here!"

"It makes sense to bring all trophies here," I replied. Remembering the General's instruction to keep the reporter happy, I framed my answers as compliments to her city. And why not? I didn't have to pretend, I really was in awe of the huge fortress. To me the structure's vast size strongly suggested it to be the legacy of some different civilization, maybe a past species, which possessed secrets of construction now lost; but that was not all: as I thought further I began to feel that despite its spooky grandeur and alien uniqueness, Neydio *fitted* in a modern sense. Its location at Latitude 60, like the Topland boundary itself, was most appropriate at this point where skis cease to be practical, where the influence of Topland culture thus reaches its natural southern limit. I gained confidence at having worked this out for myself, and briefly I wondered if I might make more use of my talent for thinking things through in an unfamiliar world. Whoa there, I smiled. Don't wobble too fast between wanting to go home and wanting more dizzying stuff. Keep your eye on the ball. The ball being –

The rarity of mobile phones! I thought back to that. Rare rather than mass-produced, the phones yet existed in their small numbers. The infrastructure must also exist for them to work; imagine, all that arrangement for only a *few* phones! It could never happen on Earth. Link this with –

The maturity of the crowd lining this procession! The way they keep back without the need for police –

Restraint.

That was the clue.

"Thus far and no further". Restraint: a kind of power that Earth did not have.

I thought of the light-sabres, the laser swords used by the characters in the *Star Wars* films. That cute fictional idea that you can restrain a beam of light, make it go the length of a sword and no further – what power it would have, if that were possible! Light-sabres, ha! I almost literally licked my lips at such breaking of rules. It was my moment of understanding, my surge in appreciation of Krothan culture. Here human beings, like the illegal stop of the Jedi sword, might say "No" to mob psychology, and so might achieve things that were humanly impossible on Earth.

Earthly behaviour knew *some* restraint, of course, but there it was always part of a trade-off. For example, on Earth you couldn't go all out for free enterprise, progress *and* social cohesion. Or liberty *and* equality. Or tradition *and* progress. Here on Kroth, well....

There's nobody to hear me, nobody to tell me I'm a prig: I can say the truth quietly to myself: here people aren't slobs.

Ahem. Harrumph. Quiet, now. Naughty, naughty. Mustn't judge people. *Not even slobs?* Shush! Who do you think you are, Duncan Wemyss? *Hee hee, nobody can hear me...*

Very much the guilty little boy, wondering when and how hard he's going to get smacked, I stared ahead as I rode, apprehensively watching the approach of the watch-towers and balloons which marked the southern, precipice-end of Neydio. The march was almost over and the procession was pooling into a magnificent square.

At its southern side reared the bulkiest of those buildings which must overlook the drop. The domed, columned pile had to be the Observatory, and the sight of its clean and stately frontage warmed my heart. Every citizen must sleep safer knowing the Observatory staff were there to monitor the great stretch of Slantland visible from that height, including, currently, the defeated and retreating Gonomong.

A figure in grey, I noticed, was standing close to Ydrad, much closer than people normally liked to come.

I peered down.

"Uncle! Typical!"

"Don't worry, the beast knows me. I didn't startle it."

I was too startled myself to inquire into this. "I mean, typical of you to show up in such unpredictable fashion! Great that you're alive – yet I'm not surprised," I added pensively. My thoughts whizzed round like over-excited midges, not only because of the joyous confirmation that I still had some family, but because Vic's presence anywhere usually gave the situation a good stir. And that was how matters were meant to be. I had renewed contact with the grinding wheels of purpose.

"Great to see you too, Mr Hero," he went on. "I am even less surprised than you – I knew for a fact that *you* were alive. We can talk later; you need to get down. I've come to take care of Ydrad while...." (I felt it coming) "....you're wanted in the Observatory. I gather His Nibs wants you to do one last job for him."

One last job. This is what I get for being naughty –

That superstitious thought shaped my latest mood:

Acceptance.

*

An orderly took me along a carpeted corridor and into a lift. As he pressed a button for the lift to ascend, I thought: *Electricity – that reminds me – I've never seen pylons on Kroth. So are the National Grid power lines all laid underground? The expense, the effort! All that infrastructure for some but not a lot of appliances! Again, restraint. That's the great secret. Capabilities taken so far and no further. Strengths are to be saved and not splurged. But saved for what?*

The lift stopped; we emerged into an open-plan warren of desks and charts, where I followed the silent orderly past hunched and murmuring officials, till we reached a spiral metal staircase.

We clattered up this, into a quite different scene.

The "dome" was a half-dome only, as though its southern half had been sheared away. The two great telescopes were therefore open to the view over Slantland. They were mounted on a high bar, maybe fifty feet over our heads, and each tube was about four feet in diameter, angled down, aimed at the landscape to the south. One of them, as I craned my neck to watch, panned slowly. The other hung motionless.

During peacetime they were (I guessed) aimed at the sky, but once every generation or so, when the Gonomong attacked, the study of astronomy no doubt had to be abandoned, and the instruments were swung to point downwards, at the southern Slope.

On the floor not far in front of me was a map table, and uniformed women with rods, Battle-of-Britain "Ops" room style, stood ready to shunt counters across it. However this table-top was slanted thirty degrees, so the moveable symbols representing enemy units had to be magnetic.

The panning 'scope above our heads must, I realized, be remotely controlled; from its eyepiece the image which it had obtained was projected down onto the plotting table, in the form of a glowing circle which I could just about see from where I stood as it slowly crept across the map surface. If I were closer, doubtless I would be able to see if and when that projected image brought updated information. The women around the table were in a position to see, and to adjust the counters accordingly.

While watching, I witnessed one such adjustment: the operator reached over and gave a slight nudge to a little block the size of a decorative fridge magnet.

Voices sounded behind me, full of confidence.

"....And yet I say, the rider will be cloaked in that field."

"Don't talk ROT, Brudenell!"

A third voice, that of the General, intervened blandly: "Major Whitton appears concerned that our theoretical discussions might result in an enlisted man being sent to his death."

A dry snort from Professor Brudenell. "Sending men to their deaths is a not unknown procedure in military circles."

"Damn your cheek," said the Major. "You know perfectly well, there are deaths and deaths."

"Er – I think," Faraliew intervened again, "in fairness to the Professor, we need to recognize that he would be quite prepared to go himself, if it came to that."

"Sir," said Whitton, ignoring this, "I have work to do. Will you excuse me?" A moment later I saw the Major stalk past me, and as he went he muttered gruffly:

"Good luck, boy."

In uncertain response, I half-raised, then lowered my arm, not having been given time to salute. Drat the man anyway – why couldn't he follow the wise Italian custom, whereby you *don't* wish someone good luck? For if you say "Good luck" to someone you imply that he's going to need it. And that need itself implies bad luck. I shrugged off my irritation and waited like a dutiful soldier, refraining from turning around, so as to avoid the suggestion that I had overheard. Seconds later came a touch on my sleeve.

Professor Brudenell turned out to be a small man who *looked* like a professor, a caricature of one, with beard and glasses and a bald dome surrounded by a straggly fringe of curly brown hair. He tugged me along without a proper glance at me; his eyes were drawn to the map table. Faraliew, however, beckoned courteously. I followed them until we came to a stop a few yards behind the busy operations map.

"Look there, Wemyss," the General muttered, "you see that concentration of the Gonomong...." and he pointed to one of the clusters of magnetic symbols on the slanting table, but instead of making further comment on it he then said: "And by the way, Wemyss, I banked on slotting in a word with you before I have to go and make my speech.... I need to be quick.... there's so much to do. Come on, we'll use that office." With me and the Professor in tow, he made for a doorway into one of the small, cluttered rooms on the edge of the main observation area. Puzzled at his rambling tone, I sat down and waited to hear what this was all about. Hadn't he just said he needed to be quick? Yet he appeared less decisive than usual, as though, perhaps, he were seeking excuses for what he planned to ask. To my astonishment he began to discourse upon the strategy of the recent battle.

I did not retain everything that he said; nor (I was fairly sure) was I expected to; the important thing for me to do was to interpret his tone, and, when he got round to the point, be ready with the right response. It was a shock, all the same, when I did finally get the message: he was telling me *that the Gonomong, though defeated, had taken quite a large number of prisoners.*

Apparently the bird-borne unit I had seen in action had not been the only one. Others had penetrated much further behind our lines. At more than one point, a successful enemy raid had bagged a haul of civilian prisoners, destined for slavery in the steep lands of the far south.

Faraliew brooded: "If I had known.... but I did not know of their bird-men, any more than they knew of our Marraspang. You may wonder at the lack of intelligence on both sides. But this isn't Earth, Wemyss!"

I thought I had better contribute something.

"I get what you mean, sir – on Earth, espionage and the media saw to it that there weren't any great technological surprises in war. People knew more what to expect."

"Precisely," said the General, and emitted a disgusted sigh. "So you see, the great victor was caught napping. Yet in a few minutes this same great victor is going to have to make a rousing speech. A proud speech – the people all expect it – and how do I tell them about the cost? The horrendous wasteful cost?"

"Stop it, sir!" I said. His eyes went wide. But the point I suddenly had to make, because it was so central to my own experience in the battle, poured forth so urgently that both he and I overlooked my insubordinate tone. "This 'waste of war' stuff is so dangerous, sir! How can war *not* contain vast blundering waste? And so you fall into thinking, *all right, I am prepared to risk death, provided it's meaningful, but not unnecessary death, no, not that* – and there it is, the trap! It's a trap," I babbled on, "because if you're disinclined to accept unnecessary meaningless death, you're going to be disinclined to fight at all. For there's no such thing as an *efficient* battle! So you reach the logical end of that thought-process – desertion."

"You've twigged, I see," Faraliew said with a haggard smile. "You're in the know. And the way out of it: have you thought that far?"

"Is to encourage the greatest fear, the fear of disgracing oneself. That's the only thing strong enough – " I stopped. I couldn't understand why he was giving me all this time. Wasn't he in a hurry? And what had I done? Into my brain came a quiet thud of comprehension.

"Duty, they call it," said Faraliew. "The determination comes from inside you."

Yes, it was all quite fair, I was caught in my own net.

It only remained for me to be informed of what I had volunteered for.

Professor Brudenell, who had not spoken for a while, now exchanged glances with the General and said, "May I explain to him now?"

"Go on, Professor. But make it short."

"Sure – sure – no need to make a meal of it. Wemyss, does the name Nathan Salterius mean anything to you?"

It did ring a vague bell. "Some legend of the Army…." I forced myself to concentrate. I must accept I was in for it.

Brudenell continued:

"Nathan Salterius, during the Rip-Mig before last, about twenty-two thousand days ago, was captured by the Gonomong. So were many others, but he was the only one to escape. Stories vary as to what happened, but the main point is, while he and his captor were riding a decapod, something happened to his captor, and Nate found himself riding that beast alone. Plenty of others surrounded him not far off – and yet he managed to make his way back to our lines. The question is, how did he avoid being seen and recaptured? My theory, which is consistent with what else we know of Gonomong psychology, is that any decapod-plus-rider combination is subsumed as a gestalt – "

Faraliew interrupted, "Put in layman's language, Wemyss, what the Professor is trying to say is this. If you ride a Gonomong steed, you are effectively disguised as a Gonomong, simply because you are doing something which only Gonomong are supposed to do. This should hold true provided you don't get *really* close, for example within touching distance. So with any luck and a reasonable degree of caution, your mission enters the realm of the possible."

Ah yes, my mission. Quite. Faraliew was doing *his* duty, after all, by squeezing the best out of me, so the least I could do was to allow myself to be volunteered.

He unrolled an annotated paper map and spread it before me on the desk. "We don't have a lot of time," he remarked. "The behaviour of the Gonomong is staying true to pattern. At the end of their last great ripple migration, they paused some miles down-Slope and made an encampment in which they sorted themselves out before accelerating their retreat south, and it seems they are doing the same this time. Their captives are there.... somewhere. We could do to know exactly where. I expect you can guess what I'm going to ask you to do."

"I'm to scout on Ydrad," I said. "Find where the prisoners are being herded. Bring back information to be used in planning a rescue raid." I heard my own words cold and clear; I saw him nod; and then more words came out of me, with a coolness which mildly surprised us both. "Before I go," I continued, "I should like to say goodbye to someone, if it can be arranged."

He lifted his brows. "Of course. Within reason. That is, if the person can be fetched in time. Who is it?"

"She is an army nurse, Elaine Swinton by name. I don't know where she is. I've asked around but I don't seem to get anywhere."

"I'll get someone to check on it. Meanwhile, you study this map while I go and make my speech," and he gave me a pat on the shoulder and left the room. The Professor remained sitting quietly, in case I had questions.

The map, and the notes, made the outline of the mission fairly plain. The information had obviously been derived from the main map on the plotting table. It showed the concentrations of Gonomong, and some question marks in red showed possible locations where prisoners might be kept.

"Not much time," I muttered.

Professor Brudenell spoke:

"You're not the only oneiro in the Topland army, and Ydrad is not the only decapod left behind by the Gonomong; others have been spotted wandering and grazing in the groves and clearings of the frontier zone."

I looked across the table at him. "So – one of the Army's tasks in the days ahead will be to forge a new reconnaissance corps from this material?"

"I believe that is the General's idea," agreed the Professor. His voice was as quietly objective as mine; we were both pieces that had been moved into our places by a grandmaster player. "Meanwhile you are to be a pioneer. You and Ydrad are available *now*."

And it was now that the Battle of Neydio was really over for me. The last shots had been fired of that battle within myself. No doubts remained as to the next path I was going to take, though I experienced a shadowy presentiment that the path was going to be very much longer, fantastically longer than Faraliew realised or intended, no matter how great the General's skill in manipulating his human resources.

Duncan Wemyss the citizen, responsible, patriotic, shrugged at these forebodings and decided: *I am the one for the job and so I must do it.* As well as the citizen there was Duncan Wemyss the sinner: the prig with his unsavoury moral gloating over the poor yobs and slobs of Earth. That has left a bad taste in his mouth, and he wants to punish or at least purge himself, by risking his life for others. Finally, weightier by far than Duncan the citizen and Duncan the sinner was Duncan the *pilot*, the steersman of self. The stormy events he's been through have created a matching force inside him, a determination to push back against the pressure, to equalize it within and without. Maybe he would adjust to peace again when he was a much bigger man, but for the moment he could no more retreat from unfinished adventure than a deep-sea diver on Earth could safely bob straight up to the surface. Push back, equalize the pressure or get the bends!

The minutes had gone by, and suddenly Faraliew was back. "Phew," he said, "you did well to miss my ramblings (wish I could have). Now, Wemyss, as to your girlfriend...." His tone became serious and, at the same time, gentle as he placed a list of names in front of me. “Missing persons, presumed captured by the Gonomong. Here….” and he put his finger on an entry near the end.

I read her name, and my throat went dry. “You mean, sir….” I swallowed and found my voice again: “Thank you, sir, for getting the information.”

He said quietly: “It does look as though you have an extra motive to locate those prisoners.”

*

Preparations went ahead during most of the rest of that afternoon. A set of saddle-bags was shaped to fit on Ydrad, and they were filled with such provisions and survival equipment as the Army experts thought suitable for a reconnaissance lasting many weeks, though it was hoped that I would return within a day or two. I, personally, had no doubt that the experts were far too optimistic, but I didn't bother to say so. Discussion might mean delay, and what was the point? Commitment – that decisive *thunk* of the guillotine that chops the past away from the present – left me happy to dispense with further talk.

I only saw the General again briefly, before I left the Observatory building. “Just one thing, Wemyss,” he added as he bustled by. “Some concern has been expressed about the way that steed stayed behind for you. Almost as though the thing were arranged.”

I did not ask him what he meant. I shrugged, “It's only a dumb beast, sir.”

“Quite so. But a dumb beast trained by its owners.”

Well, of course it was trained. Just as a warhorse is trained. I went on listening to what Faraliew was saying, but I did not concern myself with his meaning.

“And it's a special one,” he went on. “We can't see how it would profit them to plant it on purpose amongst us; quite the contrary, but we're taking as few chances as we can. Checks and balances – that's the way to proceed. You're to have a companion for your mission.”

“I'm relieved to hear that, sir.”

“A mounted companion, of course. We have managed to round up another decapod, one of the few strays left over from another part of the battle line. And we have found a rider for it: someone who, like yourself, lacks the normal Toplander's antipathy for the creatures.”

“Another oneiro?” I asked, smiling.

"In a manner of speaking, yes. Someone who's Earth memory and Kroth memory are balanced and equal...."

Faraliew's rather elliptical pronouncements caused my smile to broaden into a laugh. "You couldn't keep him out of it, could you, sir?" A lazy side of me rejoiced that I would be able to abandon responsibility for leadership of my mission.

*

Unbelievable, that I could laugh. The trusting mood I was in! Life doesn't always punish you for your faults.

My fault then was that in my delight at being reunited with my uncle, and relief at the thought that he would run the show, I took him for granted; I did not stop to think that his life would be put at risk the same as mine. It was as though I could not doubt his invulnerability; no more than a toddler, being taken to play on the beach with his parents, will think to fear for their safety.

Departure was set for after nightfall. We left Neydio and rode back down to the frontier. The motionless stars of the Krothan universe, and the lights on the summit of the Vallum behind us, looked down on two giant inchworm-like steeds which began silently to stalk southward into the unknown.

Ydrad and its companion, which was named Gnarre, made very little sound as they moved sure-footed in the dark. Vic and I were able to ride sufficiently close together to communicate in voices barely above a whisper.

After some while a blob of deeper darkness loomed ahead. "We skirt that wood," I said, and steered to the left, past the crouching of trees that so blackened the dimness all around. When it was behind us, I shone my faint red torch on the map I carried. "Over here," I said, altering course again. "The first recommended stop." I didn't mind giving the obvious orders. Vic could take over when things got complicated....

In a glade about two miles south of the Vallum we halted to wait out the night. Tomorrow would show whether Professor Brudenell's theory was correct, that we were sufficiently disguised to spy out the encampments of the Gonomong.

We dismounted, tethered Ydrad and Gnarre to a tree and spread our groundsheets. We knew that the decapods, with their dextrous front limbs, could easily untie themselves and clear off, which would abort our plans there and then; we hoped they were docile creatures, with no such inclination to abandon their new masters, but anyhow, to test their attitude was in itself an important aim of the mission.

"It looks as though they've got used to us," remarked Vic.

I didn't answer straightaway. After a minute:

"Maybe they're as daft as we are," I pondered aloud.

More silence. Where do confident, trusting moods come from? Here was I, preparing to risk my life as soon as the curtain of night should lift to expose a couple of spies to the revealing light of day. As for my reasons – they bounced along, as the torch of belief was passed from one motive to another. One moment, thoughts of duty sustained me, and I was full of adult philosophy. Next moment I felt babyish confidence in the company of an older relative who (so far as I knew) had always come out on top in life's troubles. And then, most ridiculously, I had visions of personally rescuing Elaine.

I muttered: "I seem to be taking this hero business seriously."

Out of the darkness came Vic's reply: "I heard that. I should darn well hope you are serious about it."

"It's not like me," I mused. "The whole business...."

"Get some sleep," my uncle advised. "Or turn back."

"We can't turn back."

He didn't argue that one.

I said in a low voice, "Uncle Vic."

"What?"

"Do you reckon the General was pleased to get rid of us?"

"Hmm..." I heard a shifting on the groundsheet next to mine. "He didn't want to get rid of *me.* Wanted me to stay on his staff as a permanent advisor."

"Is that so?"

"Yep. Had all kinds of plans for me – but once he realized I was determined to stand on my rights as a civilian, he made the most of my wish to go my own way." A pause. "But *you* reckon...."

I floundered a bit. "Er, what I mean is, I got the idea that he may regard me as a risk to have around. At least, when I am on Ydrad."

"Concerned about road safety, is he?"

Ignoring this typical flippancy, which was only meant to chivvy me into speaking straighter, I went on: "As though the only reason I ventured to tame a decapod in the first place, is that my mind or my will had been tampered with. That I had somehow fallen under the influence of...."

"Of what?"

"What indeed? I don't suppose he could put it into words."

"Indeed not," said Vic sardonically, "or he would have had you arrested."

"But what he can't make up his mind to arrest, he'll find some other use for. That's what he's like."

Vic considered my words. Then he said, "I wouldn't worry about old Faraliew. You tend to think of him as a super-puppet-master, but I think of him more as a mere chef de cuisine, with us in the role of the pancakes he's just tossed. He's probably forgotten about us already – though he has the politician's gift of making you seem important to him while you have his attention. But you know, Duncan, you *have* changed. I think the person who suspects you is – you."

"The battle altered my religion," I explained. "To that extent I am a different person. No need to look for 'influences' beyond that."

"What exactly do you mean?" he demanded, his voice abruptly sharper, showing keen interest.

"Er – if I go into all that – what about the need for sleep?"

"Put sleep on hold. Thrash this religious stuff out first."

So, sitting there in the darkness, I went over it all. How hitherto, until the day of battle, I had considered myself as a run-of-the-mill Christian believer. How I had continued in this way partly from habit and inertia, and partly because I had never been impressed by the arguments I'd heard against the personal character of the Christian religion: to me it had always seemed fairly obvious that, since there *is* a personal dimension to things, no credible view of reality can fail to accommodate it at the highest level. And with regard to that last point, I had always thought it particularly silly to allow a *new* horror or disaster to raise doubts about the existence of God. If you suddenly hear in the news that thousands have been buried alive in an earthquake, why should you treat this as a more conclusive argument against God than all the previous earthquakes and other horrors that you already perfectly well knew had tormented people throughout history? How can you be so daft and egotistical as to wait till *your* scene is disturbed, before abandoning your beliefs? If you're going to be like that you ought never to have believed in the first place. And yet now, here was I, going that way myself. Wriggle as I might, I could not avoid the conclusion that events had shown the truth of the old objection, "God cannot be both all-powerful and good". No matter how necessary it might be to allow mankind his freedoms and his character-building struggles, I could not accept that the ensuing agony could ever be justified. It was all very well for *me,* I had survived, but what about those who had drawn the short straw and lay mangled under the boulders of the

Marraspang? The memory of it was too much. Something had to give. All right, God is good – if you deny that, you're simply substituting the problem of Good for the problem of Evil, so you might as well call God Good – but the conclusion was one I could not avoid: *God the Good is not all-powerful.*

"Not yet, He isn't," said Vic cheerfully. "So we'll have to do our bit, as agents, commandos, conspirators, what have you. Do our bit to set God properly on His throne!"

I greeted this latest flippancy with a helpless, snorting laugh.

Then, hesitant and wondering, I asked myself: *Was* he being flippant?

A certain steely note had been detectable in the tone of what he'd said. He had no religion, or no definable religion, as far as I knew, and yet the more I reflected on his words the more I was convinced he had meant something serious.

I was afraid to ask.

Perhaps it is just as well that I did not say, at that early stage, "Uncle, what are you up to?" Sophisticated thinkers may smile, the hosts of Heaven may chuckle, at my serious reaction to his ridiculous words; but as I look back on my naïve state of mind that night, I reckon I might have done worse.

It was not too bad a curtain-raiser for the unthinkable adventure which lay in wait for Uncle Vic and myself.

THE ADVENTURE TO BE CONTINUED

IN

KROTH 2:

THE DROP

Lightning Source UK Ltd.
Milton Keynes UK
UKOW040612090113

204623UK00001B/13/P

9 781909 224308